Deadline for Lenny Stern

PETER MARABELL

DEADLINE
FOR LENNY STERN

A MICHAEL RUSSO MYSTERY

Kendall Sheepman Company, Cheboygan, MI
ISBN: 978-0-9903104-7-1

Printed in the United States of America

Bob Berg (1943-2019)
Mary Maurer (1951-2020)

It's likely just a coincidence that
these two spent much of their
professional lives with newspapers.
But it's no coincidence at all that that Bob
Berg and Mary Maurer were thoughtful,
decent people who gave to the citizens
of their respective communities,
time, energy, and support. I will miss
their friendship. I will miss the easy,
relaxed times sharing dinner and
a glass of wine. I will especially miss
the times that were not relaxing or easy,
when they stirred my mind, challenged
my political perspectives, and pushed me
to rethink my view of the world.

"Better to know more than to know less."— Lenny Stern, reporter, *The Petoskey Post Dispatch*

"Revenge is an act of passion, vengeance of justice. Injuries are revenged; crimes are avenged."
— Samuel Johnson

1

Maury Weston called this morning, said he needed me for a dangerous job. I was betting the publisher of the *Petoskey Post Dispatch* didn't want to hire me as a reporter. I told him I'd walk over.

It was a hot, steamy day even for the middle of July, so the sidewalks were crowded with tourists, eager to shop before heading to the beach. I snaked my way through them as best I could. Once out of the Gaslight District shopping area foot traffic lightened up, and I moved more easily.

The newspaper offices were packed into a two-story frame house in the middle of State Street, a short three blocks from my Lake Street office. Only a large sign on the front lawn distinguished it from so many other houses around town built in the 1930s.

I entered the building and took the stairs to the second floor. Maury Weston's office was across from AJ Lester's office. AJ was editor of *PPD Wired*, the online edition of the *Post Dispatch*, and the most important person in my life. I stuck my head in her door.

"Morning, AJ."

"Good morning," she said, smiling.

"Any idea what's going on?"

She nodded slowly. "Let Maury tell you," she said. "I love you, but this is business."

"Whatever you say, darling."

"I'll be here when you're done," she said. "Come see me."

I went across the hall to Weston's office. The door was ajar, but I knocked anyway.

"Michael," Weston said. Maury Weston was an influential member of the community, respected both for his civic contributions and for keeping the *Post Dispatch* in business (and focused on local issues).

His office had been a large front bedroom in an earlier life. Off to the side of the room was a long, rectangular cherry conference table. Three other people sat around the table. None of them looked happy.

"Let me introduce you," he said as he hauled his lanky six-six frame out of the chair at the head of the table.

First was Charles Bigelow, six feet tall, forty-something with a pencil-thin mustache on a narrow face.

"Charles is assistant to the president of Gloucester Publishing Company in Chicago."

"How are you?" Bigelow said, in a way that was both dismissive and uninterested.

"This is Tina Lawson," Weston said. Lawson was thirty or thirty-one, five-six, straight shoulder-length black hair, with green eyes.

"Tina is Lenny's agent at Gloucester."

Lenny Stern, a veteran reporter for the *Post Dispatch*, nodded when I glanced his way. Over the years, I'd given him solid leads for some juicy stories.

"Agent?" I said, and sat down. "You finally publish your book, Lenny?"

"Of course, he's published, Mr. Russo," Bigelow said. "We have a book tour scheduled. That's why you're here. I assumed you would have been told of the problem."

"I'm always late to the party," I said. "What's the problem?"

Weston jumped in ahead of Bigelow. "Lenny's received death threats, Michael."

I glanced at Lenny. "Death threats?"

He shrugged. Lenny Stern had spent enough years as a crime reporter in Chicago and Detroit to recognize a real threat when he got one.

"Because of the book?" I said.

Lenny nodded.

"Why?" I said.

Everyone was silent. I took care of that.

"Lenny?"

He hesitated, then said, "You know *In Cold Blood* by Truman Capote?"
I nodded.

"Capote called it a 'nonfiction novel.' That's what I did. All the details
are accurate. The creative part is weaving it together in a book with the
dramatic flair of a novel. To make it a better read."

"Understood," I said. "What's your book about?"

"A mob killing in Chicago, 1995," Lenny said. "I covered the story as a
reporter from the start. The name Alberto Genco ring a bell?"

"Vaguely," I said. "Mafia Don who went missing?"

Lenny nodded. "Until his body floated to the surface of Lake Michigan near Grand Haven one September afternoon. They found his gunman's body a day later."

"They ever solve the case?"

"You bet they did. But the prosecutor said there wasn't enough evidence for a jury to convict. If he'd gone to trial, it would have gutted a
powerful crime family and all its political connections. The mob paid
him off, Russo. He invented a story to cover the bribe. Pled guilty to a
low-level felony, got five years. Should have been out in eighteen months,
but he was killed in his prison cell. Raped and beaten to death."

"And you spelled all that out?"

"I did," Lenny said. "I focused on the prosecutor who didn't prosecute,
named the public officials who helped him, and the mob family who did
the killing."

"That was a long time ago, Lenny, 1995," I said. "You're being threatened now? After all these years?"

Lenny shrugged again.

"We need two things, Michael," Weston said, holding up two fingers
of his right hand in a "V" shape. "Arrange protection for Lenny, especially on the book tour, and find out who's behind the threats."

"Just a moment, Mr. Weston," Bigelow said, "Gloucester needs Mr.

Stern's book to be a success. We need him out there, we need the tour. Has Mr. Russo the experience, the temperament for this assignment? Can he handle it?"

"I'm right here," I said, "talk to me."

Bigelow put his hands flat on the table, as if he were about to leap up. He didn't. "All right, Mr. Russo, can you?"

"Can I what?" I didn't have the willpower to resist that one.

"Can you handle this assignment or not?"

"Why not hire somebody else if you need to ask that question?" I said.

"Somebody else already quit," Lenny said, grinning.

I took a moment, not that I needed one. Lenny was a good friend, after all.

"Maury, if I take the job, who do I work for?"

"You'd work for Gloucester Publishing," Bigelow said, interrupting again. "We pay the bills."

"I'm not interested," I said, and looked at Lenny. "No offense."

"None taken, Russo."

"Why'd you waste our time?" Bigelow said to Weston with a sharp wave of the arm.

"Since it's my ass on the line," Lenny said, loudly enough, "anyone want my two cents worth?"

"I would," Weston said, sounding relieved.

"I trust Russo with my life," Lenny said, "and it is my life we're talking about."

"If Mr. Russo's good enough for Lenny," Tina Lawson said, finally jumping into the conversation, "he's good enough for me. What about it, Charles?"

Bigelow hesitated, then nodded slowly, but he wasn't happy about it.

"What do you charge?" Bigelow said.

I told him. Fees, expenses, a retainer.

"Questions, Michael?" Weston said.

I leaned forward and turned toward Weston.

"Arranging protection is the easy part. I'll bring in a couple of people and set it up."

"Okay," Weston said.

"Finding out who's behind it is more difficult. Not impossible, but more difficult."

"What do you need from us?" Weston said.

"First, I want to know about the threats. Lenny?"

He shrugged. "I've had worse. A bad guy wants you dead, he usually doesn't give a heads-up."

"We can't take that chance," Bigelow said.

The man finally offered something sensible.

"No, we can't," I said. "You have a file on the threats, I assume?"

"Right here," Weston said. "And the schedule for the book tour." He handed me a manila folder.

"Do you think the Mafia is behind the threats, Russo?" Weston said.

"Be the first place I'd look."

"Then you'll take the job?"

I nodded, picking up the file.

"Oh, Mr. Bigelow?" I said.

He raised his chin in my direction, to make it easier to look down his nose at me, I'm sure.

"Leave my retainer with Maury, will you. On your way out."

2

"You really told that blowhard to leave a retainer?" AJ said, and laughed.

I'd gone back across the hall to her office. It was a smaller version of Weston's, with wood floors and an Oriental rug, but no conference table. I sat in one of two heavy captain's chairs in front of her desk.

Always the professional, AJ wore a navy suit over an ecru blouse. Her black hair curled softly above the collar. Her eyes sparkled when she laughed.

I nodded and smiled. "Better than he deserved."

"The man's just doing his job, Michael."

"He does it with a nice blend of arrogance and annoyance."

"True," AJ said, leaning back in her chair.

"You knew about the death threats?"

"When Lenny got the first ones, yeah," she said, "not much after that. After Bigelow took over."

"You think the threats are serious?" I said.

"You're the hotshot PI, what do you think?"

"Maury just gave me this," I said, and put the manila folder on her desk. "I want to read through it first, but I think Lenny sized up the threats pretty well."

"What'd I do pretty well?" Lenny Stern said from the doorway.

He was wiry, five-four, and nearly bald but for a few unruly tufts of gray hair above the ears. Lenny's face was lightly tanned and lined with experience. He wore a single-breasted, narrow lapel black suit, a white cotton shirt (not ironed), and a skinny black tie. It was his standard outfit, except for casual Fridays when he switched up for a light gray suit.

He took the other chair.

"You da man," I said, clapping my hands.

"What? What are you talking about?"

"Your novel, Lenny," I said, "that's terrific. You worked on the manuscript for what, three, four years?"

"Longer than that," he said, nodding.

"Good job," I said.

A small grin appeared. "Yeah, unless somebody shoots me."

I looked over at AJ. "Did you know about his book?"

She shook her head. "No. I mean, we all knew Lenny was writing, but news about the book came all at once."

"I didn't want to say anything until the deal was done," Lenny said.

"So you haven't read it?" I said to AJ.

"Nope."

"Would you have told me if you'd read it?"

"Sure."

"You didn't tell me about the death threats."

"That was …"

"Sure you guys aren't married?" Lenny said. "You sound like you're married. You ought to hear yourselves."

I glanced at AJ, who looked vaguely startled.

"Well, I've got work to do," Lenny said, starting to get up.

"Not yet," I said.

"What?" he said, dropping back into the chair.

"Is your book really dangerous?"

"Apparently someone thinks so."

"But it's fiction, right?" AJ said.

"Truman Capote's *In Cold Blood*. You know it?"

"Sure, the nonfiction novel."

"Well, my version's called *Corruption on Trial*," he said, and reprised the details.

AJ leaned forward, elbows on the desk.

"Help me here," she said. "A lot of books have been written about the Mafia, especially in Chicago. Historically accurate, real names, but nobody gets death threats. So why you, why your book? It was a long time ago."

Lenny smiled and put his hands out, palms up. "Just lucky, I guess."

"Not funny, Lenny, you end up in Lake Michigan like the mob guys," I said.

"Guess not," he said. "Look, it was a great story for a crime reporter, my story from the start. The newspaper pieces, op-ed columns, covering the Senate hearings in Springfield … everybody knew the prosecutor had been bribed."

"Was he?" AJ said.

"I found evidence he took a bribe."

AJ had that look in her eyes; her reporter's instincts had kicked in.

"You were the first?"

"Yep."

"But you didn't have evidence at the time it happened?"

"Nope," Lenny said. "I stumbled on it a couple of years ago. I was working on another story when, bang, there it was."

"Hard evidence?" AJ said.

"Oh, yeah," Lenny said. "Prosceutor took a bundle of cash for his wife and two boys. Proof he rigged the cover story, too. Good plan — until the guy was killed in his prison cell."

"But isn't the book out," I said, "on its way to bookstores?"

"Not quite," Lenny said. "Gloucester released excerpts, announced the stops for the tour, pre-publication stuff to generate publicity. We wrap it up in Chicago, and that's the official publication date. Copies will be everywhere then."

"Especially in the Midwest?" AJ said.

Lenny nodded.

"Do you have the evidence, the documents themselves?" I said.

Lenny nodded. "In a safe place. Only two people have ever seen the documents: Tina, and Kate Hubbell, my editor at Gloucester."

"What about Bigelow?" I said.

"No, not even him."

"Why'd you hold them back," I said, "why not use them for publicity?"

"Mobsters have long memories," Lenny said. "The mob's into a lot of things. They can reach a lot of people. If anything happens to me, my attorney gives them to Bigelow."

"Three crime families ran the town in those days," I said. "And one of them bribed the prosecutor."

"Yep," Lenny said. "If they knew for sure I had the documents, they'd offer the right price, get someone to steal them from me, and, bam, gone. Suddenly, everybody's safe ... so I held them back."

"How about that," AJ said. "You pissed off the mob. Nice going."

"There're a few public officials who don't want to see their names in print either. If the documents are destroyed, everyone has plausible deniability no matter what I put in a book."

I tapped the file on AJ's desk.

"Tell me about the threats," I said. "I'll read the file later, I want to hear it from you."

"The emails were first, then text messages and voicemails," Lenny said. "Threatened to beat the shit out of me, burn my car, that kind of thing. I've been threatened before. Usually nothing happens. If the bad guys really want to hurt you they don't give a heads-up."

Lenny's reputation was based on years of experience. He had trusted sources in Emmet, Charlevoix, and Cheboygan counties. Little of importance happened in the northern tip of the state that he didn't know — and often write — about.

"Then two guys, young punks, surprised me one night, stood me up against the car and gave my ribs a working over."

"You connected that to the book?" AJ said.

"Had to. One of them said I was sticking my nose where it didn't belong. I wasn't working on anything else at the time."

"Recognize them?" I said.

Lenny shook his head. "No. Kids in their late teens, early twenties. I'll know them if I see them again."

"What did the cops have to say?" AJ said.

"Not much," Lenny said. "They figured it for a street crime. You know, beat on an old guy for fun."

"Have they come after you again?" I said.

"Nah. But, you know, it feels like someone's following me. Where I ate lunch, when I went to the post office. I started looking over my shoulder. Checked my junk mail, *Twitter* feed, *Facebook*. Took my laptop and phone to Gilbert."

"Who's that?" I said.

"Deshawn Gilbert," AJ said. "The paper's teenage techy."

"Maury hired a student to work on your computers?" I said.

"He's a dropout," AJ said. "Seventeen-year-old Black kid who lives in Oden."

"Seriously?"

"Kid's a genius. Worked on the loading dock. Volunteered to fix the bugs in our network. He did. Maury fired the computer company and hired Gilbert."

"He find anything in your devices?" I asked Lenny.

"Nothing. Emails and texts couldn't be traced. Gilbert said they were 'unhackable,' his word."

"The 'deep web' in action?" I said.

"Guess so," Lenny said. "Threats kept coming. They've been more specific the closer we get to publication day."

"Curious the threats started before publication was announced," I said.

"Sure is," Lenny said.

"Your publisher's based in Chicago, right?"

"Yeah."

"Is that where Bigelow and Lawson work?"

"And 250 others."

"Could be a leak somewhere," I said.

Lenny nodded. "Gloucester hires media people, production, printers, transportation. Lot of people involved that don't work for Gloucester."

"You call the cops about the threats?"

"The sheriff, yeah. Full report. That's when Maury alerted Bigelow. He landed in town a couple of days later and took over."

Lenny looked at his watch. "Look, I have to be in Harbor Springs in a little while."

"The city manager interview?" AJ said.

"Yeah," he said, and stood to leave.

"I'll probably have more questions after I read the file," I said, "and we need to talk about the book tour."

"You going with me?"

"Only way to keep your ass out of harm's way," I said.

"If you say so."

"I do say so, and by the way..."

"Yeah?"

"Why'd the other guy quit?"

"Bigelow's bodyguard?"

I nodded.

"I wouldn't do what he told me."

3

"**D**o we really sound like a married couple?" AJ said.
     "Lenny seems to think so."

"Do other people think so?"

I shrugged.

"Hold on a second." AJ got up and shut the office door.

"If you want to know the truth," I said, "I really don't think about it."

"We don't talk about us all that often," AJ said. "We did that all the time in the early days."

"We were adjusting to each other back then. We don't really have many issues to talk about these days."

"Or argue about."

"That's a good thing," I said.

"Most of the time."

"Most of the time?"

"Sometimes it's good to argue things out, Michael. We do it when we need to."

"Yeah, I know," I said, "but Lenny was talking about something else, I think."

"Because we sounded married," AJ said.

"Uh-huh."

"Who was the last one to bring up getting married?"

"I was," I said.

"You were? You remember that?"

"When Frank almost died."

Frank Marshall was a retired Chicago investigator. He was also friend, a mentor, the closet thing I had to an older brother. Five years ago, he was gunned down one rainy October night on the streets of Petoskey.

AJ nodded slowly. "That was a rough time. You spent a lot of it with Frank and Ellen."

Ellen Paxton was Frank Marshall's wife and confidante.

"I saw marriage differently after that," I said, "watching them under all the stress."

"Do Frank and Ellen sound like a married couple?" AJ said.

"Never thought about it, so …"

A knock on the office door.

"Come on in," AJ said.

Tina Lawson came through the door and closed it behind her.

"Hope you don't mind," she said. "Lenny told me you were here."

AJ pointed at a chair and Tina sat down.

"I'll just be a minute," she said. "I don't want to interrupt."

"You're not," AJ said.

"I'm worried," Tina said, "scared actually."

"About the book tour, Ms. Lawson?" I said.

"Call me Tina," she said. "Look, you may know how to protect people, but I've been on plenty of book tours. There aren't many places to hide."

"It's not about hiding," I said, "it's knowing where to look, what to look for."

"Can you keep Lenny from getting hurt?"

AJ's desk phone buzzed. "Excuse me," she said. Then, after a moment's discussion, "Maury wants to see me. Take your time. Finish up."

After AJ left, I said, "There are no guarantees, Tina, if that's what you mean."

"I'm not sure what I mean," Tina said. "I'm just scared."

"I can reduce the odds of him being hurt. I can make it tougher on the people who try to hurt him."

"So you're telling me you can't prevent him being killed if someone's willing to die to do it."

Tina was right, of course, but it seemed like a lousy time to confirm her worst fears.

"It's much harder to do," I said. "Not impossible, but harder."

"Or if someone throws a bomb."

"That's not likely to happen."

"Why not? I don't understand."

"Bombs do a lot of damage," I said. "Public outrage would demand arrests, there'd be pressure on the cops, the prosecutors. Even the mob doesn't want that much attention. They'd use one or two experienced shooters."

"Professional killers?"

I nodded.

"Will you have any help?"

"Yes."

Tina waited for an explanation.

"When you're in the private eye biz," I said, hopefully with a straight face, "you know plenty of skilled people, experienced in this kind of thing."

That meant Henri LaCroix, of course. And I might bring someone else in if things got really dicey.

"Skilled, like … like … with guns?"

"Yes," I said, "but trying to kill Lenny isn't the only thing to worry about."

Tina paused, staring at me, waiting for more.

"They might kidnap him, ransom him for the documents, something like that."

"Shit," Tina said, "never thought of that. Really?"

Might be better to head off this line of questions, too.

I leaned back with my hands behind my head, trying to look relaxed enough to ease her anxiety.

"Tell me about the book tour."

"Well," she said, her face losing some of the tension as we shifted to a familiar topic.

"Lenny Stern's tour is pretty simple, and it's short. Four events in three locations, wrapping up in Chicago on the official release date of the book."

"The file Maury gave me included a tour schedule. Is that the current one?"

Tina nodded.

"Good. So where do we start?"

"Here," Tina said, "in Petoskey."

I smiled. "As fond as I am of Petoskey, it doesn't seem like a very big market to get the tour rolling."

"It isn't, but Lenny insisted. He wants to kick it off in his hometown. Where he lives and works."

"You'd prefer elsewhere?"

"Of course. Gloucester's marketing division always wants to start in a medium-sized city or larger. More bang for the buck that way."

"But not this time?"

"Gloucester wanted to sign Lenny. He insisted, they agreed."

"Got it. I want to ask you, before I forget: you're Lenny's agent, but you work for Gloucester Publishing. I thought agents represented their clients to prospective publishers. What am I missing?"

Tina smiled. "Nothing, you didn't miss a thing. Lenny doesn't have a traditional agent. I'm more like a publicist or marketing specialist. My job is to work with Lenny, to get the word out."

"Is that why your name appeared in the *Post Dispatch* story about the tour stopping in town?"

"Yes."

"Okay, so we start in small town Petoskey. Is Detroit on the list?"

"It was originally, but Lenny said no. Northern Michigan only."

"And the Chicago wrap-up."

"Yes," Tina said.

"Didn't you say three locations but four events?"

"Lenny opens just down the street, at the old Carnegie Library with an evening talk about his days as a crime reporter, the backstory on the

Mafia killings. That kind of thing. Right after the talk he'll sign copies at a table in the main room. That's two events for us."

"The talk open to the public?"

Tina shook her head. "Invitation only," she said. "From a list of VIPs, the rest of the tickets will go to supporters of the library."

"How about the book signing?"

"Open to the public. People will come and go for two hours. I suppose the signing will be tougher to patrol."

"Anyplace the public can wander in and out is harder to cover. The Carnegie talk is mostly limited access."

"So it's safer?"

"It should be," I said, "but you never know."

Tina nodded slowly, still digesting the danger that was building around her.

"The next day, he'll be at B. Humbug's Bookstore in Harbor Springs for a signing. Two days later, a luncheon at the Iroquois Hotel on Mackinac Island."

"The tour portion is over?"

Tina nodded. "Then it's on to Chicago."

"This all by car?"

"Yes."

"Even Chicago?"

Tina smiled. "Gloucester's not likely to pop for plane fare for three hundred miles."

"You usually do the driving?"

She nodded. "It's part of the job."

That's a lot of miles on the open road to worry about, a lot of opportunity for the killers to come at us. But Henri and I have dealt with that before.

"It'll be day trips up here," Tina said. "Although we might stay over on Mackinac. Chicago's three nights."

"Why three?"

"Gloucester's throwing a couple of VIP receptions. High-profile author, high-profile …"

"Hopefully high-profile book," I said, and smiled.

"You're learning," Tina said, laughing.

"Who makes the hotel reservations?"

"Gloucester has a travel staff who does that."

"Where are you staying?" I said.

"The Perry," Tina said, "I love the history of the place. Did you know it was slated to be a hospital a hundred years ago? Very cool. Anyway, they booked me at the Perry, I'm delighted to say."

"How many on the staff?"

"Two."

"Know them?"

"Yeah," she said. "Nobody new. They've been around for a while. You think one of them ... ?"

I shrugged. "I ask questions. Don't know the people, don't know the business. So I ask."

"So everybody's a suspect?"

I smiled. "Not everybody," I said, "but someone's threatening Lenny."

"And you want to know who."

"I want to stop them."

4

"**S**ounds simple enough," Henri said, "our job is to keep one cantankerous reporter from getting wacked."

We sat in the outer office, by the windows overlooking Lake Street. The July heat was in its eighth day. Sandy was at her desk, nibbling on a molasses cookie.

"Whenever you say something's simple," she said, "I get nervous."

Henri laughed. "Muscle memory, Sandy. Don't jump to conclusions."

"That's easy to do, hanging around the two of you."

"Did you tell Lenny's agent ..." Henri said, hesitating.

"Tina Lawson."

"Right. Did you tell Tina Lawson we'd take over the tour?"

"Uh-huh."

"She okay with that?"

"She understands we have to do some things our way to protect Lenny. But we have to work with the schedule set by Gloucester Publishing."

"I assume we also stick with Lenny when he's not on tour."

"Until this is over, yeah."

"Where is he now?"

"I have no idea."

"That's not a very reassuring way to start, gentlemen," Sandy said.

"Said he'd let us know when he got back to the office."

"The real danger starts when the tour starts," I said. "The people doing the threatening don't know if the tour's been canceled or not. Because of the threats."

"Unless there really is a leak at Gloucester Publishing," Sandy said. "Should we trust anybody associated with Gloucester?"

I shrugged. "I think Lawson's okay. She seems like a sharp professional trying to do her job. Besides, Lenny likes her."

"Bigelow?" Sandy said.

I shook my head. "He's probably okay. Seems too preoccupied with himself to sell out to the mob."

"That's not enough to rule him out," Henri said.

"No, it's not," I said.

"We going to set Lenny straight on how this will go," Henri said, "on and off tour?"

I nodded.

"I suppose the esteemed Mr. Bigelow will want to weigh in."

"I'll fill Bigelow in after we set it up with Lenny. Keeping his author out of harm's way is our job, not his."

"Book must be a helluva read," Henri said.

"Hey," Sandy said, reaching under her desk.

"*Voila.*" She held the book in the air. "Hot off the press. Our own copy of *Corruption on Trial.*" The large block letters of the title were superimposed over an even larger judge's gavel.

"Where'd we get that?" Henri said.

"Kid from Weston's office dropped it off," Sandy said. "Already read the introduction."

"So what do you think?" I said.

Sandy carefully placed Lenny's book on the desk in front of her, as if it were a rare first edition in the original paper jacket. She stared at it for a moment.

Henri and I sat quietly, waiting.

"I'll know better after I read it," Sandy said, glancing at each of us. "Right now, hard to tell."

"What does that mean?" Henri said.

"Look, Lenny describes ... you know, gives us the background, how he covered the mob killing in the first place, how he came to write the book."

"We know some of that," I said.

Sandy nodded. "But it was the documents," she said, "they're what did it. They filled out the story he's wanted to tell for a long time."

Sandy pointed at the book. "Once he had the evidence, he knew he'd finally write the book."

"Do you want to read it first?" I asked her.

"You bet."

"Might be something we need to know…"

"How about this," she said. "I'll email you two highlights, a summary, something. You'll have that."

Before we could quiz Sandy further, we heard footsteps. A moment later, Lenny Stern came through the door. He stopped when he caught all three of us staring at him.

"What?" he said. "What'd I do?"

Sandy held his book in the air. "Look, Lenny. My own copy."

Lenny smiled. "You got it," he said. "That's Maury's, but he can get another one. You guys need a copy right now."

"Will you autograph it for me?" Sandy said.

"I would be delighted," Lenny said, with a very theatrical bow at the waist. "I've only read the introduction," she said. "I have a quick question."

Lenny hung his coat on the hall tree and took the chair next to Henri.

"What's the question?"

Sandy leaned forward on her desk. "Finding the evidence of corruption sealed the deal…"

Lenny nodded. "To write the book."

"Yeah, I got that," Sandy said, "but why stick with it so long? You reported on the original crime, wrote the stories for the *Tribune* years ago, but never let it go. Why not?"

"You hang around cops and criminals as long as I have, you can smell a cover-up. Even if nobody spells it out, the cops, prosecutors. They all know."

Lenny paused a moment. "Proving it … that was another story."

"But when you could prove it," Sandy prompted.

"I started the book," he said.

"Anyone else know you'd started the book?" I said.

Lenny sat back. "Well, at first no one. How could they? I have all my original notes. The rest is in the paper's cloud file."

"Would anyone at the paper be interested?"

"That I was digging in the digital files?"

"Uh-huh."

Lenny shook his head. "Reporters, editors, we're always checking stuff. Nobody'd paid any attention."

"Would anyone care that you started a book on a famous crime?"

Lenny smiled. "Every reporter is writing a bestseller, Russo. Like English professors are always writing…" Lenny paused, making quote marks in the air with his fingers. "You know. The 'great American novel.'"

"You tell anyone you were working on the case?"

"Nobody to tell," Lenny said. "I was the only one who had the evidence. It wasn't any kind of big deal that I was sketching out a book."

I stood and looked out the window. There were shoppers moving here and there in the humid air. Most visitors were at the beach trying to stay cool. I was happy for air conditioning.

"It had to be a big deal to somebody, Lenny," I said. "Somebody who knew about the book."

"Lenny," Sandy spoke up. "After you started the project, what's the first thing you did? Like, where'd you go, who did you talk to?"

"Well." Lenny thought for a moment. "I might have said something to someone at work, you know, over coffee or a beer."

Sandy shook her head. "No, no, not that. I don't mean a casual conversation at work."

"How about Gloucester Publishing?" Henri said. "When did they get involved?"

"Later," Lenny said. "I'd finished most of the rough draft before I took it to Gloucester."

"Who'd you talk to first?" Henri said.

"At Gloucester?"

Henri nodded.

"Tina Lawson."

"You already knew her?" I said.

"Yeah. I met her a few years ago," Lenny said, "in Chicago. At a retirement party for my editor at the *Tribune*. She'd heard about the case, has crime writers as clients. She seemed the logical person to ask."

"Did you tell your old editor," I said, "the one who retired?"

"Never had the chance," Lenny said. "He died six weeks later. Cancer."

"I assume Tina thought you were onto something?" Sandy said.

Lenny nodded. "Murder and the mob in Chicago. It may not be a *New York Times* bestseller, but that's good enough to sell books in the Windy City."

"What happened after you approached Tina?"

"She wanted a proposal, told me how to put it together, so I did."

"You give the proposal to Tina?" I asked.

Lenny nodded.

"Who'd she give it to?"

"Don't know for sure," he said, "but Bigelow gave the project a green light."

"Back to Bigelow again," Henri said. "That guy bothers me, and I haven't even met him."

"Hell, Henri, he bothers everybody. He's an insufferable snob, but apparently he knows the business of books."

"That might sell books," Henri said. "Doesn't make me less cautious."

"Tell me again," I said, shifting the subject, "who's seen the documents besides you."

"Tina and Kate Hubbell," Lenny said. "She edited the book."

"That's it?" I said.

"Yep."

I looked over at Henri, and he nodded slowly.

"Either of them been threatened?" Henri said. "Or anything odd happen to either of them? You know, they think they're being followed, stuff like that?"

Lenny shook his head. "I would have heard," he said, "especially after I got beat up."

Lenny glanced at Henri, then at me. "Do you think they're in danger?"

"Can't be sure," I said. "We'll assume the answer's yes for now."

"Listen, Russo," Lenny said, looking at his watch, "I'm on a deadline. I have to write up an interview. What do you need from me?"

"Two things," I said. "I want to review the death threats with you and Tina, and we have to talk over how the tour's going to play out."

"I figured we'd get to that sooner or later," Lenny said.

I nodded. "Had to happen, Lenny, had to happen."

Lenny shrugged and took his coat from the hall tree. "All right. How about my office in the morning? That work?"

I looked over at Sandy.

"You're clear, boss."

"Henri?"

"I'm clear, too, boss," he said, and laughed.

"How about Tina?" I said.

"She can be there," Lenny said.

"How about Hubbell, the editor?"

Lenny shook his head. "In Chicago. But I'll make sure she's kept in the loop."

"Does Hubbell have plans to be on the tour?"

Lenny nodded. "Just the first stop at the Carnegie Library and the Chicago events at the end. Okay to go now?" he said.

"I'll be outside when you leave work," Henri said, "follow you home."

"And now it begins," Lenny said and left the office.

We were silent for a moment.

"What do you think?" I said.

"We don't know enough," Henri said.

"That happens a lot in this office," I said.

"We have the death threats," Sandy said. "Let's start there."

"Okay," I said. "You're up to bat, have at it."

"All of us," Sandy gestured with her hand in a big circle. "Us, Lenny, Maury Weston, even the dude from Gloucester Publishing, we all assume the Mafia's pissed off about Lenny's book."

"Lenny writes about a mob killing, the mob is pissed," I said. "Politicians implicated want the book to go away, Lenny is beat up, threatened. It's the logical assumption."

"Unless it's wrong," Sandy said, leaning forward. "Just suppose it's not the Mafia. Suppose it's not Joey DeMio who concocted a plan to stop publication of the book or try to kill Lenny."

"Then who?" I said. "Who else would put together a plan like this?"

Sandy shook her head. "I don't know. You guys are the detectives."

"He's the detective," Henri said, pointing at me. "I'm just along for the ride."

I pushed my chair back from the desk and swiveled around. The sun was up there, waves of heat shimmered up from the tarmac in the parking lot.

"Sandy's got a point," Henri said. "Maybe we should consider someone else is behind the threats."

"Our job's tougher if it's someone else," I said.

"How so?" Sandy said.

"The mob is fairly predictable. They always do things the way they've always done things. They're not very creative when it comes to intimidation and murder."

"Worth thinking about, Russo," Henri said. "And there's one man who'd know."

"Joey DeMio himself," I said.

Henri pointed his forefinger at me and pulled an imaginary trigger.

The DeMios — Joey and his father, Carmine, now retired — were from Chicago. They owned a perfectly legitimate enterprise, the Marquette Park Hotel on Mackinac Island. Carmine also owned a restored

Victorian cottage on the island's East Bluff. The hotel provided cover for the family's more criminal operations in northern Michigan and Ontario.

"Well, if you decide to go ask him," Henri said, "I have breaking news about Mackinac Island's favorite mob family."

"What's that?"

"'Trouble right here in River City.' Remember Ristorante Bella?"

The highly regarded Italian eatery a block down Lake Street put its tablecloths in mothballs two years back.

"Uh-huh."

"New owners. Want to guess?"

"DeMio wants a base in Petoskey?"

"It opened last week," Henri said.

"You know anything?" I said.

Henri got that look, like I'd asked a dumb question.

"It's a legitimate move."

"Seriously?" Sandy said.

Henri nodded. "Paperwork checks out. The official owner is the same corporation that owns his hotel on Mackinac."

"Is Joey using the restaurant as a cover, too?" I said.

"Too soon to tell. I suppose it's possible a move to Emmet County is separate from his more traditional business practices."

"That'll be the day," I said.

"Maybe he just wanted good pasta," Henri said.

"Funny," Sandy said.

"The Don renamed the place, too. 'Ristorante Enzo.'"

"Well," I said. "When it's time to see the man, walking down the street's easier than catching a ferry to Mackinac."

5

I swung the chair around and put my feet on the window ledge. Small whitecaps slid along the blue water of Little Traverse Bay. I spotted two single-mast sailboats moving smartly on the other side of the breakwater.

I texted AJ, "Dinner?" and put the phone down.

Sandy leaned on the doorjamb.

"Where's Henri?" I said.

Sandy jerked her thumb, hitchhiker style, toward the outer office.

"Henri," I said loud enough, "what are you doing?"

"Hold on a minute," he said.

Sandy looked back. "Be careful with my computer, if you know what's good for you."

We heard the printer come to life and start its dedicated task. Henri came in the office and sat down.

"What were you doing?"

"Looking up Petoskey's Carnegie Library," Henri said. "Interesting history. Never been inside."

"I have," Sandy said. "A couple of times."

"So have I," I said, "for a community event or a fundraiser. Never as a bodyguard."

"Where will Lenny do his book thing?"

"In the main room," I said, "his talk and the book signing. That's the way I've seen it done before."

"How many ways in?" Henri said.

"Two," I said. "The front door on Mitchell and a door on the side, where the library connects to the Arts Center."

"We should be able to cover both doors," Henri said.

"Lenny's talk will be easier," I said. "It's invitation only. That helps."

"But the doors are wide open for the signing, aren't they?" Sandy said.

I nodded. "Harder to cover depending on where they set up the table for Lenny. We'll figure out the best place to watch."

I thought for a minute, then leaned over and tapped a few keys.

"Let's see…the library…should be an event schedule. Here it is." I sat back and pointed at the screen. "How about that? We have an author presentation tonight," I said. "Woman's got a new book on gardening…" I looked back at the screen. "Taking care of flowers, shrubs, that kind of thing. I could swing by tonight, get a lay of the room."

My phone buzzed. The screen read, "Yes."

"It's AJ," I smiled. "Maybe she'd like to tag along."

I tapped her number.

"Michael," she said, "a real phone call? What's up?"

"You interested in a brief detour before dinner?"

"Would you like to be more specific? Not that I'm suspicious, or anything."

"I'm going to listen to an expert gardener who has a new book out. Thought I might learn a thing or two. Want to come along?"

Silence.

"AJ?"

"No, really, Michael, what do you want?"

"I'm serious, AJ. All about gardening. At the Carnegie Library."

"I was thinking we'd share a glass of wine, something romantic at my house."

"We can still do that," I said. "It wouldn't take more than a few minutes. We could stop at City Park Grill for a drink."

"I was thinking…are you on speaker?"

"No."

"I was thinking more along the lines of wine in the bathtub."

Sandy and Henri were watching me. I tried to keep a straight face.

"Oh…I think I get it."

"It's a damn good thing you're a detective, Russo. I shouldn't have to spell it out for you." She paused. "Wait a minute. Your interest in gardening is limited to watching me work in the garden. So this has to be about something else."

"Uh-huh."

"The Carnegie?"

"Uh-huh."

Silence again. She was thinking.

"That's Lenny's first stop on the book tour, isn't it? You want inside the building, don't you? To check out how they set it up for authors."

"You'd make a terrific reporter. Want to come along? Then some wine."

"In my bathtub?"

"Absolutely."

"I may rip your clothes off between the front door and the tub."

I tried hard to look nonchalant, edging toward blasé.

"I certainly hope so," I said.

AJ laughed. "Okay, I'll meet you at the library. What time?"

I told her and clicked off.

My office companions waited patiently for my next words.

"She loves to garden," I said, and smiled.

"If you say so, boss. I have a few things to do before I go home."

Sandy went out to her desk.

Henri looked at his watch. "Time to keep Lenny company on his ride home."

6

I walked up the steps and through the double-front door at the Carnegie Library. The large rotunda was beautifully restored, with high ceilings, wood beams and tall windows. Folding chairs, in neat rows, filled most of the floor space. They were aimed at a podium at the back of the room. People milled about, talking and laughing and waiting for the evening's presentation to begin.

Off to one side, AJ leaned against the wall. She smiled and waved when I looked over. She wore a two-piece navy linen suit over a soft pink blouse. I walked over and gave her a quick kiss.

"Hi," I said.

"Hi, yourself," she said.

I stood next to AJ and took in the room.

"Would you like my two cents worth?" she said.

"Always. About what?"

"About what? Some Philip Marlowe you are."

"I'm not Sam Spade anymore?"

"Oh, hush, darling," she said. "If they set up the room this way for Lenny, you have four problems."

I moved back a half step and gave the rotunda another look. "Is that right?"

AJ nodded slowly, but her attention was focused on the room.

"First off, the door you came in," she said, "and then that one, over there."

AJ pointed to a side door, several feet in front of us, near the middle of the rotunda.

"That one connects to the Arts Center, right?" I said.

"It does, through a narrow hallway."

"Back in a second." I walked to the other side of the room, opposite the side door. I watched for a couple of minutes as some visitors entered the library using both doors. I walked across the room and down the narrow hallway to have a look, then I went back to AJ.

"What do you think?" she said.

"Clear view of the front door," I said, "but I need to watch that hallway more carefully. Maybe they'll only use the front entrance."

"Don't count on it," AJ said, "the side door leads to a parking lot and the restrooms. That's the third problem."

Two women, one taller, thinner and younger than the other, came straight out of an Ann Taylor catalog and walked to the front of the room. Both women smiled, but they didn't really look all that happy. The younger one placed a folder on the podium and began chatting with women in the first row.

AJ looked at her watch. "Think they're ready to start?"

"Looks that way."

"Maybe we ought to vamoose before they do," AJ said.

"Okay with me, but you said four problems. What's number four?"

AJ raised her left arm and waved slowly across the expanse of the rotunda. She leaned in and spoke softly.

"You'd spot a bad guy as soon as he came in the room. But what if he's already sitting in the audience? What if the bad guy is a she?"

I nodded. "Yeah. Worth thinking about. Let's get out of here."

"Good idea."

We left by the front door as people were coming in for the gardening presentation.

"City Park Grill?" I said.

"Not a chance," AJ said. "It's my house. Did you walk?"

"Yeah. Your truck here?"

"Across the street. And it's an SUV, Russo. Would it kill your ass to call it an SUV? Just once?"

"Probably."

"It's a damn good thing I love you," AJ said, laughing … just a little.

She took my hand. We crossed Mitchell Street and climbed aboard her SUV.

"Do you mind riding in my SUV, darling?"

"I'd love a ride in your SUV, darling."

"The right thing to say."

AJ started the motor, and off we went to Bay Street. We rode in silence, AJ's hand finding mine. It was a short trip, and the quiet was both welcome and relaxing. Our workdays provided enough stimulation. We enjoyed sharing the quiet the way we shared so many things.

AJ pulled in the driveway, and we entered the house through the kitchen door.

"I have to get out of these work clothes," she said. "Wine's cold. Get the cheese out, too."

I took two glasses, a bottle of chardonnay and napkins to the living room and placed them on the coffee table in front of the sofa. I put down a plate with crackers and a brick of manchego cheese. I kicked off my shoes, poured wine into the glasses and leaned back.

The soft hum of the air conditioning was a welcome sound in the middle of the heat wave. AJ's elegant two-story Victorian needed serious repairs when she bought it several years ago. Structural updates, a new roof, the heating and air systems, came first. Then it was onto cosmetic improvements like fresh paint, inside and out. It was a work in progress, but almost complete.

AJ came into the living room wearing a familiar outfit, loose baggy shorts and a man-tailored light blue shirt not quite buttoned up the front.

She sat down and picked up a glass. "A toast."

"To what?"

"Us, and I have a question."

"Me, too."

"You first," she said, and tapped my glass with hers.

I sipped some wine. "At the Carnegie Library, you were playing private eye."

AJ glanced at something on the other side of the room.

"So?"

"Seriously," I said. "You like to help out from time to time, but you were scouting the library, too."

"Yes, I was."

"Why?"

"Lenny Stern, that's why. I have more than a passing interest in his well-being. He's our best reporter: skilled, experienced, people talk to him. He's a mentor, a coach to every rookie reporter that comes along."

I nodded. "And he's a pretty nice guy."

"No, he's not," AJ said, "he's crabby, single-minded and annoying when he's on a story. But I've made peace with that. If I need a friend, I've got you."

She leaned in and kissed me.

"I'm glad to hear that," I said.

AJ took a small chunk of cheese. "Have you told Lenny what he's in for?"

I laughed. "Tomorrow morning he'll get the details from Henri and me."

"Lucky him," AJ said, shaking her head. "He ain't gonna like it."

"We'll do the old soft-sell," I said. "Tina Lawson will be there, too."

"You think she's in danger?"

"Don't know, but only three people have seen the documents proving corruption."

"Who's the third?"

"Kate Hubbell," I said, "Lenny's editor at Gloucester Publishing."

"Are you and Henri doing your usual routine to protect them?"

I picked up my wine glass. "I thought we came to your house this pleasant evening so you could rip my clothes off without getting kicked out of the City Park Grill?"

"Any minute now," she said, "answer my question."

"Yes, the usual routine. Henri got him home safely tonight, will cover him to work in the morning." I sipped some wine. "That satisfy your curiosity?"

She nodded, smiled and took my glass away.

She swung her leg over and sat on my lap … facing me. "There."

She leaned in and kissed me, slowly running the tip of her tongue around the edge of my lips.

"That felt good," I said.

"How about this," she said, and pressed herself down on my lap, moving her hips … just enough.

I smiled.

She put her arms around my neck, and we kissed, slowly, lingering, our mouths open.

AJ tilted her head back and smiled. I reached up, unbuttoned her blue shirt and pulled it back.

"You forgot a camisole."

"Didn't want to slow things down," she said.

"Nice," I said, and gently kissed each nipple.

"Ooh, time to move upstairs."

AJ climbed off my lap, picked up the glasses and went toward the kitchen. I followed and came up behind her at the kitchen counter. I put my arms around her and kissed the back of her neck. She freed herself just enough to turn around.

We kissed again.

"Upstairs," she said.

I opened my eyes and tried to move my legs, but it wasn't working. Not sure why. I eased my head off the pillow. Oh, that's why. AJ was pushed in close on top of the covers, and sound asleep.

The sun came through the window blinds, slapping a ladder of light on the opposite wall.

I tried moving again.

"What time is it?" she said.

I lifted my head up just enough to see the clock. "Six-thirty."

"I'm going to be late for work," she said.

"Move your legs," I said, "I'll make coffee."

"Okay."

I slid off the bed, found my clothes here and there, and headed for the kitchen.

I drank coffee and watched a squirrel dance his way along the deck railing outside the kitchen window. The back of AJ's house overlooked a ravine thick with elms, evergreens and a variety of critters.

"How's my favorite lover," AJ said when she breezed into the kitchen. She was bundled up in a long white terrycloth robe, her black hair glistening from the shower. She poured a mug of coffee. "Want me to drop you at home?"

"Thanks, I'd rather walk." My apartment was downtown, a pleasant ten-minute walk through the neighborhood.

"Okay. Call me later," she said, and went back upstairs.

I put my mug in the sink and left by the kitchen door. A wall of heat hit me the second I stepped outside. If the temperature dropped overnight, it wasn't obvious at AJ's house. The July sun hung well above the trees as I moved along Bay Street. It would be another splendid day for the legion of tourists who escaped to northern Michigan each summer for a week or two, hoping someday to "live the dream" and do it "up north."

A few people had other, more dangerous plans in mind.

7

It was almost nine by the time I got to the office, a three-block walk from my apartment. I cut through Roast & Toast, picked up a *New York Times* at McLean & Eakin, and went up the stairs.

"Morning, boss," Sandy said when I came in the door. "No messages, coffee's hot."

"Thanks," I said, "but on my way to Lenny's office."

"The black blazer is a nice touch with the khakis. Aren't you warm?"

"Of course," I said. "It's July. Hear from Henri?"

"Nope."

"Me, either. He probably tagged along when Lenny went to work this morning."

"That was a good idea," Sandy said.

"Text me if anything comes up." I picked up my brief bag, left the jacket behind, and headed outside.

It was still early, and most of the shops in the Gaslight District had yet to open for the day. Tourists were someplace else, sipping coffee. I walked through downtown over to State Street.

Henri's SUV was parked across the street from the *Post Dispatch*. The side window edged down as I walked up.

"Morning," he said.

"Good morning. Is our man inside?"

"He better be," Henri said. "Told him to use the front door, in or out."

"Think he'll listen?"

Henri shrugged. "Guess we'll find out."

"Shall we go?" I said.

Henri eased himself out of the SUV and beeped the door locks.

We entered the newspaper building and walked straight down the hall to the newsroom at the rear of the recent addition. The newsroom featured larger windows and a much higher ceiling than the original residential house. Gray metal desks covered in printouts and computer monitors lined the walls. A large, square table occupied the center of the room. Fluorescent lights sprayed a harsh, bright light over the entire space. The buzz of the lights mixed with the din of voices.

Lenny's desk was off to one side, away from the door. The noise of talking dropped off as the other reporters watched us approach Lenny. Rumors had no doubt spread around the newsroom long before we arrived.

Lenny put down his phone when he saw us.

"You're late," he said. "You were supposed to be here ten minutes ago."

I decided to let that go. Henri folded his arms across his chest at glared at Lenny.

"Aren't you hot in that jacket?" Lenny asked Henri.

Before Henri could respond, I jumped in. "Is Tina Lawson here?"

"Of course, she's here," he said. "I told you she'd be here. She's here."

This wasn't going well. Be interested to know why.

"I don't want to be here forever," Lenny said. "Let's get this over with."

With that, he sprung out of his chair and headed from the room. He looked back.

"You going to stand there all day?" he said without breaking stride.

We followed him. By the time we were through the newsroom door, Lenny was standing twenty feet down the hall in front of another room.

"In here," he said.

It was a small square room, without windows. In the center stood a round, dark wood table and eight high-backed wooden chairs. Tina Lawson sat in one of them with a mug of coffee in front of her, both of her hands wrapped tightly around the mug like it might jump off the table. She had a blank look on her face, as if she were bored, or annoyed.

I introduced Henri to Tina. They shook hands as Lenny slammed the door. We took seats, but Lenny remained standing.

"All right," he said, "let's hear it."

He folded his arms, daring us to so much as say one word.

"The hell's the matter with you?" I said. "You've been barking since we walked in …"

"Damn," Tina said. "I'm glad I'm not the only one. He's …" she flung her arm in Lenny's direction. "Been yelling at me since I got in this morning. Who knows why?"

Lenny remained rigidly at attention.

"Come on, Lenny," I said. "Right now, talk to us."

"This is bullshit," he said, "bullshit."

"Okay," I said, "now that we've established that, the hell's going on?"

Lenny didn't move, but he finally looked at me.

"I don't like being handled, Russo. Don't want you telling me how to do my job, how to live my life. It's bullshit."

I shook my head slowly. "Got a job to do, Lenny."

He leaned in just a bit — for emphasis, I guessed. He didn't need it.

"Not just the tour. Every day and night. All the time. Have I got that right?"

I nodded. "Yeah, you got it right."

"It's bullshit."

"You made that clear already," I said, "doesn't change a thing."

Lenny started to say something else, but stopped when Henri stood up. He came around the table and stood in front of Lenny, a few inches away.

"A few minutes ago, you asked me if I was too hot," Henri said, as he slowly unzipped his nylon jacket. He took it off and dropped in on a chair.

Henri reached in his shoulder holster and pulled out a long-barreled .357. He held it tight, close to his body, pointed at the ceiling.

"Jesus," Tina said. "Holy shit."

"Listen to the woman, Lenny," Henri said. "This is why we're here."

Lenny grinned ever so slightly. "A little melodramatic, don't you think?"

Henri holstered the handgun. "Got your attention, didn't it?"

"Lenny," I said, and he looked in my direction.

"You're a good reporter, you have a job to do. I respect that. We won't stop you."

"But you won't leave me alone either."

"One of us will always be with you," I said. "Doesn't mean we sit in on a meeting or get in your way during an interview. But we stay close, yeah, especially when you're in the open."

"What does that mean?"

"To and from work, a meeting, interview, anything like that. We get you to your destination, then do our best to stay out of the way."

Lenny unfolded his arms. Some of the edge was gone.

"So, you're not with me every minute?"

"What I just said, Lenny. You're in the open, we're there. We ..."

Lenny raised his hands, palms out.

"Got it," he said. "I .... What else?"

"You want to sit down now?" I said.

Lenny nodded slowly and pulled out a chair.

The tension eased, but it hadn't left the table yet.

"Sorry, Tina," Lenny said. "I don't care about these two, but I shouldn't have growled at you."

Tina paused for a moment. "No, you shouldn't have," she said. "I don't get paid enough put up with that. But I accept your apology."

"All right," I said, "we've got some work to do."

Henri and I outlined our routine for covering Lenny. He listened better than I expected, considering how much he hated the idea.

When we finished, I took the manila file out of my brief bag and put it on the table.

"Now, about the death threats," I said, pointing at the file. "I read the emails and transcripts of the texts."

"I told you I've been threatened before," Lenny said.

"Well, I haven't," Tina said. "This might be the daily grind for you guys, but I sell books. I got scared. Especially the voicemails. They…" She shook her head.

I put my hand on the folder. "You read all of these?" I said to Tina.

"Uh-huh."

"What was it about the voicemails that got to you?"

"Hearing the words," she said. "It was easier to keep a distance with the emails. Just words on a page. I read true crime for a living. But hearing a voice was something… I don't know, more real I guess. It was so soft, almost quiet, measured. It was a lot creepier than a loud voice."

"You think Tina's in danger, too?" Lenny said.

I caught a glimpse of Tina's face. She tensed up at Lenny's question. It had occurred to her.

"Not in the same way as you, Lenny," I said. "She's not the public face of the revealed corruption, like you are."

"Should I feel relieved?" Tina said.

"Well," I said, "since only you, Lenny and Kate Hubbell have actually seen the hard evidence…"

"But only I know where the documents are," Lenny said.

"You think it might be a good idea to tell us," Henri said, "just in case you get popped on the way home?"

"Thought you weren't going to let that happen," Lenny said, and smiled for the first time this morning.

"Guess I'm not relieved yet," Tina said. "Have you talked with Kate about this?"

I shook my head. "Haven't met the woman."

"Want me to talk to her?" Tina said.

I looked over at Henri. He shrugged.

"You know her pretty well?"

"Yeah, pretty well."

"Keep it simple," I said, and outlined a few things Kate Hubbell needed to know before she arrived in Petoskey for the book tour. "Tell her stay alert, vary her commuting routine."

"Okay," Tina said.

"Once the tour starts," I said, "you'll be with Lenny most of the time, right?"

"Like glue," Tina said. "My job's to run interference for him, when I'm not selling books."

"Back to the documents," I said. "Your attorney has them, right? Where have you hidden them?"

"In plain sight," he said. "My attorney's around the corner at Jagger-Stovall. Know the firm?"

Before I could respond, the door opened and in walked Charles Bigelow. He didn't look happy. Lot of that going around.

8

"Someone should have told me about this meeting," Bigelow said. He was dressed in a well-fitted dark gray two-piece suit over a white shirt and solid yellow tie. His eyes were narrow and gloomy.

"You weren't invited," I said.

Bigelow straightened his frame. A power stance, no doubt.

"If you meet with my author, I'm invited. Is that clear, Mr. Russo?"

Be nice if this guy went back to Chicago, and soon.

He did a subtle double-take in Henri's direction.

"And who might you be, sir?" Bigelow said to Henri. The "sir" came out as anything but respectful.

"Henri LaCroix," I said, "meet Charles Bigelow, from Gloucester Publishing Company."

"Morning," Henri said.

"What business do you have here?" Bigelow said.

"The man keeps me alive," Lenny said before Henri could respond. "He's got a real big gun. Show it to him, Henri." Lenny muffled a laugh. He'd slipped from grumpy to stand-up comic at the first sign of a straight man.

"That will hardly be necessary," Bigelow said, and pulled out a chair. "Would one of you care to fill me in?"

Henri stared straight ahead, Tina looked at her half-empty coffee mug.

I glanced at Lenny, wondering if he wanted to chime in again. He shrugged.

"We were discussing keeping your client alive," I said.

"He means me," Lenny said, not quite smiling.

"How do you propose to do that?" Bigelow said, ignoring Lenny.

"Our job is to keep Lenny alive," I said. "We'll take care of it."

"Everything regarding my author and my book is my concern," Bigelow said. "You would do well to remember that."

"Hard for them to forget," Lenny said, but he wasn't laughing.

"Mr. Bigelow," I said, "you know about publishing books, we know how to protect people. It's what we do." I thought that sounded pretty reasonable.

"I am paying the bill for this," he said, and waved his arm over the table so as not to miss any of us.

"All right, it goes something like this," I said. "If Lenny's at home or at the office, particularly the office, he's safe. If he's anywhere else, one of us…" I pointed at myself, then at Henri, "… will be with him all the time."

"All generalities, with nothing to tell me how you plan to responsibly protect him," Bigelow said.

"For god's sake, Bigelow." It was Lenny. "Give it a rest. Let the man do his job."

I reached over and put my hand on Lenny's arm.

"Look," I said, "you could explain publishing books, marketing books. I'd get what you tell me, doesn't mean I'd understand your business. We'll keep Lenny safe because this is our business." I gestured across the table. "And Tina, we'll keep her safe, too."

"Tina?" Bigelow said, obviously caught off guard. "Is she…" he looked over at Tina. "Have you been threatened?"

"No," she said, "not like Lenny."

"But she's here, and she's with Lenny," I said, "so we assume she's in some level of danger because of that."

"You'll watch her, too?"

I nodded. "Of course."

"They think Kate might be in trouble, too, Charles," Tina said.

Bigelow's eyes widened. His mouth opened, and he sat back in his chair.

"Kate? Her, too?"

The wind had just been punched out of the man's sails. He crossed his legs, smoothed the crease in his elegantly tailored slacks, and shook his head slowly.

"I ... I hadn't thought about that."

I guessed the reality that he was in the middle of a dangerous drama had finally caught up with him. It didn't settle in easily.

Bigelow looked up, first at Tina Lawson, then Lenny Stern.

"I'm sorry," he said. "It never occurred to me that you might ... that your lives ... because of a book contract."

Tina smiled without enthusiasm. "Me either, Charles."

"Something like this isn't predictable," I said.

"But what are we going to do about it?" Bigelow said.

"You're already doing it, Mr. Bigelow," I said. "You hired us."

I'd just given him more credit than he deserved, but no point jumping on the man when he was trying to get his feet back on the ground.

"Lenny," Bigelow said, "did you know this would happen?"

Lenny sat forward and put his elbows on the table. "I didn't know, not for sure anyway. I've been a crime reporter for a long time." He shrugged. "If it makes you feel any better, it never occurred to me my book would put anyone's life in danger."

"It doesn't make me feel any better," Bigelow said, shaking his head. "Does all this, the emails, the punks who roughed you up, does this scare you?"

Lenny thought for a minute. "Yes and no," he said. "All my years on the streets, with the cops, got me used to a certain level of violence. But I can't just ignore what's happening. Somebody has it in for me — for real."

Bigelow looked over at me. "Am I in danger, Mr. Russo?"

"Hard to tell," I said, "but your name's not out there like Lenny's. And Tina's name shows up in the publicity for the tour."

"Let me ask you something," Bigelow said. "Am I in more danger here or in Chicago?" He put his hand up, traffic cop-like, before anyone could answer.

"I didn't mean that like it sounds. If I'm here with Lenny and Tina on the tour…" he glanced at Henri and me, "I assume you'll have to guard me, too. Is that true, Mr. Russo?"

That was the sharpest thing this guy's said about the whole case. He's thinking, at least.

I nodded slowly.

"I also assume that we'll all be in danger when we're in Chicago. Is that correct?"

"Lot of Mafiosi in the Windy City."

"But if I'm not here, on the tour, I mean, is your job easier?"

"Simpler, maybe," I said. "One less person to cover. How much time did you plan to spend on tour?"

"The first night at the Carnegie," Bigelow said. "I want to be here for that. We hadn't discussed the rest of the tour. I don't have to go, but I'll host the events in Chicago. Chicago should be okay."

"Why okay?" I said.

"Well, Gloucester has security services on call. They're scheduled to be at the Chicago finale anyway. They could protect us."

Bigelow paused. He was still thinking.

"So to be clear, Mr. Russo, if I'm not here, your job is less complicated."

I nodded. Maybe there was more to this guy than I'd given him credit for.

"Then it's done. I'll attend the Carnegie event and go home."

"I'll keep you up to speed, Charles," Tina said. "Texts, photos, whatever you need."

"You'll alert your security people?" I said.

"It'll be the first thing I do," he said, "as soon as I leave here."

"I'll need contact information for the security service," I said.

"I've got it," Tina said.

"It's settled then," said Bigelow as he stood up. "Well, I have work to do before I leave."

"What time's your plane?" Tina asked.

"Two-twenty."

"You flying out of Traverse City?" I said.

"Yes."

"Short turnaround for the Carnegie event," I said.

"Such is publishing."

"How are you getting to the airport?"

"Rented a car," Bigelow said. He glanced around the room. "Do you see a problem?"

"Any stops on the way?"

"No. My bag's in Maury's office. We plan to have lunch before I leave for the airport."

"Text Tina when you board the plane."

"I will."

Bigelow backed up two steps, as if unsure of what to do next. He wasn't behaving at all like the arrogant man I'd met in Maury Weston's office.

"Good-bye, then," Bigelow said, and left the conference room.

"I almost feel sorry for the guy," Henri said.

"I don't think he understood … really got what's going on," I said.

"Charles lives the business," Tina said. "It's his whole world, publishing, his life. It's all about marketing books. You just cracked his world a hard one, Michael."

"Did he read the threats, the emails?"

"I gave him the file," Tina said, "same one you have. Maybe he didn't read it."

"Or maybe the threats were only important for selling books," Henri said.

"Not anymore," Tina said.

"All right," I said, "let's wrap this up."

"About time," Lenny said, and stood up. "I'm on deadline."

"I'll be out front when you're done tonight," Henri said. "What time?"

"How about I call you?"

"Not a chance. What time?"

"Five-thirty, quarter to six," Lenny said. "Since you insist."

"I'll be waiting," Henri said, smiling.

We ended the meeting and exited the newspaper offices into the summer sun. We crossed the street to Lenny's SUV. The surface of the truck was hot to the touch.

"I'm surprised by all this hot weather," Henri said.

"I thought it didn't bother you."

"It doesn't, not after Iraq and Afghanistan. I'm just surprised, that's all. A heat wave in northern Michigan?"

"Yeah," I said. "Where you headed?"

"Picking up Margo in a while."

Margo Harris, a smart, beautiful and savvy professor of English at Bannister College, just north of town. She and Henri had been "an item," as Sandy called them, for a couple of years.

"You two have any plans?"

"We'll grab a sandwich somewhere," he said, "probably Cormack's Deli. After Lenny's done at work. Why? You have something in mind?"

"Not really, but I can't get the Carnegie out of my mind. Something AJ said."

"And that was?"

"She asked how would we know if a gunman, or woman, was already in the audience, you know, before we arrived with Lenny."

"You got an idea about that?"

"No. We're not even sure what the threat will look like."

"Hold on a minute," Henri said before opening the SUV's door, starting the motor and switching on the air. We climbed in and closed the doors. The outside temperature on the screen read 94 degrees.

"How about this? One of us keeps Lenny company, the other arrives at the Carnegie ahead of time."

I thought for a minute.

"We have to alert the library staff what we're up to," I said.

"They need to know," Henri said. "Besides, we need their cooperation." "Maybe they can keep the doors locked until we get there," I said.

"Or one of us can show up when they open the library?"

"That's a place to start," I said. "I'll call over there, see what they have to say."

"Want me to drop you at the office," Henri said, "or do you want to walk?"

I laughed. "Always rather walk, but today, I'll accept your offer. To the office."

'd spent some time at my desk catching up on calls, answering emails and occasionally staring out the window.

Sandy stuck her head in the door.

"Remember Pam Wiecek?"

"Sure, why?"

"She answered the phone at the library. Line one, boss."

I picked up the office phone. "Pam, hello."

"Mr. Russo," Wiecek said. "This is a nice surprise. It's been a while."

"At least a couple of years," I said, and explained why I'd called.

"You'd best talk to our director about Mr. Stern's event," she said. "Her name's Andrea McHale. Want me to check her schedule?"

"Please."

"Hold on, Mr. Russo, I have it right here…she'll be in tomorrow morning. About ten. Want me to leave her a note that you'll stop by?"

I told Wiecek to do that, thanked her and said good-bye.

By the time I shuffled some more papers it was almost five. The July sun wasn't going away anytime soon. But I needed to get out of there.

"I know what you're thinking, boss," Sandy said from the doorway.

"You do?"

"You want to go run. I can tell, I've seen that look before. It's ninety-three, ninety-four, boss; run tomorrow morning before work."

I turned my chair toward the window. "Good breeze off the water. Cool things off a bit."

"Then take a walk down by the bay. Feel the breeze off the water," she said, and laughed. "Just don't do anything stupid."

"Yes, mother."

I left the office and made my way through the parking lot, crossed U.S. 31, and went into the small park at the water's edge. I found a spot under a large elm tree and sat down in the shade.

Not as much of a breeze as I'd hoped for. Still, I stretched my legs out, leaned back against the tree and watched a group of teens trying to manhandle two kayaks off a trailer.

I wasn't aware how long I'd watched people playing in the summer heat when my phone buzzed.

"Hey, Henri, what's up?"

"Lenny ditched me. The son-of-a-bitch cut out on me. He's got a half hour head start."

"Where are you?"

"Out front of the newspaper."

"You checked inside?"

"Yeah, he's gone."

"Anybody there know where he went?"

"Woman at the desk said he waved good-bye on the way out. That's all."

I told Henri where I was. "Come pick me up. I'll make a couple of calls."

I tapped Lenny's line, but it went to voicemail after two rings. His inbox was either full or he was dodging calls. I tapped AJ's phone.

"Wow," she said. "Another call. I really feel important."

I told her about Lenny.

Silence.

"AJ?"

"Do you think something happened, or did he skip out on Henri?"

"Don't know," I said, "but I bet he just took off."

"But we have to know."

"Yeah. The Side Door still his favorite hangout?"

"As far as I know. There's another place some of the crew talks about. Mitchell Street Pub, maybe. I'll find out."

I saw Henri's SUV pull into a parking space.

"Henri's here," I said. "Let me know."

I tapped Lenny's number again. Voicemail.

"You try his phone?" Henri said.

"Uh-huh." I shook my head.

"He's fucking with us," Henri said. "Seeing how far he can push before we push back."

"That your instincts talking, or your head?"

Henri ignored my question. "Assuming I'm right, where would he go?"

"AJ says the Side Door's his favorite hangout."

"Would he be that obvious? His favorite bar?"

"If he's messing with us, he wouldn't care," I said.

"What are we waiting here for? Let's go."

Henri pulled out of the lot and went to Bay Street. He avoided the chaos of the shopping district as best he could, taking side streets lined with bungalows, Cape Cods and the occasional McMansion.

Henri cut it close for the stoplight at the plaza on 31 and swung into the parking lot for the Side Door Saloon.

We walked through the front door and not-so-gently pushed our way through the waiting area, which was clogging with tourists as the early dinner hour closed in.

The main room of the Side Door was a large rectangle with a few dividers to break up the space for tables. The walls were filled with memorabilia and sports bar-sized TVs. A long bar wrapped around one side of the room near the kitchen.

Lenny Stern sat on a stool at the far end of the bar. He had a beer in front of him.

"I'll go to Lenny," I said, "cover us from the other side."

Henri unzipped the nylon windbreaker that hid his shoulder holster and walked casually across the room, smiling, as if he were about to meet friends. I went around the bar and took the empty stool next to Lenny.

He glanced at me. "Hiya, Russo. What took you so long?" he said, and drank some beer.

"You think this is funny?"

He nodded. "A little bit. You want a beer?"

Henri sat at a two-top about twenty feet away. He already had a beer in hand. When I looked over, he shrugged. He hadn't spotted any trouble yet.

"Come on, Russo," Lenny said, "have a beer. It's on me. Zack, hey, Zack," Lenny shouted at the bartender over the din of the crowd. "A draft for my friend, here."

"You have to take this seriously, Lenny. Remember the threats?"

He waved me off. "I do take it seriously, but I've been threatened before. Remember me saying that?"

"Yeah, I remember," I said, "but this is now, Lenny. It's our job to keep you alive."

"Our job? Right. Where is my shadow?"

"Small table on the wall," I said, and Lenny glanced in Henri's direction.

"I know what your job is, Russo, but I know half the people in this room."

"It's the other half I'm worried about."

Bartender Zack put a tall glass with foam on top in front of me. He was in his mid-thirties, with olive skin, a shaved head and the friendly grin of everyone's most trusted listener.

"Zack," Lenny said, "you know the people here tonight?"

The bartender looked down the bar.

"Folks at the bar, all regulars," he said with a wave of the hand. "The after-work crowd." He looked out at the room. "Tables are mostly summer people. They don't like jamming elbows with strangers."

I took a drink as Zack went down the bar.

"We need to get a few things clear, Lenny. About how this is supposed to go."

"Yeah, yeah, I hear you, Russo. But I need some flexibility to move around, to do my job."

"Are you working right now?" I said. "Are you doing your job in here?"

"How about one more?" Lenny said. "Get Henri over here, we'll figure out how to keep me alive over another beer. How's that sound?"

"Finish your beer, Lenny. It's time to go."

I waved discreetly at Henri, who drained the last of his beer and walked over.

"Hiya, Henri," Lenny said.

Henri moved closer to Lenny, giving him little room to move. He put his hands on his hips.

"That was a bullshit move, Lenny."

"Where was I gonna go you wouldn't track me down?" Lenny said.

"Yeah, I'd track you down," Henri said. "Dead or alive is the question."

I took the beer from Lenny's hand, put the bottle on the bar.

"You're finished," I said. "Let's get out of here."

Lenny started to protest, but Henri grabbed him by the arm and led him to the door before he could say a word. He moved Lenny through the hungry people crowded around the entrance. I dropped a couple of twenties on the bar and followed them.

"Where's your car?" I said once we were outdoors.

"Other side of the handicap spots."

"Walk," Henri said, "in front of us."

Lenny did as he was told, not that he had much room to argue. He stopped at a maroon Honda Accord. I stayed with Lenny, but Henri moved away from us toward the front of the car. He leaned back against the fender, getting a good view of the parking lot.

"In a minute," I said, "we're taking you home. I'll ride with you." I looked over at Henri. "Anything?"

He came around the car and walked up to us. "Not sure. Over there, the beater Chevy, faded red. See it?"

I glanced casually in the direction of the Chevy.

"Two heads in the car," Henri said. "Spot them?"

"Barely," I said. "What are you thinking?"

"Just being careful."

"All right, Lenny," I said, "let's go."

Before he moved a step, I heard the noxious sound of a motor in need of a new muffler roaring to life. We looked up.

The Chevy came out of its parking spot in a big hurry. It moved fast our way, slamming on its brakes in a flurry of smoke and screeching tires a few inches from where we stood.

I pushed Lenny behind me. Henri dropped behind the Accord and drew his gun.

The driver pushed his arm out the side window and gave us his middle finger.

"You're dead, you piece of shit," he yelled as he hit the gas and went for the street.

10

Henri came around the front of Lenny's Accord, holstered his gun and walked a few steps away to get a better look. He scanned the parking lot, moving between a few parked cars, just to be sure there was no ambush vehicle waiting to catch us off guard.

"Clear," he said, but his eyes kept moving.

I turned to Lenny. "You convinced now?"

Lenny stood staring at the street, but remained silent.

"Well if he isn't," Henri said, "he ought to be."

Lenny stuffed his hands into his pants pockets and leaned back against the car. He looked at me.

"When I told you I'd been threatened before, by really nasty guys, that was true. More than once over the years."

Lenny cleared his throat.

"One night, somewhere west of the Loop, I was chasing a story. Another mob killing. I'd written several pieces for the *Tribune* with names ... politicians, local mobsters. Chicago PD loved it. Brought a lot of rats out of the sewer. But a lot of other people were pissed."

He cleared his throat again. "They caught me in an alley one night. Two of them. This wise guy stuck a .45 right here ..." Lenny put an index finger between his eyes. "Backed me up against a wall. I held my breath, waiting for it, one hand going for the .38 I used to carry."

Lenny paused, his face frozen, eyes full of remembrance.

"The crack of a gun ... so loud in that alley ... one shot to the side of the head. Somebody put the wise guy went down. His buddy ran."

"Cops?" I said.

"Yep," Lenny said, nodding. "Undercover. They knew me from the street, knew my writing."

Lenny came off the car. He took his hands from the pockets and ran them over the top of his head like he was smoothing hair he didn't have.

"I've never forgotten that night," Lenny said. "Everything's measured by what happened that night. Today, we get a couple of kids in a car?" Lenny stretched his arm out, pointing to the street. "Emmet County is not Cook County, never will be."

I started to say something, but he stopped me.

"I'm convinced, Russo, all right?" He turned to Henri. "You hear me, Henri? I'll do what you tell me from now on."

"No arguments?"

"No arguments," Lenny said. "This may not be Chicago, but that kid could have stuck a gun out the window. You guys got your ass on the line for me. Doesn't matter if I like it. No, Henri, no arguments."

We stood there, next to Lenny's Honda, in the late afternoon sun. A small black SUV pulled into the lot and parked across from us. We watched. The doors opened. Out came a woman and a man in their sixties, wearing shorts and T-shirts, both with gray hair. They grabbed each other's hand like a couple of teenagers and disappeared happily into the Side Door Saloon.

"Did you recognize the men in the car?" Henri said to Lenny.

"It all happened so fast," Lenny said. "They were young and white, at least the driver was."

"Both white, both young," I said. "Twenty, twenty-one, maybe. I might recognize the driver, not the other one."

"I think I'd know the driver, too," Henri said. "And I caught something else. A tattoo."

"You were looking at a tatt?" Lenny said.

"I was looking for a gun," Henri said, "when the driver's arm came out the window. It was here ..." He tapped his arm just above the wrist. "The number '44' inside a circle."

"Think that means anything?" Lenny said.

Henri shrugged. "Could be gang-related, could be nothing, but it's worth remembering."

"Kid had a narrow face," I said, "close-cut hair."

"The driver?" Henri said.

"Uh-huh. The other one was white. That's all I can tell you."

Two sedans entered the parking lot, drove slowly past us.

"Tourists," I said. "But it's too busy here. Time to go."

"How do you want to do this?" Henri said.

"I'll ride with Lenny," I said. "You follow."

"Do you think that's necessary?" Lenny said. "Two of you? I'm not arguing. Just asking."

"It is today," I said. "You still live in the house over on Jackson?"

"Same place, Russo," Lenny said. "I don't like buying houses."

"Know where we're going?" I said to Henri.

He nodded. "Across the highway from the hospital?"

"That's it," Lenny said.

I climbed into the Accord with Lenny, and we left the Side Door parking lot with Henri close behind. We talked very little on the way. Now that Lenny had agreed to let Henri call the shots, there was nothing to argue about. Lenny mostly grumbled about the heavy summer traffic.

"You going through Bay View?" I said when Lenny turned off the highway.

"Shortcut," he said. "I do this all the time."

"If you say so."

We meandered our way past the colorful Victorian cottages of the Bay View Association. I've been up and down these crowded streets for years, but always as a runner. Given the constant snarl of cars, delivery vans and construction vehicles, I moved faster on my feet.

Lenny turned away from the commercial area. The streets quickly turned residential. Most of the clapboard-sided houses were built in the 1930s, some single floor, some two floors. The yards were small, no wider than the house and driveway.

Lenny's place on Jackson was a square two-story with weathered tan paint in need of freshening up, brown shutters and a one-car garage at the back of the lot.

Lenny turned into his driveway and stopped, but Henri went past us, turned around, and parked a safe distance down the street.

"You're not going to walk me to the door, are you?"

I shot him a look.

"Just trying to lighten the mood, Russo. I'll do what you want."

"We go to the door together, but I go in first and check the house. Got it?"

"Like I said, no arguments."

We exited the Honda, and I watched the street while we walked to the front door. I took my gun out and held it close to my side.

"Unlock the door and wait here."

The house was small, with a living room in front, the dining room and kitchen in back. I toured those rooms, then climbed the stairs to the second floor. Two small bedrooms and a bath didn't take long to search.

"All set, Lenny."

"Okay."

"Probably a good idea to keep a sense of humor, Lenny. You might need it before we're through. You ready for the Carnegie?"

"If you mean am I ready for my presentation..." Lenny shrugged. "Sure, I've talked to audiences before, I like doing it. If you mean am I ready to be a target because the public can come and go, how are you ever ready for that? That's stressful even here in calm, relaxed Petoskey."

"We'll do our best to keep it calm."

"Is seven-thirty in the morning good for Henri?" Lenny said.

"It will be," I said. "I'll tell him."

Henri's SUV was now in front of the house. I never took my eyes off the street as I walked across the parched brown grass and climbed in the passenger side.

"Everything okay?" Henri said.

"Yeah. He's in for the night."

Henri pulled away from Stern's house. He turned on 31, and we rode in the welcome cool of his SUV to retrieve my car at the Side Door Saloon.

"You think the struggle with Lenny is over?" he asked me.

"I do. We've seen this movie before. Lenny's not the first guy we've protected who takes a while to understand the situation. Maybe they get scared, maybe not, but no matter, they finally do what we tell them to do."

Henri stayed on 31 around downtown. Traffic was thick everywhere, but we were in no hurry.

"Same question to you," I said. "Think Lenny'll give us any more trouble?"

"He's good. Besides, he doesn't scare easily."

"Which is why it took him a while to catch on."

"And he's seen worse," Henri said.

We rode patiently in the single line of vehicles along the bottom of Little Traverse Bay.

"It's just … I don't know, Russo. It's just … something bothers me."

"About Lenny?"

"Not Lenny," Henri said as the road widened to two lanes. He edged his way into the right lane as we passed the Country Club and turned into the Side Door parking lot.

"The end of this row," I said, pointing straight ahead.

Henri pulled up behind my car.

"Then what's bothering you?"

"This afternoon, here, in the parking lot."

"The two guys in the Chevy?"

"They were two young guys," Henri said.

"Barely out of their teens," I said. "Still think you can ID one of them?"

"I'll know the driver, I see him again," Henri said. "That's not it."

Henri paused, and I waited. The hum of the A/C fan droned on pleasantly inside the SUV.

"Remember when Lenny told us he'd been attacked?"

"Finally got around to telling us, you mean."

"Yeah, yeah. Forget that. But what did he say?"

I thought for a minute. "That he got beat up, a couple of guys roughed him up. What about it?"

"What else, about the guys?"

"He said they were young punks, I think."

"And today," Henri said, "in this parking lot, a couple of young punks shout 'you're dead.'"

"You think they're the same guys?"

Henri shook his head. "Nah, Lenny said he'd remember who attacked him."

"What's on your mind, Henri?"

"Four kids have come at our favorite reporter."

"Okay."

He looked over at me. "When's the last time the mob hired teenagers to do their dirty work?"

11

"Let me see if I have this right," Sandy said from her usual chair in my office. I was already on my second bottle of water after an easy, early morning run. The temperature dropped overnight, but the humidity hadn't gotten the memo.

"Have what right?" Henri said, his face hidden behind my copy of the *Times.*

"That the guys who threatened Lenny walked out of a Hallmark movie instead of *The Godfather.* Why does every tough guy have to look like Luca Brasi?"

Henri put down the newspaper. "Only the ones who work for Joey DeMio."

"I think you two distinguished gentlemen might have missed something, god forbid."

"You think she's talking about us, Russo?"

Sandy rolled her eyes. "All I'm saying is that maybe good help is hard to find, even for Joey DeMio. Maybe all the tough guys these days don't fit the mobster stereotype."

"Joey and his father," Henri said, "have relied on Santino Cicci and Gino Rosato to rough up people and deliver threats."

"Then along comes Don Harper," Sandy said.

"Good point," I said. "DeMio's new lawyer is Ivy League, top to bottom with a wardrobe to match. He delivers the threats these days."

"But Cicci and Rosato still do the killing," Henri said. "Those two kids in the parking lot, however tough they think they are, they're not killers. It doesn't fit."

"Maybe Joey DeMio didn't hire them to be killers," I said.

"Then what did he hire them for?" Henri said.

"Maybe he didn't hire them at all," Sandy said.

"Not the first time you've wondered that," I said.

She shrugged. "Maybe it's time to rethink what we're doing here."

I checked the time on the monitor. "Well, you two keep right on rethinking if you want, but I've got to go. Can't be late, since I'm about to throw a scare into the nice folks at the library."

The Petoskey District Library consisted of two buildings. The historic Carnegie was reserved for special events. On the other side of East Mitchell sat the new Petoskey Library, a two-story Georgian colonial, all red brick and white trim with a stately copper-topped cupola.

I went through the front doors into the main room, stopping at the circulation desk.

"Mr. Russo."

I turned around as Pam Wiecek crossed the large, airy room in long strides with a bright smile and an outstretched arm. She was five-six, a little thinner than the last time I saw her, wearing a pale green cardigan sweater over her shoulders as defense against the air conditioning.

"Hello, Pam," I said. We shook hands, and she leaned in and kissed my cheek.

"It's good to see you," my former client said. "Has it been four or five years?"

"Something like that, yeah. How are you?"

She nodded. "Good, very good."

But her bright eyes and broad smile told me that.

"Well, you helped turn my life around," she said. "But you're here on business."

She took me by the arm. "The periodical room's down here."

We went around the corner, past the main doors and into a square room lined with newspapers and magazines. Tall, narrow windows, tinted against the sun, let plenty of natural light into the room.

A woman was standing over a long, rectangular table sifting through a stack of magazines.

"Andrea?" Pam said to the woman who turned out to be the library director.

Andrea McHale turned around. She looked to be in her late forties, with soft features, an earnest face, and sensible shoes. Like Pam, a cardigan sweater was draped over her shoulders, held in place by a small chain like my grandmother used to wear.

We shook hands.

"Thank you for making time," I said.

"We can sit here," McHale said as Pam left the room. We pulled out two chairs at a corner of the long table.

"I'm not sure how much Pam told you," I said.

"Well, she said you were a private investigator, and you have some security concerns about Mr. Stern's talk." Her head tilted slightly as "security concerns" came out of her mouth.

I nodded. "All true."

"If you could explain ..." she said, her voice trailing off.

I did explain. About Lenny, the threats, about Henri and me.

"I see," McHale said, but she was still absorbing the news. "I suppose you have an idea ..." she paused. "First, I have to ask. Do you think something violent will happen at the Carnegie, Mr. Russo?"

I chose my words carefully. McHale had a right to know if her library and its people were in danger. But I didn't want to overstate it.

"There's a possibility that someone may try to harm Lenny," I said. "We're here to keep that from happening."

"Of course, you are," she said, but she didn't look convinced.

"Honestly," I said, "trouble is less likely to happen at the Carnegie than someplace else."

"Why do you say that?"

"It's simple, really. Too many people will be at the library that night."

"You mean, too many witnesses?"

McHale had seen the requisite number of *Law & Order* episodes. But I welcomed all the help I could get.

"Too many witnesses, sure. But these people only want Lenny, nobody else."

McHale nodded. "If these hoodlums hurt other people or damage the library, the community will demand they be brought to justice."

McHale had also read her police procedurals.

I nodded. "But Lenny Stern's an easier target, more vulnerable, out in the open, a car, on the street. It's harder to get at him inside a building with lots of people around."

McHale pondered that for a moment.

"How can I help, Mr. Russo?"

I leaned in, elbows on the table.

"Tell me about access to Lenny's presentation in the rotunda. Who comes and goes, and when?"

"We've issued tickets for that," she said. "Business and community VIPs, benefactors of the library."

"Will they use all the tickets?"

McHale shook her head. "Some people just don't come, some give them away." She stopped in mid-sentence. "Oh, I think I see. Tickets might get into the hands of the hoodlums?"

I nodded. "Nothing we can do about that. What time do you open the doors?"

"An hour before the official start time," she said.

"Is it all right with you if I show up when you unlock the doors, just take a look, hang around the door, watch people drift in?"

"Of course. What about Mr. Stern?"

"My associate will come with Lenny," I said. "When do you want him here?"

"We've already talked to him about the schedule."

"What happens after Lenny's finished?"

"Well," she said, "a few members of the audience will buttonhole him to talk." She smiled. "But that gives us a chance to clear the chairs and set up for Mr. Stern's book signing."

"You have a regular procedure for that, I suppose?"

McHale nodded. "The signing table will be at one end of the rotunda. We'll put another table, with books and a cash register on it, between the doors and Mr. Stern's table."

"Two hours to sign books?"

"Give or take a few minutes, yes. A little more than four hours start-to-finish for the evening."

I sat back in my chair.

"I think that about covers it," I said. "Will you be there?"

"Of course," she said. "Mr. Stern is a big event for the library. The attention helps with fund raising, future events, and so forth."

We stood up and shook hands.

"I heard a story that this building used to be the phone company. Anything to that?"

She nodded. "Michigan Bell Telephone Company. Back in the days when phones had wires instead of satellites."

I smiled. "Thank you, again, for making time."

"Glad to help."

"See you soon," I said, and turned to leave.

"Mr. Russo?"

I looked back at Andrea McHale. She started to say something, then paused. I knew what was on her mind, but instead she said, "Stay cool in all this heat."

12

Outside, the heatwave continued on its merry way: hot sun, heavy air, not a hint of rain. I entered the office, but Sandy wasn't at her desk.

"She left early."

It was Henri in my office. He had maneuvered my desk chair so he could put his feet on the window ledge and keep an eye on the cool blue waters of Little Traverse Bay. AJ sat in a client chair, her feet on the corner of my desk.

I took the other client chair. "Say where she was going?"

"Something about you being a real hard ass, and she'd had enough."

We laughed.

"No, really, where'd she go?"

"Dentist appointment."

"What're you doing here?" I said to AJ.

"I just needed to get out of the office, clear my head."

Henri dropped his feet to the floor and scooted the chair behind my desk.

"Here, she left these," he said, handing me several sticky notes.

I sifted through the messages.

"Anything important?"

I looked up. "Do you really want to know?"

Henri smiled. "Just being polite. You talk to the library lady?"

"Let me make one call first," I said, reaching for the office phone.

Henri grinned. "Who we calling?"

"Maury Weston."

"Don't bother," AJ said. "He'll just tell you that Charles Bigelow arrives on the last plane tonight into Traverse City. Maury's meeting the plane. Bigelow's staying with him."

"What about Hubbell, the editor?"

"She's already here," AJ said. "Drove up yesterday."

"Wouldn't the boss pop for a plane ticket?" Henri said.

AJ laughed. "She's staying with her sister, on the other side of Alanson."

"Back to the library lady," Henri said.

"That would be Andrea McHale, the director."

"She worried?"

"Concerned in a business-like way," I said.

"Good to hear."

"This is a lot more serious for her than collecting book fines."

"I assume you want me to stick with Lenny," Henri said.

"Yeah, he's finally used to you telling him what to do. No point messing with a good thing. I'll meet McHale at the library before she opens the doors."

"I'll have Lenny there on time," Henri said. "What's happening with you newspaper types, AJ?"

"We haven't organized anything, if that's what you mean. We're just going to meet at the office and walk to the Carnegie." She looked at Henri, then me. "Why are you asking? Have there been new threats?"

"No," I said. "But I need to talk to Kate Hubbell."

"Tina explained the situation to her," AJ said. "She'll be out of town with her sister when she's not with us."

"We still have to meet her," Henri said.

"Of course," AJ said. "The least we can do is show her what the good guys look like."

"How about early tomorrow?" I said.

"Maury will arrange it," AJ said.

"Hold on a second," Henri said, looking at his phone. "Lenny's done with work. I told him we'd stop at the Side Door on the way home."

Henri said good-bye and left the office.

I reached over and touched AJ's left hand. "You hungry?"

She shrugged. "Not much. But I'll get soup, maybe a salad."

"Let's walk over to City Park Grill."

We went down the stairs and turned up Lake Street for the two-block walk to the restaurant. We crossed to the other side of Lake Street at Pennsylvania Park, next door to the City Park Grill.

Once inside, we asked for a table near the front windows. The Grill began life in the 1880s, serving men only. The long front room featured wood floors, tables scattered around the room, and a high tin ceiling. Along one wall was a heavy mahogany bar. Back in the 1920s when it was known as The Annex, a local resident named Ernest Hemingway often occupied a stool at one end of the bar where he dreamed up short story ideas.

We ordered two chardonnays and glanced at the menu.

"You want to stay at my apartment," I said, "or your house?"

AJ put down her glass. "Either one would be okay, but I'll take a rain check. Is that okay with you?"

"Of course. Still have that staff meeting in the morning?"

"Uh-huh. Not quite ready for it."

I leaned over and kissed AJ softly on the lips.

"I'm always disappointed when we can't fit in time together, but it's still okay."

"That's very sweet," she said.

"We've had too much time apart lately," I said.

"Maybe it'd be easier if we lived together."

"Where we live isn't the problem, AJ. We have busy, complicated lives."

AJ slowly nodded. "Yeah, I know." She picked up her glass. "Well, here's to the big day tomorrow. Are you happy the book tour will finally start?"

I touched her glass with mine. "Relieved is more like it. We needed a few days to get ready, but it felt like a long time coming."

13

I lingered in the shower, letting the hot water slowly melt into cold. It helped. So did a light run through Bay View. Sleep had come quickly, but it was a restless night of tossing, turning, and staring at the ceiling. Too much nervous energy.

I finished off eggs, toast and coffee, put the dishes in the dishwasher and left the building by the back stairs. It was already 73°, still humid, and the sun was hot on my skin.

"Morning, Sandy," I said when I arrived at the office.

"Good morning," she said. "Don't settle in, Maury Weston's expecting you. You didn't forget, did you?"

"I remembered, Sandy."

"Then get a move on, the gang's all there."

The sidewalks became less congested as I moved away from the Gaslight District. I turned up State Street and walked into the offices of the *Post Dispatch*.

"They're in the conference room, Mr. Russo," the receptionist said as I went by.

This was my third visit in recent days to the small, humorless space the newspaper people called a conference room.

"Michael," Maury Weston said. "Come on in."

Charles Bigelow was there, and Tina Lawson and Lenny Stern. Off to one side, leaning against a bookcase, was Henri LaCroix.

Standing next to Maury was a small, dark-haired woman with freckles across the bridge of her nose, wearing a J.Crew business casual outfit.

"I'd like you to meet Kate Hubbell," Maury said, "Lenny's editor from Chicago."

We shook hands. "Nice to meet you," I said.

Hubbell's face lit up with a soft smile. She was very much the young professional, eager to learn, always looking for the next opportunity.

"I've heard a lot about you, Mr. Russo," she said.

"Fake news," I said, "all of it. Please, call me Michael."

"Yes, Michael," she said, smiling. "Tina told me you're Big Ten."

"Michigan State," I said. "You, too?"

"Illinois. Creative writing." She gestured at Bigelow, who was off in a corner on his cell. "I had an internship at Gloucester my senior year. They liked what I did, and Charles hired me. That was four years ago."

"You like editing rather than writing?"

"Well," Kate said, "I've learned a lot, for sure, but … it's not like writing. The process, I mean."

"Would you rather be writing?"

Kate shook her head. "I'm still writing. I've got two short stories circulating. One might be published."

"That would be exciting."

"But I wouldn't trade my job," she said. "Besides, Lenny's book is my first solo edit."

"Congratulations," I said. "Lenny doesn't always play well with others."

She laughed. "Not a problem," she said. "I just tell him to shut up and listen."

I started to respond just as Maury Weston rapped lightly on the conference table.

"If I can interrupt your pleasant chitchat …" In his easygoing, low-key way, Maury went over plans for the Carnegie event.

"I realize this may sound unnecessary, all of us walking to the library together," Maury said, "but I'd like us to help Michael and Henri," he gestured in our direction, "any way we can. With Charles and Kate here, well, it's additional people for two men to watch."

I noticed Henri had a satisfied, if discreet, smile. I moved over next to him.

"Your idea, I take it?"

He nodded. "Went down like a piece of cake."

"You'll stick here until they're ready to walk over?"

"Easier that way. Listen, Bigelow mentioned taking the group out for a drink after."

"Sure," I said. "If everything goes okay, it'd be a nice way to celebrate Lenny's book, relax a little."

"I think so, too," Henri said.

"All right," I said, "I'm going to slip out of here, they're all busy anyway."

I left the conference room. I had no reason to suspect I was being followed, but I chose an odd route back to the office just in case. I walked at a leisurely pace, intentionally, down Mitchell.

I window shopped at Reid's Furniture and stopped again at Dittmar's Chronotech. I glanced occasionally behind me and across the street, but I wasn't being watched, let alone followed. I continued to the alley that runs behind the Lake Street stores, cut through Roast & Toast and went up the stairs.

"Hi, boss," Sandy said. "Is everyone on board over there?"

"Seems to be."

I fidgeted away the rest of the afternoon with calls, emails and scanning the new issue of *Runner's World*. I kept looking at the time — my watch, my phone, the monitor on the desk.

"Sure you won't change your mind and come to the Carnegie?"

"I'd just as soon not spend an hour in those uncomfortable chairs. Besides, I'm lucky. I can talk to Lenny anytime I want."

"Okay."

"You're taking your gun, right?" Sandy asked.

"Probably a good idea."

"You're not going to clip the holster to your belt, are you?"

"I'll take a jacket," I said. "The Carnegie's air conditioned. Nobody'll think anything."

I went over and took a dark green nylon jacket off the hall tree.

"Stay safe, boss."

The sidewalks of Lake Street were still busy, but with people reading menus for an early dinner. There was plenty of traffic, so I crossed at the stoplight and went over to Mitchell. Not as many shoppers as Lake Street, but several bars and restaurants helped make up the difference.

I made my way to the Carnegie Building on East Mitchell and waited for Andrea McHale. A few people milled around the front of the building, no doubt waiting to get a good seat. Near the main door sat a plaque honoring Bruce Catton, the Civil War historian and Petoskey native. I'd admired his work ever since I first read *A Stillness at Appomattox* years ago. He deserved the tribute.

"Mr. Russo."

I looked up and spotted the library director waving from the doorway.

"Hello, Ms. McHale."

"Come on. Get out of the heat."

I went through the side door, and she closed it behind us.

"We won't use the back entrance for Mr. Stern's talk," she said. "Just the front door."

"Admission tickets only, right?"

McHale nodded. "But once he starts signing books, both entrances will be open to the public. The parking lot is out there," she said, pointing to the rear door. "It's closer for our older folks, if you get what I mean."

"Got it," I said.

"This way," she said.

We entered the rotunda. It was set up much as I'd seen the room for the gardening writer. The podium was at the far end, by the windows, with chairs arranged in rows reaching back to the front door. I'd already picked the best spots for Henri and me to watch the doors.

McHale moved around the room, talking with staff members, then went over to unlock the front door. She clicked the latch and turned toward me.

"We're ready, Mr. Russo."

14

I watched people pass through the door, giving over their tickets and making a much bigger deal out of selecting seats than the event required. They were mostly older adults, the ones who likely read Lenny Stern in a paper copy of the *Post Dispatch* rather than the digital *PPD Wired*. Locals and tourists alike ambled into the rotunda, filling most of the seats.

After thirty-five minutes, I recognized two men who arrived together: Frank Marshall and Wardcliff Griswold.

Marshall, a retired investigator from Chicago, was an old friend, a mentor from my early days as a private eye. A touch over six feet tall, he was trim and fit, befitting an avid runner (despite having edged into his seventies). He was dressed in resort casual: a navy polo shirt, khaki shorts and a beat-up pair of running shoes.

Wardcliff Griswold was another matter. We tangled several years ago when I helped the police investigate a murder at ritzy Cherokee Point Resort, just north of Harbor Springs. Griswold, the self-important president of Cherokee Point, made it his business to hinder that investigation using every option shy of illegal. I didn't like him, he didn't like me. Fair enough, but Frank Marshall was his neighbor at the Lake Michigan resort, so I tried to be nice. Griswold frequently wore khaki pants with little green ducks all over them. He did the first time we met, and he did not disappoint tonight.

"Michael," Marshall said, coming up to me with a huge grin. We hugged.

"AJ and I were just talking about you, Frank," I said. "How are you?"

"Training for the Great Turtle half," he said, referring to the annual October thirteen-miler on Mackinac Island. "You remember Ward, don't you?"

"Certainly," I said, acting interested and polite as I reached out my hand.

"Mr. Russo," Griswold said, condescending to shake my hand as if I were there to park his Mercedes. "I shall secure two seats while you chat," he then said, turning away.

"Be right along, Ward," Frank said.

"Didn't think you two were friends," I said.

"Ah, Ward's okay. He just has an odd priority list, that's all."

"Are you a fan of Lenny Stern?"

"You bet," he said, smiling. "Chicago was my town, too, remember?"

We took a few moments to catch up, as old friends do when they haven't talked in a while. He started to walk away, but stopped.

"Michael," Marshall said, glancing from one side to the other. "You're working, aren't you?"

"Is it that obvious?"

He shook his head. "Not to the others, but it's all the years I did the same thing. I had a gut feeling."

He said good-bye again and went off to find Griswold.

"Was that Frank?" a familiar voice said.

I turned to see AJ and the crew from the newspaper come through the door.

"It was," I said. "Where's Lenny?"

"Outside talking to someone. Henri's with him."

I nodded, and said hello to the others.

"I want to catch Frank before the talk," AJ said as Henri and Lenny walked up. "See you after."

"Anybody look suspicious?" Lenny said.

I shook my head. "Not unless our assassin has gray hair and moves very slowly."

"That's a depressing thought."

"Hello, Mr. Stern," Andrea McHale said as she walked up.

I introduced McHale to Henri.

"Nice to meet you," she said. "This way, please, Mr. Stern. We have a full house."

"Duty calls," Lenny said with a grin and a quick salute of his right hand.

When McHale took the podium, Lenny stayed off to one side.

"Good evening, everyone," McHale said, and spent a few moments on a brief biography of the evening's guest, concluding with his introduction.

"Any changes to our plan for this little soiree?" Henri said.

"Nope."

Henri nodded, then circled around the rotunda and took up a position on the opposite side of the room. I stood on the sidewall across from him. We had a good view of the entire space, both doors, and of each other.

"Good evening," Lenny said from the podium. "I'm delighted that you're here tonight, that you've chosen to spend a glorious summer evening at the Carnegie Library.

"Tonight..." Lenny paused for effect, then raised his voice and said, "Murder, mayhem, and the Mafia in Chicago. What's not to like?" He spread his arms wide like he was about to give someone a big hug. He grinned broadly, his eyes sparkling.

Scattered applause broke out. There was an air of expectancy in the room.

This was a Lenny Stern I'd never seen before, in private or in public. Never heard him use "glorious" before. Never seen him so interested in talking to people who weren't criminals or the cops who chased them. My friend, the cantankerous crime reporter, was a charming public speaker. Of course, I'd never seen him perform — and that was the right word, in a setting like the Carnegie.

"It's essential to remember that this is a true story, with real people living corrupt, dangerous lives." Lenny was off and running, revealing gruesome details and taking us along for the ride.

"So you can just imagine, can you not," he said, "the reaction of the citizenry when two bodies washed up on a pristine beach at Grand Haven, Michigan."

The way Lenny told it, I was sure the rapt audience pictured every sordid detail.

Occasionally someone got out of a chair and walked past Henri toward the restrooms. My eyes followed when that happened. I'd glance at Henri, and he'd watch, too.

"So that's my tale of crime in the city of Chicago," Lenny said, and the crowd broke into a loud and sustained applause. He smiled and nodded. After a few moments he raised an arm, quieting them down.

"It's time for questions," he said, and several hands shot into the air.

"Yes, ma-am," Lenny said.

A head of fluffy gray hair rose in the front row. She was short enough so that's about all I saw, but I had no trouble hearing her.

"Mr. Stern," the woman said. "I lived in the Windy City for thirty-five years before I retired. I remember reading you in the *Tribune*, the trouble you got yourself into…" Lenny laughed at that one. "Aren't you frightened, writing a book like this, you know, with names… accusing politicians and mobsters of murder?"

There it was. The perfect start for the Q&A. There wasn't a sound in the room. They waited for Lenny's answer. Even I wanted to hear it.

"I made a decision," he said, "that some things are too important…"

Lenny spent almost thirty-five of his allotted fifteen minutes taking question after question, until Andrea McHale moved to the podium and politely drew this portion of the evening's event to a close.

"Give us a few minutes," she said, "to rearrange the room, and Mr. Stern will be delighted to sign copies of his book."

Staff people, who'd obviously done this before, took over. Most of the chairs went out, replaced by two tables and several cartons of books. A few people approached Lenny at the podium. Henri had already moved forward to be closer.

"Michael," AJ said when she came over, "did you know Lenny was that good?"

I shook my head. "Not a clue."

"I'm as surprised as you."

Maury Weston and Charles Bigelow were standing close to Lenny's table.

"Have you seen Tina or Kate?" I said.

"They told me they'd be right back." AJ chuckled.

"What?"

"I'm sure I heard the word 'cabernet' as they walked away."

Over the next hour, a steady stream of people came through the doors and stood in line at the table.

Two teenagers, one male and one female, both white, wearing jeans and T-shirts, entered through the side door, walking right past Henri. He caught my eye as he moved in behind them while they approached Lenny.

We'd been caught off guard by teens before, so I eased in closer.

The two huddled off to one side of the table, talking quietly. When they decided to get in line, Henri moved around behind Lenny to get a better look.

As the pair approached the table, Henri caught my eye and waved me off with a slight shake of his head. I nodded, returning to my spot next to AJ on the sidewall.

The teenagers turned from the table with their very own signed copy of *Corruption on Trial* and left by the side door, clutching each other and the book with equal vigor.

Frank Marshall and Wardcliff Griswold left the table, each with a book, and walked toward us. Frank stopped, but Griswold kept right on going, never glancing our way.

"Well, it was good to see both of you," Marshall said.

"You like Lenny's talk?" AJ said.

"Very much. I'm eager to read his book." Marshall glanced over his shoulder. "I have to catch up," he said, pointing at the front door.

With less than thirty minutes left, Henri and I remained in our positions, relieved that our services were unneeded. We were waiting to wrap up as Tina Lawson and Kate Hubbell entered the rotunda and went past Henri. They laughed quietly and found two unused chairs.

"You may have been right about going for wine," I said to AJ.

Andrea McHale edged her way over. "As soon as those folks leave, we'll be finished, and I'll lock the doors." She gave a casual wave to her people stationed at the doors.

"Well," AJ said, "it looks as if the tour's off to a quiet start."

I nodded. "Be nice if it stayed quiet."

With the visitors gone, the library staff removed the last reminders of the evening's event. Lenny came over to us to get out of their way.

"You can be quite the charmer," AJ said, smiling. "The audience loved you."

Lenny came as close as I'd ever seen him to an "ah, shucks" look on his face. But he rescued himself with a shrug.

"Told you I liked doing this," he said.

"Mr. Stern," Charles Bigelow said in a booming voice, and we turned as he walked up with Maury, Tina and Kate pulling up the rear.

"You were superb," Bigelow said. "I've seen plenty of book talks in my day. You were right up there with the best of them."

"Thank you," Lenny said.

"I can't wait for the wrap-up in Chicago," Bigelow said. "A real VIP group, that'll be. They'll be mightily impressed with Gloucester's newest star. Don't you think so, Maury?"

"Sure thing," Maury said. "Gloucester's newest star."

"All right," Bigelow said, with a loud clap of the hands. "It's time to mark the occasion. I have a table waiting at Chandler's. Food, drinks, whatever you want. Shall we go?"

Before anyone could answer, Bigelow made his way toward the back door of the Carnegie. We said our good-byes to Andrea McHale on the way out.

"I'm walking," Bigelow said in the parking lot behind the Arts Center. "You all know where Chandler's is?" He looked around. "You've been there, right, Tina?"

"Sure, Charles," Tina said. "But…"

"But what?"

"Kate and I thought we'd go back to City Park Grill," Tina said.

Kate gave a thumbs-up. "We have a couple of barstools all warmed up."

"Go, go," Bigelow said. "We'll see you in the morning."

The two women took off before Bigelow changed his mind.

"Where's your car?" I said to AJ.

"At the office," she said. "I'll get it later." She put her arm through mine. "Or maybe I'll say to hell with it and walk home with you."

"I vote for that."

15

"That was a wonderful idea, darling."

"Which one?" AJ said.

"Which one? To come back here last night."

"You're just saying that because I grabbed your ass as soon as we closed the door."

"Yeah," I said. "That's probably it."

We sat at the small table in my kitchen. It was early, the sun just up, the coffee hot and strong. AJ had put on jeans and a paint-stained sweatshirt that lived on a hook in my bedroom closet.

"I assume you have time to go home and get ready for work."

She shrugged. "I don't have to hurry. Maury will be busy with Bigelow all morning. Besides, those two had a few drinks last night."

I laughed. "After a couple of martinis, Charles Bigelow's a pretty funny guy."

"He actually smiled a few times."

"Was that before or after the martinis?" I said as I refilled our mugs with hot coffee.

"Both," she said. "I assume you're headed out to run? Unless those shorts and Spartan T-shirt count as private eye undercover this morning."

"Be a more relaxing run than yesterday. The Carnegie's done, Andrea McHale was excited about the packed house..."

"And Lenny's safe."

"He is indeed. So Bigelow and Hubbell go back to Chicago today, right?"

AJ nodded. "The rest of the tour belongs to Lenny."

"Don't forget me."

"I'd never forget you, darling," AJ said, "not as long as you wear those cute running shorts."

A phone buzzed. "That's mine," AJ said, looking around.

"It's next to the coffeemaker."

She picked it up and tapped the screen. "Little early, isn't it, Maury?" She paused.

"Where am I? At Michael's. You don't ask me where I spend my nights, Maury. What's going on?"

She listened for a moment.

"I need to go home and take a shower first ... okay ... okay ... he's right here. Yeah ... tell me what ..."

As AJ listened her shoulders sagged, her face looking strained.

"Dear god," she said. "We're on our way."

AJ ended the call and looked up. There were tears at the corners of her eyes.

"What?" I said.

"Kate Hubbell's dead. Police found her body a few hours ago."

"What happened?"

AJ shook her head. "Don't know. Maury wants us at the office right now."

"What about Lenny?"

"He's okay. Maury called Henri first."

I put the mugs in the sink, switched off the coffeemaker, and grabbed a pair of wind pants. We took my car. It was barely a five-minute trip without traffic. There were two patrol SUVs out in front of the *Post Dispatch* offices. I left the car at the curb, parked behind a familiar-looking unmarked sedan.

We went through the front door and up the stairs to Maury's office. His door was open.

"Come on in," Maury said when he saw us. He was talking with Charles Bigelow, who was perched on the corner of Maury's desk. Bigelow didn't acknowledge our arrival. Tina Lawson sat in a client chair, her head down, wiping her eyes with a tissue.

AJ sat in the chair next to Tina and took her hand. Tina looked up.

"Who ..." she started to cry. "Who would 'murder' ... *kill* her?"

AJ put her arms around Tina's shoulders.

Henri stood alone, leaning next to the tall windows at the side of the office. His face was without expression. I glanced his way, and he offered a subtle nod.

At one end of the rectangular conference table Lenny Stern sat talking with Martin Fleener, Captain of Detectives with the Michigan State Police. An experienced homicide detective, a legendary interrogator, Fleener was six feet tall with angular good looks and classy taste in clothes. He was the department's most experienced cop.

Fleener came over and shook hands.

"Marty," I said. "What do you know?"

"I want to hear what you have to say first, Russo." The captain, ever the professional, was seasoned enough to know that occasional humor or sarcasm eased the rigors of his job. But not this morning. Murder didn't happen very often in Petoskey, but when it did, Fleener and Emmet County prosecutor Donald Hendricks got testy because their jobs got harder. Murder disrupted a pleasant, quiet community. The City Council pointed fingers, the Chamber of Commerce worried tourists would stay away. Worse still, on this occasion, a woman we knew was dead.

"Have you interviewed everybody?" I said.

"Between Detective Javier and me, yeah. Except you and LaCroix over there."

"Then let's talk," I said.

"We've been using the conference room at the end of the hall," Fleener said, turning away. "You too, LaCroix. Let's go," he added without looking back.

"Stay here till I get back," Henri told Lenny.

The grizzled crime reporter nodded. He was clearly shaken.

Henri and I followed Fleener down the hall. I felt as though I'd spent more time lately in the *Post Dispatch* conference room than in my own office.

Fleener closed the door, and we took chairs at one end of the table.

"I heard you two were in charge of security," Fleener said, glaring at each of us. "How's that going?"

There was no good answer to that question, so I said, "What happened to Kate?"

"No, no," Fleener said. "You first, Russo. From the top."

I reprised the basics of our assignment, starting with the email threats and Charles Bigelow. I knew Fleener well enough. He'd interrupt if he had a question or thought I'd left something out, intentionally or otherwise.

"You have anything to add?" Fleener said to Henri.

Henri shook his head, slowly.

"So what happened?" I said.

"One shot, back of the head. Small caliber, probably a .22, but we'll wait for the report."

"Assassinated?" I said. "A book editor?"

"I assume it's tied to the Stern threats."

"I would, too," I said. "But she just arrived, so who would know she was here?"

"And that she was connected to Lenny and Gloucester Publishing."

"Someone's watching Stern," Fleener said. "In walks Kate Hubbell."

"Then you have to wonder, why kill her and not Lenny?"

"Who found her?" Henri said.

"Sheriff's deputies. Routine patrol, called it in."

"Then you got a call," I said.

"Usually the way it happens."

"Where was she found?" Henri said.

"West Conway Road. Behind a small warehouse." The area was a small industrial park just off US 31, north of town.

"Was she killed at the warehouse?" I said.

"Too early to tell," Fleener said. "But we didn't find a car at the scene."

"Somebody took her off the street?" I said. "After she and Tina Lawson split up?"

"Apparently," Fleener said. "Lawson left her at her car and walked back to the Perry. We checked, found the car parked at a meter on Lake Street. Had it towed in. We'll look it over."

"Okay if we talk to the others?"

Fleener nodded. "Be my guest."

"Was Tina Lawson the last one to see Kate alive?"

"As far as we know right now," Fleener said. "We're still working the area."

"Not much to go on."

"One more thing," Fleener said.

"What?"

"A four-foot length of line was tied around her neck."

"Strangled?" Henri said.

"That's just it," Fleener said. "No marks. It was tied loosely."

"If a bullet did the job, why the rope?" Henri said.

"Wouldn't be the first time the mob sent a message," I said.

"Yeah, but what's the message here?" Fleener said.

"The eyes see, the mouth talks," I said.

"That might fit if she was actually strangled," Fleener said.

I shook my head. "Makes no sense, Marty."

"Got to be a connection," Henri said. "Has to mean something, or why bother?"

"Could be the killer's trying to throw us off," I said.

"The mob's an in-your-face bunch," Fleener said. "It doesn't waste time on clever."

"Yeah, I get that. But Henri's right, Marty, it has to mean something."

"We'll have to think on it," Fleener said. "I'll put it in the system, see if it hits a match."

"Anything with the rope?" Henri said.

"It's a section of line, like they use on boats."

"Could have come from a dozen places around here."

"We'll check anyway," Fleener said.

"Any suspects?" I asked.

"Not yet," Fleener said. "We'll start with the threats to Stern. So who do you think's been threatening northern Michigan's favorite reporter?"

"You know about his book?"

"I do now," Fleener said.

"Chicago, murder, and the mob," I said. "The Baldini crime family's in the middle of the action. And we know who runs the family."

Fleener took in some air and let it out slowly. "Guess we start with Joey DeMio."

"He'd be my first choice," I said.

Fleener looked at his phone, swiped the screen.

"Have to get back to the office. What's the next stop on the book tour?"

"Harbor Springs, two days," I said.

"Okay," Fleener said. "Anything else?"

I shook my head.

"You'll give me a heads up, you think of anything, right?" Fleener said.

"You'll be the first to know," I said as the captain left the conference room.

"You held out on a couple of details," Henri said.

"That bother you?"

"Of course not," Henri said. "I figured you had your reasons."

"What would we have told him? Some teenager with a tattoo tried to scare us? He'd laugh. Let's find something solid before we take it to Fleener."

16

"What's next?" Henri said.

"Lenny and Tina. Let's talk to them first."

We returned to Maury's office. He sat at the small conference table with Lenny. No Bigelow, no AJ, no Tina.

"Where're the others?" I said.

"Charles went to pack," Maury said. "Tina and AJ went out front."

"You taking Bigelow to the airport?"

Maury shook his head. "Two of our people will do it in the company van."

I glanced at Lenny, who seemed to be staring off somewhere.

"You okay, Lenny?" I said.

He shrugged, but his face looked tired and drawn. Absent was the mischievous grin of the street-hardened veteran crime reporter.

"I want to catch Tina and AJ," I said. "Stay here 'til we get back, Lenny. Okay?"

"No argument from me."

We found Tina alone out front of the building. She sat on the steps in the sun, her knees pulled up, tissues clutched in her hand. Henri and I sat down with her.

"Hi," I said.

"Hi," Tina said. "AJ went home to get dressed for work."

"Feel like talking?"

"I've been talking since the cops woke me up this morning."

"I know. Just a few more minutes."

"Sure." She sounded too tired to argue.

"You and Kate walked off last night..."

Tina nodded. "City Park Grill."

"Tell me about it," I said.

"There's not much to tell," she said, shrugging her shoulders. "We sat down, drank some wine... Kate only had one glass, she had to drive to her sister's..."

Tina froze for a moment. "Oh, my god. Her sister. I should tell her."

"The police will do that, Tina," I said.

"But I..."

"The police have done this before, Tina. It'll be all right."

She stared across the street, like she'd spotted something interesting.

"They won't forget?"

"They won't forget. It's part of their job."

"Lousy job."

"Some days, yeah," I said.

"I guess that'll be okay."

"Do you know Kate's sister?"

"We only met once, but I still think..."

"You can call her later if you want."

Two uniformed officers left the building, walked to a patrol SUV and drove off. The three of us watched them intently, as if witnessing something quite important.

"Tina," Henri said, "did anything odd or strange happen at the restaurant?"

"Like what?"

"Anything. Anyone hit on you? Did you pick up anyone?"

Tina sat up straight. "I'm not sure that's..."

"Tina," I said. "We're not prying into your personal life, but we need to know about last night. That's why Henri asked. Somebody knew you and Kate were there."

She turned my way. "You think we were followed?"

"It wasn't a coincidence, Tina."

"But why Kate?" she demanded, the tears coming again. "Why not me?"

"I don't know."

"Tina." It was Henri. "Did you talk to anyone while you were there?"

She was quiet for a moment.

"There was one guy, kind of cute."

"Tell us."

Tina described the man — older, business dress, expensive haircut. Obviously not one of the tough-guy teenagers who tried to scare us in the parking lot.

"I had another glass of wine," she said. "I could walk."

"To the Perry?" Henri said.

Tina nodded. "I walked Kate to her car, it was across the street from the bar."

"Did you see her drive away?"

"The police asked me that, too … I didn't look back. Don't know why. I just … went to my hotel and climbed into bed."

"Until the police woke you up this morning?"

"Uh-huh."

We talked a while longer, took from Kate what we thought might help, which wasn't much.

"Henri's going to keep an eye on you," I said. "The hotel isn't the best place anymore."

"You haven't talked to AJ, have you?"

I shook my head. "No, why?"

"I'm staying with her as long as the book tour's in town."

"You are?"

She nodded. "We talked about it this morning. She said it would be okay with you."

"It's a great idea."

"I'll ride back and forth to the office with her."

"I'll take it from there," Henri said. "You're with Lenny and me most of the time anyway."

Tina gently rubbed her eyes.

"Is there anything else?" she said. "I need to talk with Charles before he leaves for Chicago."

"Not right now. Thanks," I said.

"Okay," she said, and went back inside.

Henri and I sat for a few minutes. The sun was almost too warm. We'd have to retreat into air conditioning sooner rather than later.

AJ's Explorer pulled up to the curb across the street. She got out and walked over.

"Have you seen Tina?"

"Inside. She'll be safer staying with you. Good idea."

"I thought so, too," AJ said in a matter-of-fact way, and entered the building.

"Okay," Henri said. "We've talked with Tina. Let's see what Lenny has to say."

We found him right where we left him, sitting in Maury's office.

"Maury had a meeting," Lenny said. "He said we could use his office."

Henri and I took seats at the table.

"I suppose you want my take on last night?"

I nodded. "Go ahead."

He shrugged. "I have no take on last night. Henri made sure I got home after we left Chandler's."

Henri nodded as Lenny talked.

"I locked the door, and that was that."

"Nothing?" I said. "No calls, nothing?"

He shook his head. "Until Henri called early, said he was on his way over. Told me to stay inside, away from the windows."

"I checked the yard when I got there," Henri said. "All clear. We drove two cars over here."

"I've been in the building all morning."

Lenny sat back in the chair and tugged on his right earlobe. "She was just a kid," he said, glancing at Henri first, then me. "She was smart,

I knew that first time we met. She knew how to handle the book, you know, the edits, the changes, all of it. She was just a kid. Why kill her?"

"Thought you might have an idea about that," I said, but Lenny seemed lost in the violence of the night.

"I know why they're pissed at me ... I nailed their asses, got the evidence to back it up. Why Kate? I wrote the goddamn book."

Lenny took a deep breath and let it out slowly. "Look, I'm on deadline. I'll be at my desk." He glanced at each of us. "Okay?"

"Sure," I said as Lenny eased himself out of the chair and left the room.

Henri and I sat quietly for a moment.

"What's next?" Henri said.

"Joey DeMio's next. Like Fleener said, we should start with the man himself."

"Fleener might not like it if you talk to him first."

"We ask different questions."

"Which means you don't care if Fleener likes it or not."

I shrugged.

"I'm not sure anymore," Henri said.

"If DeMio's behind this?"

"Yeah, but it's time we found out."

17

"**Y**ou think it's smart to go over there alone?" Henri said. He sat on the couch in my apartment, feet on the coffee table, hands clasped behind his head. I'd taken a shower, dressed in khakis, a short-sleeved shirt and beat-up Brooks running shoes.

"I'll go in easy," I said, taking a bite out of a large, red McIntosh apple. "Just to talk. See what Joey has to say."

"Okay, but Joey's not going to just say, 'Yeah, I killed Stern's editor.'"

"He won't have to. His reaction will tell me all I need to know."

"It's not his reaction I'm worried about," Henri said. "His gunmen, on the other hand ..."

I shook my head. "I'm not going to threaten the man, Henri. Said I'd go in easy. Ristorante Enzo's a public place, lots of people around."

I finished off the last of the apple. "First, I need to find out when Joey'll be there."

"He's at Enzo now," Henri said. "Table in the back corner of the room."

"Sure about that?"

Henri nodded. "Made a couple of calls while you were in the shower."

"Of course you did. He alone?"

Henri shook his head. "Not alone, but neither Rosato nor Cicci are there."

"He's without his favorite gunmen?"

"Hard to believe, isn't it," Henri said, looking disappointed. He'd been needling those two for years, and seldom passed up an opportunity.

"I don't get it," I said. "Joey doesn't move without cover. You don't suppose he's trying to go legit with this move to Petoskey?"

Henri laughed. "Joey's probably washing dirty money along with the dirty dishes."

"It wouldn't surprise me."

"You'll carry your .38?"

"No. Probably be searched. Better to do this clean."

"Don't know about you, Russo."

Henri paused. "When you going?"

"Don't see any point waiting. Sooner we rule Joey in, the better."

"Unless we rule him out," Henri said, dropping his feet to the floor. "Tell you what, give me ten minutes to put my car across the street."

I shook my head. "No need for that."

"Maybe not, but it's too late for a lunch crowd. The place could be empty."

"Except for Joey's people, you mean."

"Exactly," Henri said. "I'll sit in the car, watch you go in, hope you come out."

"That's encouraging."

"How 'bout I come to the rescue when the shooting starts?"

"I'd appreciate that," I said. "Well, get a move on."

Without a word, Henri was off the couch and out the door. I followed him a few moments later. He'd have his car in place at the restaurant by the time I arrived on foot. Such is street congestion in the Gaslight District in July.

I walked two blocks to Bay Street. Cars and trucks inched their way through the narrow streets. The sidewalks were full of people who'd collected in town for a steamy day of shopping. I turned on Lake Street and spotted Henri's SUV parked near a fire hydrant, almost across from the restaurant.

The driver's window slid down, and he looked over at me with no sign of recognition. The window went back up.

The restaurant occupied a narrow space in the middle of the block. The front door sat between two large windows. Heavy maroon curtains held up by thick brass rods covered the lower half of each window.

Above the door hung a simple sign, red letters over black: *ENZO*.

I went inside and waited for my eyes to adjust to the dimly lit interior.

The room was a narrow rectangle, front to back, with a long, heavy bar of wood and brass on the wall to the right. Small tables filled the space across from the bar, with larger tables at the back of the room. The previous iteration of an Italian eatery, Ristorante Bella, was mauve carpet and white tablecloths. Ristorante Enzo was oak floors, dim lights and red-checked tablecloths. The mellow strains of Frank Sinatra's rendition of "Lady is a Tramp" filled the dead air usually taken up by noisy diners and hustling waiters. The feel was all 1950s New York rather than 21st century northern Michigan.

Leaning on the bar near the door was a tall, gangly kid in jeans, a watch cap atop a thin face, baggy print vest barely concealing a large shoulder holster. Jimmy Erwin: a teenage shooter from Indiana I'd last seen being hauled off the streets of Petoskey in handcuffs.

"Jimmy," a voice said from the back of the room.

Erwin stepped away from the bar and moved in front of me. He put his hands on his hips and nodded.

I spread my arms out to each side and he frisked me, moving from arms to torso to legs.

"He's clean," Erwin said, loud enough to be heard in the back of the room.

A few feet down the bar stood Roberta Lampone (AKA Bobbie Fairhaven), tall and angular, her black hair pulled into a ponytail. Her face said sorority girl, her body said Army Rangers, Afghanistan and Iraq. Her father, and before him her grandfather, ran the Lampone crime family, a frequent Windy City competitor of the DeMio family.

I nodded as I went by her toward the back of the room. A beam of light spread out on the floor, cast beneath saloon-like swinging doors fronting the kitchen. The staff was busy cleaning up after lunch and prepping for dinner. Muffled conversations blended with banging pots, whirring mixers and noisy fans.

At a four-top in the right rear corner sat Joey DeMio and Donald Harper.

DeMio took over the Baldini crime family after his father, Carmine, retired to spend more time on the front porch of his East Bluff cottage on Mackinac Island. Joey's typical outfit — dark slacks, silk t-shirt and gray V-neck — always seemed more suited for someone hosting a cocktail party, rather than running drugs or prostitution rings. His salt-and-pepper hair was brushed back, like his father's; his face featured close-set oval eyes, framed in an olive complexion. Joey didn't react as I approached the table.

Not so for Harper, the family's Ivy League lawyer. He stiffened as I came up. I couldn't read his face. Was it derision or irritation? Did it matter? He looked every bit the part of an attorney featured in *Vanity Fair*. Expensive suit; sharp movie star features, rimmed glasses. The works.

"Joey … Don."

"Counselor," Joey said. "Sit."

I pulled out a chair, aware that the two empty chairs put my back to the room, to Lampone and Erwin.

"Nice place."

"First visit?"

"Yeah, I don't get out much. It's got a good feel, Joey, a city feel."

I thought I detected a small smile.

"Surprised you opened a restaurant here," I said. "The island could use an honest Italian menu."

Joey shrugged. "Petoskey's a good town."

"You looking to expand your reach to the mainland?"

"Mr. DeMio's vision for business expansion is not limited by geography."

That was Harper.

"He's guided by a sense of community need and opportunity."

"Did they teach you to talk like that at Harvard, or do you make it up as you go along?"

"Yale, Mr. Russo. Y-A-L-E." A vivid reminder to a Big Ten guy like me that the distance between our schools, between us, was calculated in more than just miles.

I started to say something, but Joey interrupted.

"What can I do for you, counselor?"

I leaned forward, elbows on the table.

"I've got a problem."

"And you've come to me."

I nodded.

"Why do you think I can help?"

"You might be the problem."

Harper glanced toward the front of the room, toward Erwin and Lampone. It was a subtle move, but I caught it.

Joey caught it, too. "Easy," he said while looking at Harper, loud enough for the others to hear.

"I might be your problem, counselor?"

"You heard about the murder last night?"

Joey nodded ever so slightly.

"The woman who was killed, Kate Hubbell. You know her?"

He shook his head.

Joey was holding back. He wasn't sure where I was going with this, so he was being more cautious than usual.

"You know Lenny Stern, the reporter?"

A nod.

"You know about his book?"

"Why don't you tell me?"

I did.

"Stern writes about a couple of floaters, you come to me? You think I dumped the bodies in Lake Michigan?"

"The bodies were wiseguys from Chicago, Joey. Scores were settled, public officials were bribed. Lot of killing in those days. You know that."

"What's that have to do with me?"

"You were part of it, Joey. Not you exactly, but your family. Carmine ran the family then."

Joey flinched just a bit at the mention of his father's name.

"Stern used to write about us. When I was growing up. They'd drink Anisette, Stern and my father, and talk. Then Stern would go and write it all down."

Lenny knew the Chicago crime families in those days — DeMio, Lampone, Fanucci — and wrote about them, but I never suspected he was on drinking terms with Carmine DeMio. *Damn sure I'm going to ask him about that.*

"Stern wrote about the Lampones, too," he said, gesturing in the direction of Roberta Lampone, still standing at the bar with Jimmy Erwin. "And about old man Genco and the Fanucci family."

"Are you seriously suggesting Mr. DeMio is responsible for this woman's death?" Harper said. "Because she's connected to Stern's book?"

I ignored Harper, who seemed more agitated than Joey about this discussion.

"Joey, you're the only guy I know travels with gunslingers. You're the only guy I know wrapped up in the business of the Chicago families who knew the politicians Lenny wrote about."

Silence.

I turned and looked toward the front of the restaurant.

"Where are Rosato and Cicci? You never go anywhere without your gunmen."

"Our employees are of no concern to you, Mr. Russo," Harper said.

He was easy to ignore, so I did, again.

"You hiring younger gunslingers these days, Joey?"

He offered a response somewhere between a grin and a smirk.

"My father feels more comfortable with familiar people. They can't be two places at once, so we brought in some new people."

Maybe Joey had given me an opening…

"Next thing you know you'll be hiring teenage boys to do your dirty work."

"Do I look that stupid?" Joey said.

"When you gonna send a couple of kids to gun down Lenny Stern?"

"That's enough," Harper said.

"Like you did Kate Hubbell."

"You're done here."

I glared at him.

"Harper, ever think I might not be talking to you?"

"Shut up, Russo," Joey said. "He's right, your time's up. You walk in here, accuse me of murder, you're done." With that, Joey made a small movement with his hand. Erwin and Lampone quickly moved to stand just inches behind my chair.

"Escort the gentleman to the door," Harper said.

18

"You went in there alone, without a gun, and accused Don Joey of murder?" Sandy said. We sat in the front office, Sandy at her desk, Henri and I in chairs by the Lake Street windows.

"He wanted to do it easy," Henri said, gesturing at me with his thumb, hitchhiker-style.

"What do you mean, easy?" Sandy said. "You're not supposed to let him do stupid shit like that."

"I was all set to run in when the shooting started," Henri said.

I laughed.

"Be quiet, both of you," Sandy said. "You sound like frat boys again. This isn't some college prank after the big game."

"I didn't really accuse Joey…"

"Close enough," Sandy said. "These are dangerous people you're messing with."

"Henri doesn't think Joey's people killed Kate Hubbell."

"What's that got to do with anything?" Sandy said, sounding exasperated. "DeMio's always dangerous. I need another job."

"Thought you liked this one?" I said, trying to be serious.

"I do like this one. But I'd like you to live long enough to sign my next paycheck." Sandy's voice trailed off as she shook her head.

I had no witty response, no humor to minimize the violent people we'd been dealing with.

"Much as I hate to admit it," I said, "you're right. I thought I was being careful, but…"

"And we're back at it tomorrow," Sandy said.

I looked up. "Tomorrow?"

"The Harbor Springs bookstore? Stop number two on the tour? Jesus, boss, get your head in the game, will you?"

We were quiet. I stood and looked out the window. The late afternoon sun put one side of Lake Street in the shade — to the appreciation of the tourists, I was sure.

"Russo?" Henri said.

"Yeah?"

"How 'bout I run over there and have a look?"

"To Harbor?"

Henri nodded. "Look at the layout, the bookstore, the street."

"Good idea," I said. "The threats, even Lenny getting beaten up ..."

"Then Kate was killed," Henri said.

"It's a different game now," I said.

"I hope both of you remember that," Sandy said.

"Where will you be in a couple of hours?" Henri said.

"Not sure. Probably with AJ. Text me when you're done in Harbor."

"Speaking of done," Sandy said, "you have anything else for me, boss?"

I shook my head. "See you in the morning."

Sandy turned off her computer screen, gathered up her shoulder bag and went for the door. We heard her go down the steps.

"One thing's bothering me," I said.

"Only one?" Henri said.

"Maybe two things. Something Joey said when I accused him of hiring teenage boys."

"Which you did intentionally."

"Of course, to get a reaction. So Joey says, 'Do I look that stupid?' Something like that."

"He was insulted by the question."

I nodded. "Right. It came off the top of his head."

Henri sat forward, elbows on his knees. "You think Joey really didn't know what you were talking about?"

I shrugged. "Well, he knew Kate had been killed, he said so ..."

"But after that, you lost him."

"Maybe I was too quick to blame Joey for this. We seem to do that when anything bad happens around here."

"They've made themselves easy targets, don't forget that. Joey's people do bad things. He's at the top of Fleener's list, too, and he's a good cop."

My phone buzzed, and I took a look. "AJ's leaving for Chandler's."

"That's my cue," Henri said. "Off to beautiful downtown Harbor Springs."

I dialed back the air conditioning, and we left the building. The shade on my side of the street was welcome for the short walk up Lake Street.

Chandler's is a comfortable restaurant tucked into a small courtyard behind Symon's General Store. The main room was a long rectangle, a bar on the left, tables large and small scattered in the rest of the space.

"Hey, Michael," Jack said from behind the bar. He'd been serving drinks from that spot for as long as I could remember. "AJ's already here." He pointed to the back of the room.

AJ waved from a four-top in the corner, and I went to join her.

"Hello, darling," she said.

I leaned over and kissed her. "Hello, back. What's that?"

"Chardonnay."

I turned toward the bar and pointed at the glass. Jack waved back.

"How're you doing?" I said as I sat down.

"Work was fine, but Kate Hubbell was all anybody talked about. Most of them never met her, but that didn't matter. She's dead, we're all feeling it."

Our waiter, a short, stout man in his twenties, put down a napkin and my wine. "Another glass, Ms. Lester?"

"With dinner," she said.

He nodded, and we ordered dinner, the duck breast for AJ, walleye for me.

"Any more news on Kate?"

I shook my head and described my trip to see Joey DeMio.

"Sandy's right, Michael."

"About what?" I said, sipping some wine.

AJ leaned in, her face taut, eyes narrow.

"Stop, just stop. Damn it. I'm not in the mood for your Sam Spade routine. I'm too tired, and Kate Hubbell's too dead.

"I didn't mean ..."

"Bullshit. I know you too well. You always feign ignorance when danger's in the air. You ... you thrive on it, Michael. I just can't stand to hear it right now. Kate's murder ..."

AJ sat back. She was done, for now, but the tension in her face remained.

I put my hands out, palms up, and nodded.

"All right," I said. "I'm sorry ..."

"Sorry doesn't do it. Kate's got a bullet in the back of her head. It hasn't been twenty-four hours yet. Treat the risk seriously for a minute, will you? I don't give a damn if Joey has new bodyguards. You made a serious mistake walking in there alone."

I remained silent. I had no answer for her.

The waiter put our dinners on the table and left another glass of chardonnay for AJ. I cut off a piece of walleye. AJ picked up her fork and stared at it for a moment, like she wondered of what possible use it might be. We sat quietly and sampled our dinners.

"I accept how you earn a living, but ... but there are times when I ... I tolerate it, but right now, Kate's dead." She picked up her wine glass, but put it down before taking a sip. "Sometimes you shove it in my face, Michael. You do. That time ... that time you and Henri went after Conrad North and his gang ... walked down the middle of the fucking street like cowboys in a shootout. It wasn't a goddamn movie, Michael. I wanted to yell at you ... at both of you."

I hesitated.

She caught it and glared at me. "Would it have done any good if I had?"

19

AJ and I sat at the table and were quiet. Odd for us. I ate some of my dinner while AJ moved food around her plate. We always had much to say, much to discuss, but words didn't come easily this night. We didn't even comment on our dinners. Not like us at all.

"I get scared, Michael. You scare me. Not you ... exactly. Your life can be dangerous. Violent people. I know that. Then ... I remember that call in the middle of the night, when you'd been knifed in an alley ... !"

"I was attacked ..."

"Just listen, will you? I need you to listen. I know damn well you were attacked, but in the hospital ... you were groggy. I stood there and heard the doctor say if the goddamn knife went just two inches the other way ..."

She sat back, pushed her plate to one side, picked up her wine and took a drink.

"Now you go to DeMio's alone? You could have vanished, right there, in the middle of town, the middle of the day. The man's capable of that with a snap of his fingers. I don't know what makes me crazier, your movie-hero bravado or being afraid you'll end up in Lake Michigan."

I wanted to say something, anything. Anger was one thing, but listening to her fear was painful. But I kept my mouth shut. We'd treaded lightly over this territory before, without coming to any understanding or accommodation.

The front door opened, and Henri entered the restaurant. He waved greetings to the bartender as he walked over, pulling out a chair.

"Michael, AJ."

Our waiter put a Molson Canadian down. "Anything to eat, Mr. LaCroix?"

"I'm fine," Henri said, glancing at each of us. If he detected tension in the air, he said nothing. He knew us well enough, knew when it was best to leave it alone.

Henri took a long pull on the Molson and waited.

After a slow minute, I said, "What did you find out in Harbor?"

"You mean Humbug's Bookstore? Or the street?"

"Both."

"You've been to Humbug's?" Henri said.

I shook my head.

"It's a small store, square," Henri said, moving his hands as if to create a diagram. "Two floor-to-ceiling windows on either side of the front door."

"That's not good," I said.

"Shelves crammed with books lining the walls. Tables with bestsellers, local authors, Michigan history are arranged in the middle of the floor."

"Any idea where they'll put Lenny?"

"Uh-huh," he said. "You're not going to like it."

"No?" I said.

"There's a tall stool and a podium in the window to the left of the doorway."

Henri was right, I didn't like it. Lenny Stern was vulnerable enough. In stores, libraries, on the road. But placing him in the bookstore's front window endangered our author, not to mention the audience that would come to listen or other customers in the store.

"One shooter with an automatic pistol could do a lot of damage," Henri said.

"I'll talk to the owner or manager tomorrow," I said.

"Try to get Lenny out of the window."

"See what I can do," I said. "After you deliver Lenny to the store, you decided where you'll be during his talk?"

Henri nodded. "Across the street, Café Java. I'll get a table on the patio right in front. Good sightlines. Easy to see fifty, sixty feet up and down the street."

The waiter came by and removed our plates. I folded my napkin and put it to one side. AJ sat quietly, sipping her wine.

"What's up, Russo? What're you thinking?"

I wasn't sure if Henri meant about AJ and me, or was asking about Humbug's Bookstore. I played it safe.

"You've got it all figured out?" I said.

Henri nodded.

"You'll set it up as best you can?"

"Of course."

I was quiet.

"I'll ask again," Henri said. "What're you thinking?"

"What if the gunmen who show up don't belong to Joey DeMio? Suppose they're not professionals."

"What?" It was AJ, finally in the conversation. "What're you talking about?"

"Not sure," I said.

"If not Joey's gunmen, then who?" she said.

I shrugged.

"We haven't gotten that far, AJ."

"Well, maybe it's time to think about it. Why'd you change your mind, Michael?"

"I haven't changed my mind, but it was something Joey said."

I reprised Joey's annoyance at my question about hiring teenage gunmen.

"Then figure out who hires kids," AJ said, her irritation had not yet receded.

Henri shot a glance my way.

"Don't look at him," she said, pointing at me. "I'm pissed at everything right now, especially him."

"Okay," Henri said, sounding uncharacteristically sheepish.

"The question stands," she said, looking at both of us. "Who hires kids to kill people?"

"It has to be someone not on our radar screen," Henri said.

"Are you sure you turned the radar on?" AJ said. "You've been focused only on Joey DeMio."

"I'm not letting Joey off the hook just yet," I said.

"So do two things at once. You guys ought to be good enough for that."

I glanced at Henri, who shrugged.

AJ glared at me. "Are you going to shrug, too, or come up with a name?"

Before I could respond, Henri said, "One thing about tomorrow ... in Harbor Springs?"

"I'm listening," I said, relieved at the change of subject.

"We'd better assume we're watching for teenagers, too."

"Professionals could be young," AJ said. "What about that new body-guard, the one you saw at the restaurant today?"

"Jimmy Erwin," I said.

"He's barely twenty," Henri said, "but he is a professional, with a track record to prove it."

"Those two kids who tried to scare Lenny in the parking lot that day are a long way from being Jimmy Erwin," I said. "I'd bet they didn't kill Kate Hubbell."

"And you can bet they won't be sent to Harbor Springs tomorrow, either," Henri said.

"Are you sure they'll try to get at Lenny tomorrow?" AJ said.

"No," I said. "The whole thing might come off without a hitch, but we have to assume they'll try. If not at the bookstore, on the street, or on the way over from Petoskey."

"I'll stay off the Harbor-Petoskey Road," Henri said, referring to the most direct route between the towns. "Maybe I'll head north first ... come in the back way."

"Lenny needs to be at Humbug's at least thirty minutes before his talk."

"We'll arrive on time."

"Tina will be with you, right?"

"She will, indeed," Henri said, draining the last of his Molson. "All right, I'm on my way to get Lenny."

"Is he still at the office?" AJ said.

"Yeah. He's working late since he'll be gone tomorrow."

Henri said his good-byes, and we were, again, alone.

Our discussion about Harbor Springs seemed to have diverted some of the tension. I wasn't sure how much, but I didn't like where AJ and I had left it when Henri joined us.

"AJ..."

"I know ... I know, Michael. You don't have to say it."

"Yeah, I think I do."

"Maybe you do, but not right now. Okay? I'm too ... I'm mad at you, I love you, I'm scared. It's all mashed together." AJ took a deep breath and let it out slowly. "You've got a tough day tomorrow."

She eased herself out of the chair. She came around, leaned in and kissed my cheek. "G'night."

20

I took Beach Road, the scenic route, into downtown Harbor Springs. It ran along the bay, the sandy beach on one side, ornate Victorian cottages of the Wequetonsing Association on the other. The beach was dotted with colorful towels, water toys and vacationers of all sizes, shapes, and ages.

I left the car in the lot across from the New York restaurant, walking up State Street. I spotted Café Java three doors down Main Street, across from Humbug's Bookstore. I crossed with the light and walked to the coffee shop. Four small two-top tables took up patio space on either side of the shop's front door. All of them were occupied, but lunch hour was nearing an end. Henri had no doubt figured a way to be at one of them during Lenny's afternoon appearance. I stood for a moment, looking up and down Main Street. Henri was right. He'd have a clear view in both directions, and of the bookstore itself.

I waited for traffic to clear, crossed the street in the middle of the block, and entered Humbug's Bookstore. The space was even tighter than I imagined after listening to Henri's description. I glanced at the shelves crammed with books, the tables crowding the floor, but my attention was drawn to the podium in the front window. White folding chairs had been set up close to the podium.

Lenny would entertain folks with his back to the street, less than three feet from the glass. An easy target if the shooters didn't care how many other people they shot up.

"Mr. Russo? Michael Russo?" a woman said, hidden by two piles of books.

"That's me," I said. "Private eye to the literati."

She came from behind a table, and we shook hands.

"Eleanor Cosworth," she said, staring at my loose-fitted print shirt. "I was alerted that you were a smart aleck."

"You have good sources."

"I've heard all about your Philip Marlowe heroics."

"I've been leaning toward Harry Bosch myself," I said. "Weird guy."

"The kind folks at McLean & Eakin filled me in."

"You bookstore people sure are a clannish bunch."

"You have no idea," she said, as her eyes wandered over my shoulder toward the front door.

Eleanor was close to sixty, with a cheap haircut and sad green eyes. The badge clipped to the breast pocket of her maroon blazer displayed her name, and below it, "Manager."

"Where is he?"

"Who?"

"Who? Leonard Stern, that's who."

"He'll be here in a few minutes. He's with my associate, they're on the way."

"He's our first bestselling author, you know. Right here in the store. This is our chance to make a name for Humbug's. Do you understand?"

"Understood. Yes, ma'am."

"We begin at three sharp, you know."

"He'll be here on time. Promise."

"The talk will last about thirty minutes, Q&A another twenty, the rest for signing books."

"Yes, ma'am."

"Now, Mr. Russo, you must be no more than a fly on the wall."

"A fly on the wall?"

"Yes, yes. Out of the way," she said, with a dismissive flick of the wrist. "We don't want you to interfere with our customers, after all."

"Look …" I took a quick glance at her name badge again.

"Look, Ms. Cosworth, what plans do you have for your customers if trouble starts?"

She straightened her shoulders. "Trouble?"

"Yes, trouble."

"I'm not sure I understand."

"Ms. Cosworth, you know that Lenny Stern has received death threats?"

"Certainly."

"Do you understand what that means?"

"Of course I do," she said. "Gloucester Publishing wants to gin up sales, get better press coverage for the book tour. Good marketing, I'd say."

Ms. Eleanor Cosworth, manager of Humbug's Bookstore in downtown Harbor Springs, was in for a shock.

"The threats are very real, Ms. Cosworth."

She looked at me, but said nothing, just a small twist of the head.

Reality was about to sink in.

"You're telling me ... this ... this isn't the marketing department?"

"No, ma'am," I said. "Lenny Stern wrote a book about a Mafia killing."

"I read his book, Mr. Russo," she said, in a voice that was condescending. "I'm not sure the world needs another yarn about the Mafia."

"Since you read it, Ms. Cosworth, remember he named names, accused mobsters, public officials, candidates for office. And he's got evidence that might put some of them in jail."

Eleanor absentmindedly began scratching a small spot on her forehead.

"The bad guys will make a run at him," I said.

"You mean, try to kill him?"

I nodded. "Yes, ma'am. It will happen. We just don't know when. At one of the stops maybe, on the road. The men coming for him want only two things, to kill Lenny and get away."

Cosworth took a deep breath. "So shooting a few of our customers wouldn't matter to them?"

I shook my head. "I'm afraid not."

"I saw the news … does this have anything to do with the woman they found dead?"

The grim news had made its way through the fog of selling books.

"Her name was Kate Hubbell. She edited Lenny's book."

Eleanor's left hand went to her mouth. "Dear god," she said. "Can you stop this?"

"I can cut the odds of people being hurt, but if you're looking for guarantees, there are none."

"So was that woman killed because she was a threat like Mr. Stern, or was she in the wrong place at the wrong time?"

I shrugged. "We're not sure." Even as I said it, my gut was uneasy with her question. I wasn't sure why.

"What are you going to do?" Eleanor said.

"I make myself visible. They see me or my associate, better if they see both of us. They know if they try to hurt Lenny, they'll pay a price."

"You'll kill them?"

"If I have to, yes. Better if I don't have to."

"You mean that might be enough to scare them off?"

"It might be, yes, if we're lucky."

"But wouldn't they try to kill him at the next stop on the tour, or the stop after that?"

"Yes, ma'am."

"You just have to wait for it?"

"Well," I said. "We try to be ready, but yes, ma'am."

"You live a dangerous life, Mr. Russo."

21

I poured a cup of coffee from a small carafe at the back of the store, sat in one of the white chairs, and waited for Henri and Lenny. Eleanor's question stuck in my head. Was Kate Hubbell simply in the wrong place, or was she a threat to the bad guys, too? I pushed the question aside. My concern had to be Lenny Stern.

I still didn't like putting Lenny at that podium in the front window. Maybe we had time to change things up. I took my coffee and went to the sales counter.

"Ms. Cosworth?"

Eleanor looked up.

"I'm worried about the front window."

She nodded, but didn't say anything.

"Can we move the podium and the chairs?" I said. "Away from the window, I mean. It shouldn't take long."

"It wouldn't take long at all, but where would you suggest I move them? This is a small store," she said, like she wondered why I needed to be told. "Floor space is very valuable."

"I appreciate the complexities of retailing," I said.

"I doubt that you do, but it was nice of you to say that."

"It's only while Lenny's here," I said. "I'll help you move them all back."

"I know you're trying to be nice," she said, "but you'll just have to work with what we have."

I looked around again, as if the podium and chairs had rearranged themselves. They had not. I thought — not for very long — about constructing another line of persuasion. The neat, orderly world of Eleanor Cosworth did not appreciate disruption.

"Mr. Russo? I have a question with ... ah, all due respect. Do you have any help, or are you on your own?"

With his usual sense of good timing, Henri LaCroix entered the bookstore.

"The front door," I said with a tilt of the head. Cosworth turned around.

A few steps behind Henri were Lenny Stern and Tina Lawson. They were dressed professionally in honor of the occasion, but their demeanor suggested caution. And neither of them was smiling.

I introduced Eleanor Cosworth, and greetings were shared all around. Eleanor stared at Henri, probably wondering why he wore a green nylon windbreaker on such a hot day. She'd finally caught on why I needed a loose shirt. Of course, she might have been sizing up Henri for the task at hand.

"So, you've come to help take care of Mr. Stern?" she said.

Henri smiled. "That's my job, keep everybody safe."

"Um, I have a question," Eleanor said, "for you, too, Mr. Russo."

"Sure."

"How do you know?"

"Know what?" I said.

"The men who want to hurt Mr. Stern," she said, nodding in his direction. "How do you know who it is?" Her face looked confused, uncertain. "I can't imagine two men wearing masks will rush the store with guns blazing."

Perhaps the book lady was sharper than I thought. She'd begun to analyze the situation.

"No, ma'am," I said. "That's not likely."

"Do you ... I'm not sure how to ask this, but do you, you know, profile people?"

"You mean," Henri said, "look for black or brown guys wearing hoodies?"

Cosworth looked at the floor, a bit sheepishly, and nodded. "Kind of like that, yeah."

Henri shook his head and said, "We don't rely on stereotypes. If we did that, Stern might get killed, us too. We know what to look for because this is what we do."

Cosworth nodded slowly, letting that sink in.

"Mr. Stern," she said, turning his way. "I didn't mean to be rude. We're very excited to have you at Humbug's this afternoon, but this … this, what should I call it? This situation you're in has me a little nervous."

Lenny smiled. "Me, too, Ms. Cosworth. I'm nervous, too." He reached out and took her hand. "But that's why Michael and Henri are here."

Eleanor and Lenny then exchanged a few minutes of book-related stories, as if we weren't there.

"Well, if you'll excuse me," Eleanor said, "I have some details to see to before we get started."

After she was out of earshot, Henri said, "It's bullshit, Russo. Not that I'm telling you anything you don't know."

"Yeah."

"He's going to be in the window, isn't he?"

"Yep," I said, as Lenny turned around and looked at the setup.

"Won't she move the podium?"

"Nope."

"Want me to talk to her?" Henri said.

I shook my head.

"Bad news, Russo."

"What are you guys worried about?" Lenny said. "I'm the target in the big glass window."

I was sure Tina was listening, but she seemed detached, her eyes glassy, but that wasn't unexpected. She had not yet recovered from the emotional trauma of Kate Hubbell's murder.

"Why don't we just tell the book lady to move the podium or Lenny walks?" Henri said.

Lenny jumped in. "No, no. She's depending on us, on me. Small stores like this struggle. We can't disappoint its customers."

I took a deep breath.

After a moment, Henri said, "How 'bout this..." he glanced at the podium, the tables on the floor. "What if we move the podium and the chairs to the middle of the store? We could slide those two tables over, put them in the window."

I looked around. Lenny, too.

"Think she'd go for it?" Lenny said.

"Let's ask," I said.

"No." It was Lenny. "Let me ask. She might do it for me."

"Go for it," I said.

Lenny nodded and went over to the sales counter. A few moments later, he returned with Eleanor. He had a small grin on his face.

"All right, Mr. Russo," Eleanor said. "We'll move the podium."

"Henri and I'll do the moving, Ms. Cosworth. Just tell us where."

She did. The podium and chairs sat in the middle of the store. The tables went to the window. Eleanor seemed satisfied enough, and returned to the sales counter.

"Well, Henri?" I said.

"At least Lenny's away from the window."

"What about outside?"

"I'll head across the street in a few minutes," Henri said. "Have you explained the ground rules to Eleanor yet?"

"Thought I'd wait for Lenny and Tina, do it once. I think we finally got through to her that this is serious."

I called out to Tina and Eleanor.

They walked over.

"We have to explain a few things," I said, and looked around.

"Is there somewhere we can talk, Ms. Cosworth?"

"In the office," she said, pointing to a long plaid curtain covering a doorway behind her.

"I'll be outside," Henri said. "Text, Michael."

We retreated to her office, a tiny space with barely enough room for a desk, a dented filing cabinet, and an ancient desktop computer.

I looked at my watch.

"We have less than twenty minutes," I said. "Any idea how many people will attend?"

Eleanor shrugged. "Fifteen. A few more if we're lucky on a sunny summer afternoon."

"All right," I said. "I have a few ground rules for Lenny's presentation. I want the three of you to listen carefully. We don't want any more people getting hurt. This is all new to you, but Henri and I have dealt with this kind of thing before."

Lenny and Tina stood quite still, Eleanor was fidgety.

"First, you do as I tell you, starting now. Lenny will be at the podium, of course, but you, Tina and you, Ms. Cosworth, stay away from the front of the store. I don't want you anywhere near the windows. Am I clear?"

"Um, I have to introduce Mr. Stern," Eleanor said, "from the podium."

"Be brief, then head for the back, okay?"

Eleanor nodded.

I explained a few more basics. "All right, you do as I say, no questions, no hesitation. Clear?"

Tina and Eleanor nodded at the same time.

"Lenny? You on board?" I assumed after the Carnegie he would be, but I had to ask.

He nodded. "I don't want anyone else hurt because of me."

"This isn't your fault, Lenny," I said.

"Feels that way."

"No, Lenny." It was Tina. "I've been with you from the beginning. You were the one who thought the book might be dangerous. I knew that going in, so did Kate."

"I never thought anyone would die. Scared, maybe, but killed? You're all my responsibility. I got you into this, you and Kate…"

"Lenny," I said. "It's no one's fault. Tina and Kate are professionals, just like you. You had the story, the three of you worked on the documents. Kate edited the manuscript. Tina took care of organizing everything else. You were in it together."

"We're with you by choice, Lenny," Tina said.

"Aren't you scared?"

"Of course I'm scared, Lenny, but you have an important story to tell. You convinced us of that, and Kate and I signed on."

Lenny looked less convinced than Tina did. But it was too late for that.

"Mr. Stern?" Eleanor Cosworth said. "Come with me, please."

22

Most of the white chairs were filled as Eleanor Cosworth approached the podium, with Lenny Stern a few steps behind.

"Welcome to Humbug's Bookstore," she said. "I hope you're as excited today as I am." If Eleanor was nervous about the danger on the street, she offered no evidence of it. Her introduction of the bookstore's special guest was succinct, interesting and, happily, brief.

"Good afternoon," Lenny said as he absentmindedly straightened his skinny black tie. "Thank you for coming to Humbug's on this beautiful summer day."

I eased my way to the window and stood off to one side. Henri had taken up a position at a small table on the patio of Café Java across the street. He sat with a mug of coffee, looking no different than any other patron. Henri casually glanced in both directions as he sipped coffee.

The heart of downtown stretched three blocks, from Johan's Bakery at the corner of State and Main to Turkey's Café at the east end of the street. Between here and there, small two-story clapboard-sided buildings, painted white or a variety of pastels, housed mostly retail shops featuring trendy clothing, high-end sports gear, and glamorous jewelry. Most of them had recessed doorways that could hide one or two men. The newer buildings, red brick structures, housed banks and the real estate office. No one would loiter around a bank. Too suspicious.

Henri had done his homework. He knew where to look, which nooks and doorways would help shooters blend in with a street full of tourists.

I glanced out the window. Waves of heat slowly climbed off the pavement. Tourists, wearing odd hats and colorful shorts, moved deliberately from store to store, eating ice cream, sipping cold drinks.

If the gunmen came, would they tote an automatic pistol in one hand, a Coke in the other?

"This seems like the perfect day to talk about mayhem and murder, doesn't it?" Lenny said with a broad smile and a wave of the arms. He'd resumed the role of engaging entertainer I'd witnessed at the Carnegie Library. Better he should focus on his audience than any looming threat from the street.

"I covered the Mafia for more than ten years..."

I waited and listened as Lenny drew his audience into his tale of corruption.

"This is the most explosive story in years," he said. "Heads will roll, careers will end." I sure hoped Lenny's career — or head — wasn't one of them.

My phone buzzed. I glanced at the screen.

"Heads up."

I moved to the edge of the window. Something had caught Henry's eye. He was looking down the sidewalk, his hand close to his chest, a finger pointing east. Not sure what... then I saw him, too. He stood in front of Regency Jewelers, a half block down, looking at the window display.

The man wore a loose-fitting print shirt hanging over the waist. One hand was wrapped around a can of Pepsi, the other was in a jeans pocket.

I tapped a thumbs-up emoji to Henri. He remained at the table, not wanting to make himself too obvious until we found out if our man was alone. Experience taught us that, more often than not, a second man was nearby.

I tapped, "One?"

"So far."

Lenny was almost through with his presentation. Forty minutes or so left for questions and signing books before I could yank him away from the front of the store and move his twelve-person audience elsewhere.

Tina Lawson paced from side to side at the back of the store. Not sure she was even listening to her client. I looked around, but Eleanor Cosworth was nowhere to be seen. Good.

"Thank you for the kind applause," Lenny said, "and for being so attentive. I'd be happy to take a few questions."

I strained my neck as best I could to see down the street. It was too soon to leave the store. I didn't want a second man to see me before we found him.

"Got him," my screen read. I figured Henri would spot the other shooter first.

"Claxton's," he wrote. The women's clothing boutique was two shops down from the bookstore, my side of the street.

"Can't see him."

Henri called this time.

"He's tucked into the doorway," Henri said, "like he's waiting for somebody inside."

"Another baggy shirt?"

"No. Skinny black T-shirt."

"How do you hide a gun underneath a T-shirt?"

"You don't," Henri said. "He's carrying a small attaché case."

"What do you think?"

"I think it's a break-away Uzi."

"Thank you for your interesting questions," Lenny said as he wrapped up the second portion of the afternoon. "Some thoughtful insights, too. Well, I'd be delighted to inscribe my book for anyone who's interested."

"Kill a lot of people with an Uzi," I said.

"Right about that," Henri said. "My baggy shirt likely has a pistol."

"My guy still there?" I said, straining to see out the window.

"Yeah. Same doorway. He's been in one place too long."

"Professionals haven't used the Uzi in years. Think they're amateurs?"

"Be my guess," Henri said. "Get an Uzi pretty cheap these days."

"Big trouble anyway you look at it. Amateurs panic at the worst times."

"Hold on," Henri said. "Baggy shirt's on the move."

I looked hard. "I see him. He's still on your side of the street. Walking your way."

"How do you want to play this?"

"Let's see where your guy goes first. If he moves to the bookstore, that's one problem. Might be … wait, he's just about to you."

Henri put down the phone and unzipped his nylon windbreaker as the man walked by.

"He's a kid," Henri said.

Baggy shirt stopped across Main Street from his buddy on my side.

"Okay," Henri said. "One on each side of the street. What do you think?"

"I can't see them both."

"I got good lines, Russo. I could take them both quick, right now. But bad shit could happen fast."

Henri paused. "Don't want to wait too long, they might have itchy trigger fingers."

"Let's run a two-man on them," I said.

"Been a long since we did that," Henri said. "I might be out of practice."

"You're never out of practice. It might just keep them from shooting. But if they do …"

"I'll kill them both," Henri said.

"You ready?"

Henri clicked off, left the café and started down the sidewalk, walking fast, straight toward baggy shirt. When he got close enough, I went out the door and turned right, walking fast toward my man with the attaché case.

They spotted us.

Henri pulled up ten feet short of his man and stared at him. I did the same with my guy. We made sure our guns were visible, not drawn, but very visible. That's all.

My guy blinked first. He backed up two steps, then spun and ran. I followed.

Henri's guy took off down a side street and out of sight, with Henri close behind.

I was ten, twelve feet behind my guy when he turned on Spring Street heading toward the harbor. I cut the corner tight at Graham Real Estate, and collided with a middle-aged couple I never saw. The three of us landed hard on the cement. A large paper shopping bag exploded, and its contents slid across the sidewalk into the street.

"Sorry, sorry," I said as I struggled to get on my feet. I glanced down Spring Street. My guy was already a block away and moving fast.

"I got to go," I said, pointing. "Sorry."

The man, on his knees, pulled at my khakis. "Not so fast, you sonofa-bitch." He grabbed a handful of my shirt, and the buttons tore away.

The woman screamed. "He's got a gun, Harry!" Then, even louder, "It's a gun, Harry!"

I heard another voice — male — loud, deep, harsh.

"Stop. Right there, stop. Hands over your head. Now."

The voice wore a uniform.

I raised my hands.

"I'm a private investigator licensed to carry firearms in the state of Michigan."

23

"I want this hooligan arrested," the man said. On his feet, he was angrier and bolder with a cop around. He shouted at the officer, "He attacked us!"

The officer, handgun at his side, never took his eyes off me. He was medium height, stocky, with a serious face. His nameplate read, "Leon Flores."

A second officer, taller and leaner than the first, came up quickly. He moved beside the frightened couple, easing them a few steps away.

"That man has a gun, officer," the woman said, her voice trembling as she edged closer to him.

"Yes, ma'am. Stay here, please," the tall cop said as he moved toward me.

"I called for backup," the tall one said.

"The sheriff?" Leon Flores said.

"Yeah."

"Against the wall," Officer Flores said. I stretched out, hands on the wall of the real estate office.

His partner reached under my torn shirt, carefully pulling my .38 out of its holster.

All the excitement had drawn a small crowd of spectators. They kept a discrete distance.

"ID?" Flores said.

"Left rear pants."

"Slowly," he said, "so we can see your hands."

I came off the wall, held my shirt out with one hand and reached for my wallet with the other.

Flores holstered his gun and took my wallet. He found what he was looking for. "He really is a PI, Harry," he said, showing the documents to his lanky partner.

A sheriff's SUV stopped across the street, near our audience. A deputy eased himself out from behind the wheel and crossed the street to join the fun.

"Gentlemen," the deputy said.

"Leon Flores and Harry Bales," my cop said.

"Here for the summer, officers?" the deputy said. The Harbor Springs police brought in additional officers each summer to help during the busy tourist season.

Flores and Bales nodded in unison.

"Hands down," the deputy said to me. Then addressing the police, "So, what do we have here, officers?"

Flores held up my gun, and explained how all of us ended up on a Harbor Springs street corner on a humid July afternoon. He handed my wallet to the deputy. His nameplate read, "Isaac Lasher."

"So…" he glanced at the license, "Mr. Russo…Petoskey, huh. I've heard of you." He pulled out a notebook and flipped a couple of pages, then said, "Hold on."

Deputy Lasher walked a few steps away, took out his phone and tapped the screen. When he finished, he came back to us.

"Now, Mr. Russo, why were you running so hard? Somebody chasing you?"

"I was doing the chasing. The guy went around the corner." I pointed down the side street.

"There was nobody else." It was the man again, not shouting, but still angry at having been knocked over. "He attacked us, plain and simple."

"Please, sir," Officer Bales said, turning toward the man.

"You want to tell us why you were running after somebody?" the deputy said.

I needed to leave Henri out of this. I wondered if he'd caught the kid he went after.

"I'm on the job. Hired to protect a man named Leonard Stern..."

"The reporter?" Deputy Lasher said.

"The same."

He looked around. "Then where's Stern?" He sounded skeptical.

I pointed down Main Street. "At Humbug's Bookstore."

"But you're here," the deputy said.

He listened patiently as I told him about Lenny, the bookstore, and why I was running.

Deputy Lasher looked at the tourist couple, then at his colleagues and said, "Officer Flores, how 'bout you go to the bookstore. Collect Mr. Stern and bring him back here."

"Will do." Flores turned on his heels and left.

"Officer," the deputy said. "Keep our private eye here company, will you? I want to chat with these nice folks." He nodded in the direction of the couple.

"Not planning on running off, are you?" Officer Bales said.

I shook my head. "Hadn't thought about it."

He smiled, and put his hands behind his back, rocking gently back-and-forth on his heels.

After a few minutes, Deputy Lasher waved at the couple as they ambled off down the street.

"They calmed down now?" Officer Bales said.

Lasher shrugged. "Think so."

"Think they'll file a complaint," Officer Bales said.

"I doubt it," Deputy Lasher said. "I apologized for the city and told them Mr. Russo, here, was just doing his job."

"Which job was that?" I said.

"Keeping the good city of Harbor Springs safe for visitors like themselves." He smiled.

"Good choice."

"Just barely," Lasher said. "You're the guy ran them over, remember?"

"Uh-huh," I said. "What's next?"

"Well, let's talk to Mr. Stern first," he said, "then we'll see …"

When he stopped in mid-sentence, Office Bales and I took notice. Officer Flores was coming our way. Alone. No Stern, no Lawson.

Deputy Lasher threw me a sharp look. "Was there a problem?" he said when Flores got close enough.

Flores shook his head. "Lady at the bookstore confirmed the reporter and a woman were there."

"Who's the woman?"

"Tina Lawson," I said. "Works for Stern's publishing company."

"The reporter and the woman left with another man …" Flores said.

"That'd be my associate, Henri LaCroix."

"Do you know…" Lasher started to say, but his phone beeped. He took it out and read the screen.

"Mr. Russo," the deputy said. "How about we take a ride to the road patrol building? It's just over …"

"I know where it is. Why?"

"Captain Fleener will meet us there. Shouldn't take long."

I'd heard that one before.

24

"I'll be in touch, officers," Deputy Lasher said. The three men exchanged good-byes, and Officers Flores and Bales returned to their beat on Main Street.

"You have a car?" Lasher said.

"Down by the marina," I said.

He considered that for a moment. "How 'bout you ride with me?"

I thought about objecting.

"I'll see to it you get a ride back."

More than anything else, I wanted to talk with Henri. It wasn't worth arguing about my car. We went across the street, and climbed into the patrol SUV.

Deputy Lasher said only a few words on the way to the office, which gave me time to think. Henri had obviously made it back to the bookstore to hustle Lenny and Tina out of town. But what happened to the guy he was chasing? Hell, what happened to the guy *I* was chasing?

The road was thick with traffic. The quaint charm of the houses along Main Street, the privileged life on the fairways of Wequetonsing Golf Club, casually devolved into strip mall storefronts near the airport. The Richard L. Zink Law Enforcement Center, housing the road patrol offices, was a contemporary building with smart roof lines and not a tacky cement block in sight. Its second most notable feature was that it sat across the Harbor-Petoskey Road from Johan's Burger Express.

Deputy Lasher turned in and parked in the "official" area.

"This way," he said, pointing to a side entrance.

"Never gone in that way," I said.

"First time for everything."

He led me down a corridor with several doors on one side, the holding cell on the other.

"Here," Lasher said, opening a door to an interview room. "Have a seat."

The windowless room was about ten-by-six, with a small table and two chairs. I pulled out a chair as the deputy closed the door. I considered my torn shirt, with its missing buttons, and shook my head. Hardly the most professional dress for the job. I was momentarily tempted to call Henri, but walls, especially these walls, had ears (and electronic eyes).

I was replaying the events of the day when my attention was drawn to muffled talking out in the hallway. Moments later, the door opened.

"Why am I not surprised," I said as Captain Martin Fleener came into the room and closed the door. He leaned back against the doorframe, hands in the pockets of his immaculately tailored suit, and stared at me without expression, as if he were trying to decide what to order at a restaurant he didn't like. His eyes moved, and his head tilted slightly.

"You look like you ought to be in the drunk tank across the hall."

"A tourist took exception to meeting …"

"So I heard," Fleener said as he took the other chair.

"What are you doing here, anyway?" I said.

"I'm a cop. The building's full of 'em."

"Nice you brought your sense of humor," I said. "Seriously, why'd the deputy call you?"

Fleener hesitated; I waited.

"I put out the word after Kate Hubbell's murder. If you pop up …"

"You get a call."

Fleener put his hands out and smiled. "*Voila.*"

"The deputy catch you up?"

Fleener nodded. "His boss, too. You want to give me your version? Before and after the cops showed up on the street corner."

I did.

Fleener thought for a moment. "Strange," he said, "that the officers heard about Henri LaCroix from the woman at the bookstore. You never said a word about him. Why is that?"

I shrugged. "I don't know."

Fleener didn't consider that for very long. "Like hell," he said. "You were shielding Henri because you had no idea what happened to him, or where he was."

I leaned forward on the table and laced my fingers together. "Maybe."

"So you haven't talked to Henri yet?"

"No chance," I said. "Deputy Lasher insisted I ride over here with him."

"Henri obviously didn't get picked up like you did," Fleener said. "The guy he was chasing got away, that what you're thinking?"

I nodded. "Seems likely."

"But you don't know."

"Not for sure, no," I said. "When do I get out of here?"

"You're free to go anytime."

"What about the sheriff?"

Fleener took a deep breath. "You're my case, remember? They don't know how lucky they are to be rid of you."

"Any trouble with the tourists I ran over?"

Fleener shook his head. "I had Deputy Lasher follow up, just in case. No trouble."

Fleener slid his chair back and stood up. "Come on, let's go."

"My car's downtown."

"Of course, it is. I'll drop you off."

Fleener's dusty black sedan, looking hopelessly dated in a row of shiny cop SUVs, was parked outside the door.

He beeped the locks, we got in, and I told him where to find my car. "Think they'll ever give you a shiny, new SUV?"

"You can always walk, you know."

"Sorry I asked."

We left the parking lot and headed downtown.

"Why don't you get Henri on the phone, see what he has to say?"

I hesitated, like I wasn't listening.

"What's the matter, Russo? I'll find out one way or the other."

"True." I pulled out my phone.

"Where are u?" I tapped to Henri.

"Your office. u?" he tapped back.

"Riding with Fleener. wait for me."

Fleener turned off Main Street to avoid the congestion of downtown. He took East Bay Street along the water to the parking lot.

"Thanks for the lift," I said, opening the door.

"You meeting Henri?"

I didn't answer.

"Is he with Stern at the paper? Maybe your office?"

I put one leg out the door.

"I'll tail you," Fleener said. "I do that a lot."

"I'll be in touch."

"I'm going to find out, remember?"

I glanced back at Fleener. I remained in my seat and closed the door. "Mind if I let Henri know you're coming? He wouldn't appreciate the surprise."

"Suit yourself."

I texted Henri about our not-always-welcome visitor.

"You know," Fleener said, "something's bothering me."

"About the bookstore and the cops?"

"Well ... let's see about Henri first."

25

"**Y**ou can't be serious?" Sandy said. We were in the front office, Sandy at her desk, Fleener and Henri seated uneasily next to each other at the front window, me in a client chair from my office. Lenny Stern and Tina Lawson were safely tucked away at the offices of the *Post Dispatch* for the rest of the day.

"The tourist called you a hooligan," Sandy said, laughing. "Who says 'hooligan' anymore? It's so … *West Side Story*."

"Cut the poor man some slack, will you?" I said. "I probably ruined his vacation."

"Nonsense," Sandy said. "He'll be telling that story for years. And they got a personal apology from the sheriff."

Henri and I offered separate accounts of the events of the day. I went first. Rank had its privileges, I guessed.

When I'd finished all eyes turned toward Henri. He glanced sideways at Fleener.

"Look," Fleener said, "we're on the same side in this, like it or not."

"What side is that?" Henri said. It was as much a statement as a question.

These two had been at each other for years. Henri didn't trust cops; it was in his DNA. Martin Fleener regarded Henri as trouble afoot. But they held a begrudging respect for each other … as long as the air was clear between them.

"What side is that?" Fleener said, with an edge in his voice. "What side? How about the side with no more killing on city streets, no bodies dumped behind warehouses. How about that side?"

"All right, all right," I said. "It's been a long day. Take it down a notch, both of you." I paused. "You're up, Henri. What happened when you chased the other guy?"

Henri leaned forward in his chair.

"I got a quick look at you running down Main Street, but my guy went up the side street, at the fudge place …"

"Across from the real estate office?"

Henri nodded. "He was light on his feet, quick, but I caught him in less than a block."

"Recognize him?" I said.

"No, will if I see him again."

"But you caught him?" Fleener said.

"Yeah … put him on the ground."

"Then how'd he get away?"

"Had to let him go," Henri said.

"You let him go?" Sandy said, her mouth open.

"Really pissed me off to do that. Bunch of people in a parking lot, behind the library, started yelling at us … at me, 'Let him go. Call the cops.'" Henri shook his head. "Didn't want to be there if cops were on the way. Half a block down, my guy almost ran me over coming out of a parking lot. Old beat-up Ford Ranger truck, dirty red."

"Would you recognize it again?" Fleener said.

"I can do better than that." Henri went to Sandy's desk, took a sticky note, wrote on it, and handed it to Fleener.

Fleener looked at the note, then at Henri. "Vanity plate?"

"You bet."

"What was it?" I asked.

"Letters and numbers," Henri said. "RC space 44."

It happened again. That click in my gut. Familiar, I thought … but I lost it. "Can you run the plate, Marty?"

Fleener held the slip of paper up. "Yep," he said. "Back in a minute." Fleener took out his phone and went to the hallway.

"People put crazy things on those plates," Sandy said. "Nicknames, colleges, could be anything."

Fleener returned to his seat next to Henri, a small notebook in his hand.

"The vanity plate is registered to the Cavendish Company of Gaylord..."

"Spell it, Marty," Sandy said.

He did, then said, "Cavendish has three officers, Sylvia, Daniel, and Walter, all named Cavendish. The company owns six vehicles, three trucks and three cars, including a 1980 Ford Ranger. I'll email the specifics."

"I pulled up the website," Sandy said, leaning toward the screen. "The Cavendish Company...let's see, industrial supply stuff... pipe fittings, pumps, pressure gauges, gaskets. Some history...founded in the '20s, blah, blah, blah. Okay, here, bought by Sylvia Cavendish in 2000. Daniel Cavendish is president, Walter is marketing and production." She leaned back. "You can read the rest, if you want to."

"Industrial supplies? Gaylord?" Henri said, and shrugged. "Well, at least we found the truck."

"All right," Fleener said. "I have a question for you super sleuths."

"We're in trouble now," Sandy said, rolling her eyes.

"Ignore her," I said. "What's the question?"

"Today, at the bookstore, the two men?"

"What about them?"

"You both described them as young, right? Probably early twenties?"

Henri and I nodded.

"But they weren't the same two who tried to throw a scare into Lenny Stern the other day at the Side Door?"

"I only got a quick look at one of those guys," Henri said. "The man I chased today wasn't him."

There it was again. It clicked...

"My guy wasn't at the Side Door either," I said.

"Well, that means we have three, maybe four, men involved in this," Fleener said. "And they're all young, you say."

We nodded again.

"Then I have to ask the question again, who hires kids?" Fleener said.

"We know Joey DeMio was pissed when I suggested he hired teenagers."

Fleener shook his head slowly. "So you told me, but pissed or not, DeMio is still on top of my list."

"But it looks more and more like it could be someone else," Sandy said.

I nodded. "Sandy might just be right."

"Don't jump to conclusions," Fleener said.

"We shouldn't consider other people?" I said.

"Of course, we should," Fleener said, "just not yet."

"Your point is?" Henri said.

"My point is," Fleener said, "an old tried-and-true investigative tactic is to look for the most obvious lead, then eliminate it before looking for the next most obvious lead."

"Obvious around here is Joey DeMio," Sandy said.

"I'd like to know if the guys in Harbor today were Joey's," I said.

"So would I," Henri said.

"You weren't sure last time, Russo," Fleener said. "Make sure this time."

Henri and I both looked at Fleener. "What?" he said.

"You okay with us doing that?" Henri said.

Fleener scratched the side of his forehead. "Lot of paperwork on my desk."

I paused for a moment, glancing at Henri.

"Just do it quick," Fleener said.

"Can you find Joey?" I said to Henri.

"He's at Ristorante Enzo," Sandy said. "At least he was a few minutes ago."

"How do you know that?" I said.

She reached for a sticky note. "His attorney, Harper, called just before you got here. Joey wants to see you. Didn't say why."

"Check and see if he's still there," I said.

She nodded, walked into my office and closed the door.

"Just take it easy with DeMio, will you?" Fleener said. "I don't want to get a call you're in another police station."

"Do my best."

Sandy returned to her desk. "The lawyer said he's still there."

I looked at Henri. "Well, what are we waiting for?"

"That's my signal to leave," Fleener said, moving toward the door. "I'll see if we got anything on the Cavendish Company."

"Hold on, Marty," I said. The fog in my head was lifting.

"The plate," I said.

"'RC 44.' What about it?"

I turned to Henri. "That day at the Side Door. Didn't the guy have a tattoo?"

Henri froze for a moment. "On his arm, a '44.'"

"That's too bizarre a coincidence even for me," Sandy said, with more than a touch of sarcasm.

"A gang tatt?" Henri said.

"Could be," Fleener said. "Got a guy in Lansing I'll talk to."

"Thought all that was in the NCIC database?" Henri said.

"It is, but this guy's a walking institutional memory when it comes to gangs in Michigan."

"I think we finally have a lead," Sandy said.

26

After Fleener left the office, I picked up my iPhone to tell AJ I'd be late. I didn't look forward to the call. Tension in our relationship was a recent arrival. We both felt it. It didn't feel good.

"I have to see Joey DeMio."

"I suppose you're going to the restaurant alone again," she said. The resentment of the other night lingered. I heard it in her voice, in her assumption of how I'd do my job, of not being careful.

"Henri's going along," I said. He nodded from the other side of the desk.

"Glad to hear it," she said, not sounding all that pleased.

"Okay," I said.

"Let me know you're all right after."

We said good-bye, edgy and uncomfortable.

Sandy said, "You all right? Is everything okay?"

I took a deep breath. "Sure."

"Boss, if …"

"Let it go, Sandy." That was too sharp.

She nodded and kept quiet. But the look on her face? She didn't buy it.

"Come on, Henri. Let's go see the man."

We started down the street for the two-block walk to Joey's restaurant. The late afternoon sun had shifted itself behind some of the taller buildings just enough to drop a bit of welcome shade on our side of the street.

"Joey might get testy, you tagging along."

"Don't care if he does," Henri said. "Besides, when's the last time you saw Joey go anywhere without one of his gunmen nearby?"

We went through the front door of Ristorante Enzo. Big band music of the 1950s shared the air space with the clatter of dinner prep in the kitchen. A tall man with chubby cheeks, very little hair, and a white apron shifted glasses behind the bar.

Even in the muted ambiance, I spotted Joey's gunmen, Jimmy Erwin and Roberta "Bobbie" Lampone leaning on the bar, looking serious. Both of them stepped away from the bar when they spotted Henri.

Jimmy took two more steps, toward me.

"No gun," I said, putting my arms out. It would have been foolish to try to conceal a gun from these guys anyway.

Henri pulled back his nylon jacket, revealing his handgun. "How you doing, Jimmy?" he said.

Erwin nodded.

"Let 'em go," Joey DeMio said from the back of the restaurant. He sat at a four-top with his legal eagle, Donald Harper. They occupied two chairs, with their backs to the rear wall. The cautious seats.

I went up to the table. Henri stopped at the end of the bar, a few feet away from the table. He could survey the entire floor.

"You inviting me to dinner, Joey?" I said, smiling.

"This is business," Harper said. "I told the broad this was important business."

I took a step closer and put my hand out, index finger pointing up. "Listen. You hear that?"

The music had eased into the vocals of Frank Sinatra. *"That's why the lady is a…"*

"I wouldn't let Mr. Sinatra call Sandy a 'broad,' Harper. You don't get to either."

Harper stiffened. "Now look, Russo…"

"Don," Joey said. "He's yanking your chain. Forget it."

Harper stayed quiet, but his icy stare told me he didn't like it. Good.

"Sit down, counselor," Joey said. "We have to talk." Joey still remembered I was actually a lawyer.

I took a chair across from them. "What's so urgent?"

"You want a drink?" Joey said. "What about you, LaCroix?" Joey paused. "Gianni," he said to the bartender, but Henri waved him off.

"No, thanks," I said. "Why the phone call?"

"Think of it as protecting my interests," Joey said.

"What interests would those be, and why should I care?"

Joey leaned forward, arms on the table. "Heard you had some trouble in Harbor Springs."

"Word travels fast."

Joey shrugged. "I make it my business to know."

"What happened in Harbor threatens your interests?"

Joey nodded. "Everything around here's my business, *capisce*?"

"So you are involved in this?" I said. If I sounded surprised, I was.

"I told you last time ... you sat right there," he said, pointing at me or the chair. "I told you those teenagers weren't my men. Told you I didn't know what you were talking about."

"Convince me otherwise."

"I hire men, serious men, experienced men, to work for me," Joey said. "Not schoolboys."

"What about them?" I said, nodding in the direction of a young Lampone and younger Erwin.

I didn't figure Joey caught the irony that Roberta Lampone was a woman.

"Unless they happen to be very good at what they do."

Joey leaned sideways, to see around me. "Jimmy?"

Erwin lifted himself off the bar and walked to the table.

"Mr. DeMio?"

"Jimmy, you heard anything about kid shooters, teenagers? On the street, you heard anything?"

Erwin shifted from one foot to the other, nervous. "Wouldn't know about that, Mr. DeMio. Lot of guys think they're shooters."

Joey offered a wave of his hand, and Erwin retreated to his spot at the bar.

Joey tilted his head, waiting for my response, like I should be satisfied. Maybe I was.

"Let me ask you this," I said. "Since everything, so you say, is your business. Anybody else running a gang around here?"

"A gang trying to muscle in on us?" Joey said. "Nobody's stupid enough to try that."

Harper jumped in, saying, "What Mr. DeMio means is that our business is unique. That we have no competitors."

Joey smiled. "Man's got a point, counselor."

"Uh-huh," I said. "But you know who to ask when you need guns."

Joey shrugged. "LaCroix knows who to ask, too. Isn't that right, LaCroix?"

Henri stared at the opposite wall like he hadn't heard the question.

"You knew how to find those two," I gestured at Erwin and Lampone, "when you needed fresh guns to replace Cicci and Rosato."

"Will there be anything else, counselor?"

I glanced at Harper, then Joey. "You called me, remember?"

Joey nodded. "Don't forget, counselor, as long as your interests don't conflict with my interests . . . don't let that happen."

"I'll give it serious thought, Joey," I said, and slid my chair back. "One more thing, you ever heard of the Cavendish Company? Out of Gaylord?"

Joey shot a quick glance at Harper, but I caught it. Neither man recognized the name. Joey shook his head.

I stood, and Henri moved away from his end of the bar. So did Jimmy Erwin.

I moved past Henri, who followed me toward the door.

"Take it easy, Bobbie," I said to Roberta Lampone, but her eyes remained on Henri as I went past.

"You too, Jimmy," Henri said as he went by.

Jimmy Erwin nodded.

Once outside, we walked up Lake Street with the cool of shade on our side.

"What do you think?" I said to Henri.

"Is Joey being straight, you mean? Hell if I know."

"Well, you can guess, damn it."

Henri pulled up, almost stopped. I slowed until he was next to me again.

"What's up, Russo? First Sandy, now me. I don't care about your ..."

"Then why are you asking?"

Henri stopped a few steps from McLean & Eakin's front window. We edged ourselves to the curb on the crowded sidewalk.

"You've made cracks to me before, you'll do it again. But we're on the job right now, your head's someplace else. That worries me. We assumed Joey would be easy, but we didn't know. We never know. Those two guns leaning on the bar were working, too, you know."

"Yeah."

"You talked to AJ before we left the office. You barked at Sandy. And the other night at Chandler's ... you and AJ. What's going on?"

"Not sure," I said. "Leave it alone, will you?"

Henri nodded slowly. "I'll leave it alone, Russo, unless ..."

"Unless, what?"

"Unless it gets in the way. Unless your mind's not on the job. I don't want to go up against men with guns, you not focused. Are we clear?"

"We're clear."

We stood quietly, uneasily. Henri and I've always seen the world the same way. We've only argued about how to get the job done.

The uneasy moment passed slowly.

"You asked me if Joey was straight with us?" Henri said, breaking the awkward silence.

I nodded.

"You're the one said Joey's after Lenny. What do you think?"

"Doesn't add up, Henri. Not anymore. Joey's hands are dirty, but I don't think he's behind this."

"Then who is?"

"Let's see what Fleener's gang expert turns up about '44' first."

"Okay," Henri said. "You gonna call AJ?"

"Uh-huh."

"Make nice, Russo."

27

Henri walked away up Lake Street, and I went upstairs to the office. Sandy was gone for the day, but she left a sticky note with two unimportant messages. I sat down and tapped AJ's number.

"It went okay, I take it?" she said.

"Yeah. I cleared up a couple of things about Lenny's book tour, that's all."

Silence. We often shared silence. We were comfortable with it. But not this time. This time it felt forced.

I spoke first. "Yeah, Joey doesn't like the idea we think he's behind this."

"So you've said."

Our conversation was lifeless, perfunctory. Fear drove AJ's conversation the other night.

"I think Joey really didn't have anything to do with Kate Hubbell's murder."

"You've said that, too."

I thought I was being helpful, filling her in like I'd done so many times before.

"I'm going to run over to Palette Bistro," I said, "get something to eat. Want to meet me?"

"I just made a sandwich," she said. "Thought I'd catch up on a little work. Busy day tomorrow."

"All your days are busy, AJ." That sounded frustrated. Well, I was frustrated. "Put the sandwich in the refrigerator. We'll split a couple of small plates."

"I ... I'm not ..."

"Don't you want to meet me, AJ?" That didn't sound much better.

"Michael, it isn't about ..."

"What is it about, AJ?"

"It isn't about meeting you. It isn't that."

"Then what?"

"Don't get pissy with me, Michael."

"I'm not ... I'm trying ..."

"Trying what?"

"To figure out the other night, AJ."

"The other night? You're pissed right now."

"I just ... I just asked if you were hungry."

"You're not listening to me."

"You said that the other night, AJ."

"I meant it then, too."

I stopped. This wasn't good — I wasn't sure what I was talking about or reacting to. Did AJ know what she was talking about? I wasn't sure. Our conversation, if that's what it was, needed to stop. Right now, it needed to stop, or it would get worse.

AJ was quiet, too.

After a few moments, I said, "Kate's memorial is tomorrow. Over in Indian River."

"Yes."

"Are you going?"

"Lenny wants to write the piece himself. About the service."

I should have just said good-bye and let it go at that. I should have.

"I didn't mean were you going as a reporter."

"Maury'll be there, too," she said, sidestepping my comment. "Charles Bigelow flies in tomorrow morning."

I didn't care about Bigelow's travel schedule, not right now.

"Okay, well, I need to eat," I said, having little else to say.

"Me, too."

We said a halfhearted, uncomfortable good-bye. Like Harold Pinter had written the lines.

I dropped the phone on the desk, pushed my chair back and spun around. The deep blue water of Little Traverse Bay gave off wavy trails of late-day heat. A catamaran, all gleaming red and silver, caught the wind and slid effortlessly west toward the sun. I reached down, grabbed my holster from the bottom left drawer of the desk, and clipped it under my shirt.

I needed a glass of wine, or a nice single malt. And food. I locked the office, went down the stairs and up Lake Street.

How did our wires get so crossed? Was it AJ? Me? Did it matter? Sandy thought something was wrong. Henri did, too, although his concern was as much professional as personal.

Henri analyzed matters from every possible angle while I, more often than not, trusted my instincts. I usually did all right by trusting them, but they didn't help much on the phone with AJ.

I'd only walked half a block when the professional, experienced side of my gut instincts kicked in.

I'd picked up a tail.

He was out there, but where? Across the street? In the alcove behind Symon's General Store? I turned the corner at Cutler's and went down Howard. I kept a steady pace. No need to tip him off. Haven't spotted him yet, and I'm good at spotting a tail.

I'd chosen not to take the short way through the parking lot. I wanted the fresh air of a longer walk to help me let go of the tension. Now it also gave me more time to spot the tail. The holster on my hip didn't feel as bulky as it did a few moments ago.

I stopped at Mettler's, just another shopper checking out men's clothing in the window. I glanced over my shoulder. Nothing. I slowly moved to Fustini's window and tried again. Nothing. But I wasn't wrong. The tail was good, knew what he was doing. Anybody that good was a pro, and not likely to try anything stupid on a busy day in the Gaslight District.

I walked into Palette Bistro, a contemporary restaurant on two levels featuring huge windows for gawking at the activity on the bay while dining. Tourists often snapped up the window tables, which left the lounge for locals. I took a seat at the end of the bar near the front window. The room was empty except for two women at a small table. They were in their twenties, dressed for business and enjoying each other's company while sipping from long-stemmed glasses with little umbrellas in them.

I had a clear view of the patio and the street. If he was out there, I'd spot him sooner or later.

"Good evening," the bartender said, placing a small napkin in front of me.

"What can I get you?"

I ordered an Oban and asked for a menu. I sat slightly turned on the stool to give me an easier view of the door and out the window.

"Here you go, an Oban, neat. Small plates on this side," she said, pointing at the menu.

"What are they drinking?" I said, nodding in the direction of the two women.

"Fru-fru drinks." And before I asked, "Fruit juices with a bolt of alcohol at the bottom," she said, and walked away.

I tasted the first soothing drink of scotch and put the glass back. A couple with a small child in a stroller braved the heat and humidity to sit outside. The sidewalks of Bay Street were less crowded than Mitchell, so it was more difficult for a tail to hide. I still didn't spot him.

"Any decision on food yet?" the bartender said, leaving a setup and a glass of water.

I ordered the crab cakes and a side salad.

"Shouldn't take long," she said, and went to check on the umbrella drinks.

I enjoyed the first bites of crab cake and ordered a second drink. About the time I wondered if my instincts had failed me, a familiar figure slid his way into the bar. He was tall, six feet at least, and skinny as a pencil;

you had to wonder if he'd had a good meal recently. A gaudy print shirt at least two sizes too big hung well below his hips. He wore the same shirt the last time I saw him. At Ristorante Enzo.

"Well, hello, Jimmy Erwin."

28

"**M**ind if I sit down?" Jimmy Erwin said. He stood perfectly still, keeping his hands where I could see them. He knew I'd be watching.

I nodded, and Erwin took the stool next to mine.

"Doesn't seem like your kind of place, Jimmy."

His eyes did a quick reconnoiter of the room, stopping briefly on the businesswomen.

"Never been here."

"Buy you a drink?" I said, when the bartender arrived.

"Labatt Blue."

After the bartender left, I said, "See anyone following me out there?"

I already knew the answer, but I couldn't resist.

"Keep the glass," Jimmy said to the bartender when she dropped off the Labatt's.

Jimmy smiled. "When'd you pick me up?"

"On the corner, by Cutler's."

He nodded slowly. "But you didn't really see me, did you?"

I shook my head.

He took a short pull on the beer. "You just knew I was there."

I nodded.

Jimmy smiled. "You're good, Russo. Give you that."

"Joey DeMio tell you to tail me?"

Jimmy shook his head.

"Then what're you doing here, Jimmy?"

Jimmy took another short pull on his Labatt's. Either this guy didn't

153

drink much, or he was being very cautious. My money was on cautious. Gunmen are always cautious if they want to live longer than the next guy.

"Wanted to give you a heads-up," he said.

"That so." I took the last bite of my crab cakes and pushed the plate away.

"Thought you might be interested …"

"Why were you following me, Jimmy?" I was getting impatient.

"I wasn't following you," he said, drawing out the word "following."

"No?"

"Checking to see if you were being followed."

Didn't expect that. He had me curious now. Was he moonlighting, picking up a few extra bucks?

"Why do you want to know if I'm being followed?"

"Mr. DeMio wants to know," he said. "Told me to keep an eye out, see if anyone's on you."

Joey DeMio was not a generous man. His interest in my welfare had little to do with me. This was something else.

"You know what's going on?"

Jimmy shrugged.

I thought for a minute. "People will blame Joey if another body turns up." I sipped some Oban. "That's it, isn't it?"

Jimmy shrugged again.

"Yeah, that's it," I said. "He doesn't give a shit about Lenny Stern or me. He just wants to avoid trouble."

Jimmy moved the Labatt's bottle around in a circle, but he didn't take a drink.

"So, I've got myself a bodyguard?" I said. "You going to shoot a guy who tries something?"

"Only if I have to," Jimmy said.

The couple on the patio finally called it a night. They slowly ambled away toward Howard Street, dad holding the baby, mom pushing the stroller.

"How long you going to hang around, Jimmy?"

"When Mr. DeMio says stop, I stop."

"And you'll stay in the shadows, right?"

"Easier to spot trouble that way."

The bartender delivered two more fru-fru drinks. The women raised the glasses, laughing their way through a toast.

"Got a question for you, Jimmy."

He waited, still moving the beer bottle around.

"That story, the one about you and some gunman in Gary." Jimmy Erwin had cut his teeth on the streets of northwest Indiana and Chicago's south side.

"Cal Hawley," Jimmy said in a dismissive tone. "Wore a black eye patch. Thought it made him look tough. He was stupid tough."

"Tough and dead," I said.

"Nah," Jimmy said. "Stupid and dead."

According to Martin Fleener, Hawley, a street punk older but not wiser, drew down on Jimmy Erwin one night in Gary, middle of East 8th. Real western movie. Jimmy put two in Hawley and walked away. Officially, no one saw or said anything, not that the cops spent much time on it.

Jimmy glanced in my direction, but remained quiet. He seemed to be examining the colorfully labeled liquor bottles neatly lined up behind the bar.

"Lot of stories on the street," he said. He shook his head slowly, lost in thoughts all his own. "Especially those streets ... Gary, Chicago."

He slowly lifted the Labatt's and took a drink. He might have finished half the bottle. Cautious.

"Remember," Jimmy said after he put down the beer. "I'll be around until Mr. DeMio says I'm done."

"I heard you the first time, Jimmy."

"The memorial service, tomorrow in Indian River?" he said.

"You'll be at the church?"

Jimmy nodded. "Got to keep an eye out." A thin smile appeared for a moment.

I waved the bartender away when she gestured regarding another round of drinks.

"Why are you being so generous, Jimmy, telling me this?"

"You'd have caught on sooner or later. Could've gotten ugly, you and LaCroix don't know why I'm hanging around."

Jimmy hesitated, looked straight at me. "I owe you," he said. "You got me out of that mess with Mr. North, probably kept me alive."

Jimmy Erwin worked for Conrad North in Petoskey a couple of years back. Henri and I tracked North and his gunmen to a back street in a deserted section of town. Only intervention by the State Police Tactical Unit stopped an ugly, bloody showdown.

"You don't owe me a thing," I said. "You were in handcuffs that night, last time I saw you. Henri's the one who got you out of there, Jimmy, not me."

"Same thing," he said. "Cops had me. Next thing I know, a lawyer shows up and takes care of it."

"And now you work for Joey."

"For Mr. DeMio, yeah." Jimmy slid off the barstool, giving the room another quick once-over. "Thanks for the beer."

I watched Jimmy move across the patio and up the block. He was smarter than I gave him credit for when he worked for Conrad North. But smarter didn't guarantee a longer life. His world was filled with dangerous people and short lives.

I signed the check, put down a tip, and left for home. My apartment was around the corner on Howard. I walked past my front door to the edge of the grass, looking over Little Traverse Bay. The sun was trying hard to drop below the horizon on the other side of the water.

I took out my phone and thought about calling AJ. I wanted to talk to her, to hear her voice, but last time hadn't gone well.

I took a deep breath and called Henri instead.

"How about we meet at the office at eight-thirty?" I said when he came on.

"Kate's memorial service at ten?"

"Yeah. You'll pick up Lenny first?"

"And Tina," he said, and clicked off.

There'd be time to tell him about Jimmy Erwin in the morning.

29

I waited by my car in the lot behind the office and sipped coffee. The sun was hot as it hung above the buildings. I was finally acclimated to steamy days. Never thought I'd say that. Northern Michigan drew you in with its pleasantly warm days and refreshingly cool evenings that often required a sweater. Those evenings seemed like a charming memory.

I'd run the neighborhood streets early to avoid the worst of the heat, but it was anything but relaxing. I spent too much time thinking about AJ, about the disquiet that had slid between us. A morning run usually cleared my head of stress or helped me brainstorm a particularly thorny case. This morning's run did neither. Henri's concern that I wasn't focused on the job was more real than I cared to admit.

It was still too early for retail shopping in Petoskey, but a few people wandered the streets or headed to Roast & Toast for coffee. Henri's SUV came around the corner, pulled into the lot and stopped. The tinted passenger window slid down.

"Morning, Russo," Lenny Stern said. His skinny black tie was cinched tight, his wispy gray hair flattened behind his ears. His idea of getting dressed up to deliver a eulogy at Kate's memorial service.

"Lenny," I said.

"Good morning, Michael," Tina Lawson said from the seat behind Lenny. Her eyes were puffy and red, her hands clutched tissues.

"Hello, Tina."

"Shouldn't be much traffic this early," Henri said. "We going up US 31 to Alanson?"

"Easiest way. Want me to lead, or you want to take it?"

Henri shook his head. "I'll drive, you ride," he said, pointing at the passenger seat. "I watch the road, you just … watch."

"Get in the back seat, Lenny," I said, opening his door. He swung his legs out and went around to the other side.

"Are we going to have trouble on the way to the church?" Tina said. She seemed startled by the idea, even though we'd been stuck in the middle of trouble for a while now.

"Just being careful," I said, as calmly as I could get away with.

"We don't want to be surprised," Henri said. "That's all."

I climbed in the passenger seat, closed the door, and we were off.

Henri went up Howard, turned on Mitchell at the old J.C. Penny store, and drove through town. Traffic was light over to 31. The fairways of the Petoskey-Bay View Country Club were crowded with golfers, mostly men, in colorful, baggy shorts and an array of visors and summer hats to shield them from the sun.

"You have your remarks ready for the service, Lenny?" I said.

"What can you say when she was too young to die?"

"Well, if anybody can do it …"

"Yeah, yeah. I jotted a few things down last night."

We rode in silence up 31 and out of town. As we passed Crooked Lake, I turned around and said, "Meant to ask you something, Lenny."

"What's that?"

"Talked to Joey DeMio the other day …"

"Not exactly breaking news."

"He told me you used to pal around with Carmine in Chicago, when his old man still ran the Baldini family."

"We didn't pal around, exactly."

"What would you call it, then?"

"We'd drink some wine, eat some pasta. You know, stuff like that."

I'd been at Carmine DeMio's table before, only at his invitation, only on business, and only when his business and mine overlapped. Carmine was not a generous man unless it suited him to be so.

I'd known Lenny Stern a long time. His reporting and my job sometimes involved the same people. In all that time, he'd never said a word about Carmine DeMio that might have been taken as personal. I wondered why. By the time we slowed for traffic in Alanson, I concluded there could be only one reason.

"Lenny?"

He stopped writing in his notebook. "Yeah?"

"All those stories you wrote about the mob in Chicago."

"What about them?"

"Was Carmine a source?"

"Carmine DeMio, long-time mob boss? A press source about the Mafia? Seriously, Russo?"

"Lots of phony astonishment, Lenny," Henri said, "but you didn't answer the man's question."

"Does it really matter, Russo? The Don's retired. He reads books on the front porch of his Mackinac Island cottage all summer."

"I don't care if he tossed you tips, Lenny. What I don't like are surprises. I'm involved with Joey; that means Carmine, too. And Carmine's still a dangerous man, if he wants to be. He reads books on the porch, but two gunmen are only twenty feet away. I need to know as much as I can. I'll live longer that way."

Henri inched his way through a mesh of cars and trucks in Alanson. He turned at the light and went east on M-68 toward Indian River, heading for Transfiguration Episcopal Church.

"I haven't even seen Carmine in, hell I don't know, two, three years. The last time was probably on the island, the Jockey Club or the Gate House. He likes those restaurants."

"Anything else I should know?"

"No," Lenny said, a touch of annoyance in his voice. "Didn't seem important, what happened in Chicago a long time ago. I'll remember you see it differently, Russo."

"Do we know where the church is?" Tina said, changing the subject.

"About a half mile short of the light at US 27," Henri said, pointing at the nav screen.

"Didn't you tell me you'd met Kate's sister?" I asked Tina.

"Once. Lois joined Kate and me for breakfast in Brutus."

"The Camp Deli," Henri said, phrased in a way that suggested a favorable critique. "Gone but not forgotten."

"She's quieter than Kate, shy maybe. They were really quite fond of each other, comfortable together. That was obvious when you were with them."

"How'd she end up in Indian River?" I said. "Weren't they from Indiana?"

"Evansville," Tina said. "Lois won a scholarship to Northwestern, the year before Kate took off for Champaign-Urbana. Lois met a messed-up guy, from what Kate said. From Indian River. He dropped out, Lois followed him. He dumped her."

"Familiar story," Henri said.

"Uh-huh," Tina said. "Kate and I hit it off. We were both rookies at Gloucester. She was eager to learn, be a professional on the way up. Living in downtown Chicago was a world away from southern Indiana. We learned the business together." Tina let out a small laugh. "We learned about life in Chicago, too. I liked her. So sad." Tina put the tissue to her eyes, holding it there.

Our ride across M-68 was happily uneventful. Around the south end of Burt Lake we passed driveway after driveway that disappeared into the woods, leading to lakefront houses. It was a familiar northern Michigan saga. Many of the original clapboard-sided summer cottages had been replaced over the years by more expansive and expensive year-round houses. The quaint charm of another small summer community had vanished.

"On the right," Henri said. "The church."

I looked up as Henri slowed, turned off the highway, and followed the curvy drive up into the woods. Three cars were parked away from the walkway that led to the traditional red doors of an Episcopal church. Several more cars and trucks dotted the lot.

A black Chevy Tahoe with heavily tinted windows sat by itself in the last row, shadowed by overhanging trees.

"We've got company," Henri said.

30

"What's the matter? What do you mean?" Tina said, startled by Henri's comment.

We had arrived at Transfiguration Episcopal Church twenty minutes before Kate Hubbell's memorial service. By church standards, Transfiguration was a new parish, founded in the 1950s. It was not until the late 1960s that services were held in the new, contemporary building tucked in the woods near Burt Lake State Park. With tall, peaked roof lines, slender windows, and a bell tower above a covered walkway, it blended comfortably with its surroundings.

"The black SUV, by the trees," Henri said. "Little obvious just sitting there."

"It's Jimmy Erwin," I said.

"Who's Jimmy Erwin?" Tina said.

I recounted my time with Erwin at Palette Bistro.

"Is that right?" Henri said. "And that's why we have Joey DeMio's gunman here this morning?"

"Don Joey's worried about being blamed for a crime?" Lenny said. "That's one for the books. You think it's bullshit?"

"Can't be sure," I said, "but I'll cut Joey some slack on this one. If he has no stake in Lenny's saga of corruption, he has every reason to not want Kate's murder tied to him."

"So Erwin's going to be with us for a while then," Henri said.

"Seems that way," I said.

"I have to find the priest before the service starts," Lenny said, opening the rear door. "Meet you inside."

We exited Henri's SUV as a white Chrysler 300 pulled in behind us. The doors opened and out stepped Maury Weston and Kate's boss, Charles Bigelow from Chicago.

We said our hellos as Bigelow greeted Tina with a comforting hug. She cried softly into his shoulder.

"I'm sorry," she said to no one in particular, and he patted her back.

"When did you get in?" Lenny asked Bigelow.

"Flew up this morning. Maury filled me in over breakfast."

"I asked Charles if he thought the book tour should continue," Weston said.

Lenny stared at Weston, then Bigelow. "Seriously? You might cancel?"

Bigelow put his hands out in a gesture implying things ought to be taken easily. He'd come a long way from the arrogant, insufferable man I first met in Weston's office. The pain of death, the fear of attack, has a way of changing people.

"We're just talking about it," Bigelow said. "Nothing's been decided, but we need to discuss it."

"I'm against it," Lenny said. "Lunch at the Iroquois ... it's the last stop."

"Except the wrap-up in Chicago," Bigelow said.

"You've got your own security people in Chicago. That one's all VIPs, Charles. You don't want to quit on them, do you?"

"I don't want to quit the Iroquois either, Lenny, but we're still going to discuss it after the funeral."

"Well, you goddamn better make up your mind, Charles. Mackinac's on for tomorrow, I plan to go."

Lenny spun around. "Have to find the priest," he said, and walked quickly away from us.

"He's right, Charles," Tina said. "We can't quit on Mackinac Island, or Chicago. The book's still going to come out, isn't it?"

Bigelow nodded. "Of course."

The parking lot was more than half full of cars, trucks, and SUVs. Some people were dressed in business wear, others in clothes more suited to a day off, but variety of attire was the norm for northern Michigan gatherings.

The church bell echoed in the woods. "It's almost time," Tina said. We joined the other mourners and entered the church. People ambled down the red carpet on the center aisle and fanned out into dark wooden pews. Charles led our little group into a pew a few rows back from the altar. Lenny rejoined us and took the outside seat. Henri remained near the door, off to one side.

Piano music, hymns probably, softly filled the air. A small table sat in the middle of the aisle, in front of the altar. On it was a sky-blue ceramic jar. Kate Hubbell's ashes.

Tina leaned in close to my ear. "The first row, other side on the end. That's Kate's sister." I only glimpsed Lois Hubbell's curly black hair through several rows of mourners.

I turned toward the back of the church. The pews were about half full. Alone, in the last row, sat Jimmy Erwin, looking somber, arms folded across his chest.

A door opened to one side of the altar as I turned around. The music faded away. The priest, who I assumed to be the rector of Transfiguration, walked slowly forward and welcomed everyone to the service.

He opened a prayer book. "I am the resurrection and I am life …"

The quiet in the church was interrupted only by the occasional sniffle or cough, and people shifting around in their seats.

"Comfort us in our sorrows at the death of our sister …"

It was clear that the priest hadn't known Kate, but he cared enough to personalize his remarks.

Lois Hubbell walked slowly to the front. She spoke of growing up with her sister in Indiana, of leaving home for different colleges, of Kate's love of writing.

After Lois sat down, Lenny Stern left the pew and went to the altar. He pulled a few sheets of notepaper from his inside jacket pocket and flattened them on the lectern. Lenny looked out over the pews and ran a hand over his hairless head. The mourners watched him and waited, but they were restless, out of sadness or, perhaps, needing to return to work.

Lenny cleared his throat.

"Kate was too young to die."

He began as he began his columns: sharp, precise, direct. He had our attention now. He grabbed us by the neck and didn't let go for fifteen minutes as he talked about Kate — the woman, the friend, the professional.

"I'll miss her. We'll all miss her." Lenny rolled up his notes and returned to his seat.

Following the post-communion prayer, the pianist played soft, peaceful music that filled the church.

"Let us go forth…" the priest said, and the service was over.

By the time I stood, neither Henri nor Jimmy Erwin was anywhere in sight. We joined the other folks and moved out of the church. Some people gathered in groups of three or four under the shade of the trees, talking, sometimes laughing. A few lit cigarettes.

Henri had created his own group of two, with Jimmy Erwin, near Jimmy's SUV. They might have been two old friends of the deceased renewing an acquaintance. I knew better.

31

The solemn music faded as we left the church. Tina Lawson took hold of Lenny's arm as we approached Henri's SUV. She smiled, gently kissed Lenny on the cheek, and turned to watch the mourners return to their vehicles.

"That was some eulogy, Lenny," Charles Bigelow said, as he and Maury Weston walked up. "A little strong for rural America, don't you think?"

"Don't sell the folks up here short, Charles," Lenny said. "They don't dress like urban types, sometimes don't sound like them either, but they've got heart and passion, and they care about each other. As much as I love cities, the energy, the life, living up north is special. I can get a city fix when I need one, a few days here, a week there, but I thrive on living here."

Leonard Stern never ceased to amaze me. Lenny the man, the tough crime reporter who cut his journalistic teeth on the streets of Detroit and Chicago, felt more at home on Little Traverse Bay or Pennsylvania Park in northern Michigan. I knew too many people who tried to make that work but missed the mark. Lenny never tried. It was who he was, what he thought, and how he felt about the places he called home.

"Hard to argue with that, Charles," Maury said.

Bigelow put his hands out. "All right, all right. I didn't mean … Lenny just sounded, I don't know, a bit too harsh for a memorial service."

"We appreciate candor and honesty," Maury said, "even at a church service."

"Well, I liked it," Tina said. "You captured the Kate I knew."

"I know a lot of people in the business," Lenny said. "But I really liked

Kate. We spent a lot of time getting the book ready...getting to know each other." Lenny paused and looked out toward the woods. "I never had a daughter, but if..."

"You were wonderful."

Lenny put his arm around Tina's shoulder. "Thank you."

"Michael, who's Henri talking to?" Maury said, gesturing toward the other side of the parking lot.

"His name's Jimmy Erwin," I said. "Gunman for Joey DeMio."

"Ah, the DeMio clan," Bigelow said. "Father and son. Chicago gangland at its finest."

"That's them," I said.

"Do you think he came here for Kate?" Tina said.

"He's working," I said. "Joey ordered it. To keep an eye on all of us."

Before Bigelow could ask, I explained that we doubted DeMio was behind the threats to Lenny Stern, and that Joey didn't want to be blamed for Kate's murder.

"But you still don't know who murdered Kate?"

I shook my head. "But we've got a few leads."

"Anything Lenny can write about?" Maury said, smelling a story.

"Give us a few days," I said. "That okay with you, Lenny?"

"My instinct is to write..." he shook his head. "But I don't want anyone else hurt. Do what you have to to find these guys. Okay with you, Maury, we hold off?"

"It is this time," Maury said. He glanced at his watch. "Time to get you to the airport, Charles."

With that, Bigelow and Weston said their good-byes.

As they drove away from the church, Henri came over. A few moments later, Jimmy Erwin drove out of the parking lot.

"Nice service," Henri said. "You ready to go?"

"Just waiting for you," I said. "Everything all right with Jimmy?"

Henri nodded. "He's okay."

"I thought you said he worked for the Mafia guy," Tina said.

"He does," Henri said. "But Jimmy sticks to his word."

"You trust him?" I said.

Henri thought for a minute. "This time, yeah. Jimmy says he owes us for getting him out of that mess with Conrad North."

"If he thinks so," I said, and shrugged.

"Lois," Tina said, and waved at Lois Hubbell who walked with two women toward the cars. "Michael, come with me."

Lois walked toward us.

"Lois, this Michael Russo. The man I told you about."

"Thank you for coming today," she said, reaching out her hand.

We shook hands.

"I'm sorry for your loss," I said. "I wish we could've met under better circumstances."

"Me, too, Mr. Russo," Lois said. "I hope you find out who did this to Kate."

"We'll do our best," I said.

"I know," she said, offering a soft smile. Lois gave Tina a brief hug, thanked us again from attending the service, and walked away.

"All right," I said to Tina. "Back to Petoskey."

We rejoined the others, climbed into Henri's SUV and left Transfiguration Episcopal Church behind us. Traffic was light along the south end of Burt Lake all the way to Alanson. Not so on US 31. Henri merged into a long line of cars and trucks headed south, and we patiently listened to Interlochen classical music.

"I suppose you two have a plan for Mackinac tomorrow," Lenny said.

"Of course, we do," Henri said without further comment.

After a moment, Lenny said, "You want to let us in on your plan?"

Silence.

"You want to tell them, Russo?"

"Tell them what?"

"About tomorrow," Lenny said. "Our plans for the island and the Iroquois Hotel?"

"Sorry," I said, "I was reading a text from Marty Fleener." I closed the screen. "Okay, tomorrow. Henri and I will pick you up, both of you."

"The luncheon starts at noon," Lenny said. "They want me there a half hour ahead."

"We'll leave in time to catch the ten-thirty Shepler's ferry," I said. "You'll have an hour."

"That'll work," Lenny said.

"The text from Fleener," Henri said. "What'd he want?"

"He talked to his guy in Lansing," I said.

"The gang expert?"

"Uh-huh."

"Anything helpful?" Henri said.

"He said we'd talk later."

"You mean like street gangs?" Lenny said, before I could answer. "This have to do with Kate?"

"Maybe," I said. "Remember the Side Door, Lenny? In the parking lot? When the two guys tried to scare us off?"

"I certainly do," Lenny said.

"One had a tattoo," I said.

"Sure, a '44' on his arm."

"Well, a '44' showed up on a vanity plate. 'RC 44.'"

I reminded Lenny and Tina of the guys we chased away from the author event in Harbor Springs, of their rusty old Ford truck and license plate.

"The plate was registered to a business in Gaylord, the Cavendish Company. They make…"

"What'd the plate say?" Lenny said, grabbing the front seat back. "The vanity plate, what was it again?"

"'RC 44,'" I said.

"The vanity plate, 'RC 44?'"

"Yeah."

"You've got to be kidding," Tina said.

"What are you two talking about?" I asked.

"I put it in the book," Lenny said, clearly agitated. "Either of you half-assed detectives even read the damn thing?"

"What're you talking about?" I said, ducking an embarrassing question.

"The Chicago prosecutor," Tina said, not quite laughing. "The pivotal man in Lenny's book. His name was Ramsey Cavendish, you know, like RC on the plate?"

I turned sideways, toward the back seat.

"Let's not get ahead of ourselves," I said. "We're talking Gaylord, not Chicago."

"Cavendish's widow moved to Gaylord after Ramsey died in prison," Lenny said. "Faded out of sight."

"What's the widow's name?" I had an empty feeling I already knew the answer after Fleener ran the company through DMV.

"Sylvia."

"DMV lists three names for Cavendish Company vehicles," I said. "Sylvia, Daniel, and Walter."

"You guys should've read my book. Daniel and Walter? They're Sylvia's sons."

32

Our obedient line of cars snaked its way past the always-crowded boat ramps at Crooked Lake, but I hardly noticed. On this bright July day the lake was clogged with sailboats, jet-skis, and power boats. But I hardly noticed them either.

I sometimes missed important details because they moved too quickly or they were a jumble of ragged pieces. No excuses, no one to blame but me this time. And we had a copy of Lenny Stern's book.

Once back into town, we swung by the *Post Dispatch* building to drop off Tina and Lenny to the safety of their offices.

"You know, Russo," Lenny said as he climbed out of the rear seat. "Stop thinking like a detective for a minute. Don't analyze so much. The goddamn pieces, they're telling you what to do next."

"Enlighten me," I said.

"That would be Cavendish Company. I made the connection between events and the Cavendish family years ago. You just figured it out," Lenny said, and slammed the car door.

Henri eased his SUV away from the curb and headed for Lake Street.

"That wasn't good," I said.

"If you mean Lenny's book, no, it wasn't good," Henri said.

"We could hardly scare up a clue, two, three days ago." I scrolled through my email. "Found an email from Sandy. On the book. Here's another one."

"I got them," Henri said. "Haven't read them yet."

"We had Lenny's book in the office, for chrissake," I said.

"Too late to worry about it now," Henri said. "But it gave us new pieces, more details."

"We don't know if, or even how, they fit together," I said. "The pieces don't make any sense."

Henri let me out in front of the office and drove off.

"Damn, boss," Sandy said after I'd filled her in. "It sure makes sense now, but... we dropped the ball. Wish I'd been sharper."

"Join the club," I said.

"Want me to call the Cavendish Company?" Sandy said.

I nodded. "See if president ... forgot his name."

"I have it," she said, sifting through a stack of papers. "Daniel, Daniel Cavendish."

"Well, see if president Daniel Cavendish has a few minutes this afternoon for a private eye from Petoskey."

I went to my desk and texted Marty Fleener about the Cavendish connection.

"Text me tomorrow," he sent back, "might have something."

I hadn't given much thought to Lenny's tour stop at the Iroquois Hotel, but keeping him safe on a trip to Mackinac Island was a less complicated problem. The area was contained, unlike the northern tip of the mitt. The bad guys had to hit us on the way to Mackinaw City or back. Once at the Shepler's ferry dock, it was too difficult to hide. On a ferry, impossible.

"You're on Daniel Cavendish's schedule at two-thirty," Sandy said from the doorway. "Talk to the receptionist ... her name's Sally Peck. You'll find her just inside the front door."

"She ask why I wanted to see her boss?"

Sandy nodded. "As all good assistants should. I gave her the usual 'a name came up in an investigation' excuse, and that was that."

Over the years, I've learned most people are intrigued when a private eye knocks on the door. It was "just like on TV," they'd say. People were usually eager to talk, at least the first time. But I wasn't sure what to expect from the Cavendish folks.

I tapped Henri's number. "Where are you?" I asked when he came on.

"Just ordered a sandwich, why?"

"Road trip to Gaylord. You want to come along?"

"Of course."

I explained what and when.

"Things to do. I'll meet you there."

I finished up some paperwork and made one call. I checked the time. It wouldn't take that long to drive over to Gaylord.

"I probably won't be here when you get back. Dad's got a doctor appointment."

Sandy had lived with her widower father since her mother died. They shared a classy 1920s clapboard-sided two-story on the water at Crooked Lake, a few miles north of Petoskey.

"Is he okay?"

"Sure. It's his annual Medicare Wellness checkup. Happens every July."

"Good to hear," I said. "I'll see you in the morning."

"Are you leaving for the Mackinac luncheon from here?"

"Yeah. We're riding with Henri."

Sandy returned to her desk, and I stared at my iPhone ... again.

I wanted to call AJ, text her at least, before heading to Gaylord. I did that all the time, keeping her aware of when I left town, especially if I was working a case. We learned the hard way during the troubles with Conrad North that danger can strike anywhere, even in the most banal places. AJ worried about me differently after that. It wasn't simply fear, she told me, it had become a nagging sense of dread. I tried to reassure her, but it was just so many words, and she knew that.

AJ gave me a heads-up if she left town, too. That's what partners did.

But when we talked yesterday, she seemed uninterested, even annoyed that I was bothering her. I couldn't tell if she didn't want to hear from me, or if hearing from me made it harder to push away that feeling of dread.

I looked at the keypad and shook my head. I slid my phone into a pocket, said good-bye to Sandy, and walked out to the car.

I opened the driver's door and waited for some of the heated air to rush out. I fired up the twin-turbo six and switched the A/C on high. I tapped in directions to the Dickerson Road address for Cavendish Company. There was only one reasonable route to Gaylord; happily, the nav system thought so, too.

I joined the endless line of cars and trucks on Mitchell, then motored past the hospital and Johan's to US 131 South out of town.

Traffic was thick and steady, especially near Walloon Lake and through Boyne Falls. Not that I expected anything different at the busiest time of the summer. At some invisible place just south of Boyne Falls, US 131 added "Old Mackinaw Trail" to its name, staying that way when I turned east on M-32 for Gaylord.

Once Lenny connected a family business in Gaylord to his story of corruption and murder in Chicago, we were onto something solid for the first time since the threats started. But we still had a long way to go … rusty old trucks, vanity plates, teenage tough guys with tattoos, and a manufacturing company. It all added up to what?

By the time I passed the lush, green fairways of the Gaylord Country Club, traffic had slowed to a crawl all the way through town as visitors peeled off at Home Depot, Panera Bread, or Starbucks. When the nav system squawked at me, I turned on Dickerson Road at the Shell station. About a quarter mile past the end of the airport runway, I spotted a gaudy green-and-red sign that read simply, "Cavendish."

The building was a large, flat-roofed cinderblock structure that stretched back off Dickerson Road for a hundred yards. The side of the building was lined with a long row of huge overhead doors. Several trailer trucks were being loaded at the doors.

The office section of Cavendish Company was an A-frame assemblage tacked onto cinderblocks in an effort to reflect the alpine theme of Gaylord's buildings, adopted to make the town stand out from other northern Michigan resort communities. The shops and restaurants along Main Street did a better job of masquerading as chalets than the Cavendish building did.

I parked in the small lot at the front of the building, several spots down from Henri's SUV. He slid the driver's window down when I came up.

"Want me to come in?" he said.

"Sandy made an appointment for me. Let's not scare them just yet."

Henri nodded, and the window went back up.

I went through the double front doors into a large square room with a tile floor. On one side were four uncomfortable looking tubular chairs with orange seats; on the other side, an office-functional gray metal desk. The hum of the air conditioning tried unsuccessfully to blend with the raspy noise of the fluorescent lights.

"Hello," said the woman at the desk. She was in her early twenties, with shoulder-length brown hair and soft eyes. "How can I help you?"

"Are you Sally Peck?" I said.

Her face lit up. "Yes, I am," she said, emphatically and confidently.

"I'm Michael Russo. I have …"

"An appointment to see Mr. Cavendish," she said.

"Right."

Sally leaned forward a bit. "Are you really a private eye?"

I nodded. "I really am."

"Could I see some ID?" She tried to sound serious, but her request came across as curiosity.

I pulled out my leather holder and showed her my license.

"Wow. Just like on TV."

33

Sally Peck picked up the receiver of her museum-piece desk telephone and punched one of the plastic buttons at the bottom. The button lit up. I didn't think they still made phones like that.

"Your appointment is here, Mr. Cavendish," she said, and put down the receiver. The button's light went out. Clever.

"Would you have a seat, Mr. Russo?"

I moved toward the other side of the room. I had just figured out how to make the uncomfortable chair work when a door opened and out came a pear-shaped man in his mid-thirties, with an oval face, round eyes, and a narrow widow's peak at the front of his receding hairline.

"Mr. Russo. Daniel Cavendish," he said, extending his hand. His ill-fitting black suit needed a tailor, or he needed more time at the health club.

We shook hands.

"Come on in," he said cheerfully, and went into his office. "Have a seat," he said, closing the door behind me.

Cavendish's office was a slightly upscale version of Sally Peck's. It was bigger, but without windows or fluorescent lights. His desk was some type of heavy, dark wood. A matching conference table sat to one side. It was large enough for six upholstered chairs. A banker's lamp, complete with green shade, sat at each end of the table.

I sat in an upholstered client chair in front of his desk. Cavendish leaned on the desk, laced his fingers together, and smiled.

"Well, Mr. Russo, I have to admit I'm curious what brings a private investigator all the way over from Petoskey."

Cavendish seemed almost as eager to chat as Sally Peck.

"Your name came up during an investigation."

"My name?"

"Well, not you, personally, but Cavendish Company."

"Really? In Petoskey?"

I nodded. "Emmet County."

"How so?"

"The driver of one of your company trucks may have witnessed a crime in Harbor Springs."

His eyebrows came together, his head tilting slightly.

"One of our trucks? You sure?"

"An old Ford Ranger, red. Sound familiar?"

Cavendish nodded slowly. "Could be someone else's truck. Why would you think it's ours?"

"It's registered with a vanity plate, RC 44."

Cavendish sat back in his chair. His right hand moved up and lightly scratched the side of his face. He wasn't smiling.

"It's your truck, right?" I said.

He leaned over, picked up a phone receiver just like Sally Peck's, and punched a button. It lit up, too.

"My office," he said. He paused. "Yes, now." Not angry, insistent.

"The Ranger is one of your trucks?" I said again.

Cavendish put his right elbow on the desk, hand up, the index finger pointed in the air.

"A moment." Not angry, not insistent. Like he'd hit the pause button.

The moment lasted no more than fifteen seconds. The office door opened. I stood and turned toward the door. In came a man, not quite six feet, lean, with an angular face anchored by dark-rimmed glasses.

"Mr. Russo," Daniel said, "this is Walter Cavendish, our Director of Marketing and Production."

Walter moved across the room effortlessly and economically. His handshake was firm.

"Mr. Russo," Walter said, in a voice both sharper and less amiable than his brother's.

"Shall we move to the conference table?" Daniel said, gesturing to the side of the room.

"I'm fine right here," Walter said. His single-breasted black blazer over a gray silk T-shirt seemed more suited for downtown big city than main street northern Michigan.

"Daniel?" Walter said. That's all he said, all he needed to say. Daniel was president of Cavendish Company, but it was clear who was in charge.

"Mr. Russo is a private investigator from Petoskey," Daniel said.

Walter pulled back the sides of his blazer and put his hands on his hips. He listened silently as his brother filled him in. He remained silent once Daniel was finished, waiting to see what I had to say. He was used to being offered information, not offering it.

I didn't care, I wasn't interested in playing that game.

"That was your company truck in Harbor Springs," I said. It wasn't a question.

"What crime are you talking about?" Walter said, ignoring my comment. "That you think one of our people witnessed."

"Street crime," I said. "Two people were attacked in the middle of the day. Downtown. It was a company truck."

"One of ours?"

Daniel, the amiable front man of Cavendish Company, had become irrelevant. Walter had simply taken over, ignoring his brother, making no effort to include him.

"We got the plate," I said. "RC 44. It is yours."

Walter nodded. "And you think that means what?"

That was the first empty thing Walter had said. He was stalling. Sooner rather than later was always a good time to push.

"The vanity plate," I said. "What's it mean?"

"Our late father," Walter said. "Ramsey Cavendish, 'RC.' He ordered the plate a long time ago."

Walter shot his brother a quick glance, but I caught it. Walter's first indication that Daniel was not being completely ignored.

"After dad passed, we kept it," Walter said. "Seemed like a good idea."

"What about the 44?" I said.

"I have no idea," Walter said.

Another glance his brother's way. The first one could have been nothing more than the brothers remembering their father. The second one? A mistake.

I turned toward Daniel.

"Did you ever hear your father mention the plate?"

"Beg pardon?"

He had to be listening. It was a reach, but I hoped to catch him off-guard.

"Did your father … ?"

Daniel hesitated, shoved his hands into his pants pockets. "No … don't think so. No. I'm sure … no."

He didn't sound all that sure to me, but before I could invent another question, brother Walter stepped in.

"A license plate, Mr. Russo? We're really quite busy this afternoon — that is, if you have nothing better to be curious about."

He had me there: curiosity was all I had left. For now.

"Well, I appreciate your time, gentlemen," I said. "I'll find my way out."

Walter got to the door first, opened it and said, "Have a good day."

I waved good-bye to Sally Peck and went outside into the afternoon heat.

I cranked up the A/C for a faster cool-down as I pulled onto Dickerson Road.

I didn't bother replaying my time with the brothers Cavendish, hoping to remember some nugget of conversation. This time, only one thought ran around and around in my head.

Why did Walter Cavendish lie?

34

"So," Henri said. "You're still alive. How'd it go?"

I told him.

"See you in the morning," Henri said, and drove away.

I took the back way, south of the airport to Alba Road, avoiding the late-afternoon congestion in downtown Gaylord. Once on US 131 to Mancelona and Kalkaska, I had little choice but to join the train of vehicles for the ride home. But it gave me time to think.

Walter Cavendish lied, that much was clear. Even "why" seemed clear. He wanted to throw me off the track. Who picked the vanity plate? Just dad having a bit of fun. Why did the company keep his license plate? Well, it was dear-old dad's, after all.

I didn't buy it. Maybe Walter assumed his folksy explanations would satisfy me. It was a simple task to check the death records. If a company driver did witness a crime, Walter had to worry the police would eventually come calling. Likely he knew the local cops and thought he could take care of it.

The ride to Petoskey seemed longer than usual, probably because I was in a hurry. I took the stairs two-at-a-time. Sandy was gone for the day. I knew that I rummaged around her desk at my own peril, but Lenny's book was there someplace. He'd sent her a pre-publication copy, one with "not for sale" slapped on the front cover, "uncorrected proofs" on the back.

Luckily, *Corruption on Trial* was hiding in plain sight under yesterday's copy of the *Post Dispatch*. I sat in Sandy's chair and scanned the email summaries she sent about the book. Helpful stuff, but I needed more detail. I opened the book and dug in.

It was right there in Chapter 18. Ramsey Cavendish died in prison, beaten to death in his jail cell. No suspects.

I leaned back, carefully put my feet on Sandy's desk and kept reading.

Ramsey's widow, Sylvia, and her boys, Daniel (age 10) and Walter (age 9), sold the family home on Chicago's Gold Coast and moved to northern Michigan. Sylvia bought a less-than-successful manufacturing firm in Gaylord. They lived quiet lives, as she, and later her sons, built the Cavendish Company into a successful business well-positioned to take advantage of online sales during a time of a rapidly expanding global economy and its demand for industrial supplies.

All of which made for an interesting story of success in the wake of tragedy, but it didn't answer my question. Why did Walter Cavendish lie? Ramsey Cavendish was long dead when somebody chose a vanity plate for the battered Ford truck.

I read on for a while, but learned nothing helpful. About the time I thought I should give up and head home, the office door opened.

"Hi," AJ said, and closed the door.

It could have been an hour or a week since we'd been together. It didn't matter, I always reacted the same way. My heart skipped a beat.

She hesitated, then crossed the room to sit opposite from me in one of the client chairs next to Sandy's desk.

"Hi," I said.

"I stopped at McLean & Eakin on my way home. Thought I'd see if you were still here."

I nodded and smiled. I didn't care why. I was happy to see her.

She reached out and touched the back of my hand. "What are you reading?"

"Lenny's book."

AJ smiled. "Uh-huh. He told anyone who'd listen that you and Henri could be, and I quote, 'dumb shits.' I didn't have a chance to ask him why."

"Neither of us read his book. We missed an important detail."

"A real clue?"

"Yep," I said, "and helpful."

"Want to fill me in?"

I shook my head. "Not right now."

"No, not right now." AJ waited a moment. "Michael, I don't like this. I'm uncomfortable. Where we are ... the distance."

"I don't like it either, AJ. We're not used to ... to this."

"No, we're not."

"How did we get here?"

"Does it matter?"

I nodded. "I think it does. It feels ... no, I feel ... like you're being critical, judgmental about the way I do my job."

"I'm not judging you, Michael." She shook her head slowly. "I'm not."

"It feels that way."

AJ sat back and looked away, at the wall, maybe, or the large aerial photo of the Mackinac Bridge that occupied most of the wall space. I waited.

"I'm afraid, Michael ..."

"That I could get hurt?"

"Hurt? You've been hurt before. I don't want ... night is the worst time, did you know that? The middle of the night ... I wake up ... Marty Fleener's banging on the door."

Her eyes were wet. And sad.

"AJ ..."

"What if I never see you again? You go off ... to an alley or a deserted house ... you'll die in the street, alone."

"It's what I do, AJ. It's dangerous sometimes."

"Well, hell, I know that ..."

I closed the cover of *Corruption on Trial*. She'd gone another place, alone.

"AJ ..."

"I don't want you to be a dead private eye, Michael. I'm angry."

AJ looked startled, just for a moment, at what she'd just said.

"Who are you…"

"Who am I mad at?"

I nodded, but didn't say anything. I felt bad for her, for her fear. I stayed silent for a few moments.

"I'm mad at you, Michael. You."

Tears trailed slowly down her face. She sat still. I wanted to ask why, but that would not have been a helpful question.

"But… but I'm mad at me. Really mad at me." She took a tissue from a box on Sandy's desk. "I don't want you to be a dead private eye," she repeated.

AJ looked as sad as I'd ever seen her. It broke my heart to see her so despondent, to feel her in such pain.

"Would you rather I be a lawyer again? Divorces, wills?"

She was quiet.

"I'm really a good investigator, AJ."

"That's because you want to be a good investigator, Michael. There's a difference." She wiped tears away and took a deep breath.

"I'm really mad at me… for being scared. I want to push the fear away." She shook her head slowly. "That won't work, not really. I have to find a way to accept it, live with it.

"I wish I could tell you how to do that," I said.

"I have to do it myself, dammit, I don't need…"

She stopped, waited a moment, then turned toward me.

"Sorry," she said. "That wasn't fair. I'm sorry."

I reached over and took her hand. She squeezed it.

"I want to figure out a way… a way through it, Michael."

I nodded, but I didn't know what was in her head, only what she said. I felt pretty sure not interrupting was a better idea than jumping in too soon.

"Michael." She glanced around the office, as if it were filled with people and she didn't want them to hear.

"Michael, come home with me. I know you have to leave early for the island."

I nodded.

"I want ... I just want to feel you next to me, feel you ... inside of me. I want to put my arms around you and just ... I want to do that."

35

"What time is it?" AJ pulled the sheet away from her face just enough so that I heard the question. I'd already slipped out of bed, grabbed my clothes, and put on coffee.

"Almost six-thirty." I leaned over and kissed her on the cheek. "I'll have some coffee, then get going."

"Want me to drive you home?" AJ was sitting up, leaning against the headboard, holding the sheet across her chest.

I shook my head. "The walk will feel good. Don't have time to run."

"You have your .38, don't you?"

"Uh-huh, and I'll pay attention, AJ, promise."

"You anticipated my next question."

"I did. Meet you in the kitchen?"

"I'll get my robe," she said, flipping the sheet back and getting off the bed with more theatrical flair than was necessary.

I smiled. "Beautiful."

"So you said last night ... more than once."

I was leaning against the kitchen counter working on my coffee when AJ walked in. She tightened the cinch on her long, white terrycloth robe. I filled a mug with hot coffee and handed it to her.

"You're not worried about the walk home?"

I selected my words carefully. I didn't want to launch into another contentious discussion of my job. For one thing, I didn't have time. Mostly I didn't want to spoil the moment.

"I'll be careful about every move we make until this is over," I said.

"But experience has taught me that some places are more dangerous than others."

AJ sipped coffee. "Walking home this morning is less dangerous?"

I nodded. "There's no Lenny, no Tina. The car's at my apartment. Being here was not predictable, not scheduled."

"But leaving for the island this morning is on Lenny's public schedule."

I nodded again. "Anyone can read it."

"Want more coffee?" she said.

"Wish I could stay..."

AJ put down her mug, took two steps, put her arms around me and pulled me close.

"Please don't take this the wrong way, Michael," she said softly, with her face close to mine. "I still have to work through this ... this stuff."

"Yes."

"Thank you."

We kissed good-bye, and I left by the side door.

The sun had a good start on its arc through the morning sky. I moved along at a decent clip, feeling beads of sweat under my shirt. It was a four-block walk to my apartment from AJ's restored two-story above the ravine on Bay Street. I'd walked this route many times, often under the pressures of a case. Shooters only had a few spots to try something without giving me a lot of warning. I kept my eyes moving, watching for the odd, the unusual.

I didn't take AJ's comment the wrong way. I knew she had to sort out the fear, to deal with the anger. She wouldn't be happy until that happened. But being together overnight was a pleasant diversion for both of us.

I took a fast shower, then put on a polo shirt and fresh khakis. I decided on a lightweight blazer instead of a loose shirt to cover my .38. The author luncheon at the Iroquois Hotel was resort-dressy, unlike book signings on the mainland.

I left my car at home and ate a banana on the two-block walk up Howard to the office.

"Good morning, boss," Sandy said when I walked in the door.

"Morning, Sandy," I said. "Did your father do okay at the doctor?"

She laughed. "Passed his Medicare checkup with flying colors. I'm sure he gave only the best answers."

"To get done faster?"

"That's it," she said. "What time is Henri picking you up?"

"In a couple of minutes. Any messages?"

"Nope, you're good," she said. "Text when you're back from the island, okay?"

"Sure."

"Boss?"

I looked back from the door.

"Be careful."

I picked up a coffee at Roast & Toast and left for the parking lot by the back door. Henri's SUV was in the alley, waiting.

"Good morning," I said as I climbed into the front seat. Lenny and Tina were in back.

Henri took the usual route to Division, then US 31 north for the fifty-minute drive to the Mackinaw City ferry docks. We rode along without much idle chitchat. Lenny scanned his notes, Tina checked her email, Henri and I were, well, alert.

"Michael." It was Tina. "I have a theory I want to run by you. You, too, Henri."

We were a few miles south of the airport in Pellston. Traffic was steady.

"Go ahead," I said.

"Wait a second, Tina," Henri said. "Michael?"

"Yeah, I see it."

"How long?"

"Ten minutes, fifteen maybe."

"What's happening?" Lenny said.

"Black Tahoe, right?" Henri said to me.

"That's the one."

"Do we have a tail?" Lenny said.

"We do," Henri said.

"Can you tell who it is?"

"No," Henri said. "We'll keep driving, see what he does when we get to the dock."

"Sorry, Tina," I said.

"No, no," Tina said. "Your job comes first." She paused.

"You have a theory?"

"So, we've talked about Kate's murder. Why kill Kate?"

"Yes."

"You weren't sure. Lenny and I weren't sure."

"I'll say it again," Lenny said. "I wrote the goddamn book. Why kill Kate?"

"It's the documents," Tina said.

"All the evidence is with your lawyer," Henri said. "Right?"

"It's not the documents themselves, you guys," Tina said, "it's us. The Mafia wants to kill us, shut us up."

I thought again that maybe the mob wasn't after anyone, but that someone else was. The bookstore owner in Harbor Springs asked if Kate was killed for a reason, or — was she just in the wrong place at the wrong time? I wasn't convinced by Tina's theory.

"I don't get it," Henri said. "If they kill two of you, three of you, the damn book gets even more publicity, more attention after it's published."

"So what?" Tina said. "They shout 'prove it' or 'fake news' or sue Gloucester Publishing for making it up to sell books. Somebody will get the ball rolling, I don't know, a former office holder, one of the Cavendish people. Somebody puts it on *Facebook*, *Instagram*, it wouldn't take much to ruin the book, muddle what it exposes."

Henri eased up on the gas as he went through the stoplight at US 23 in Mackinaw City. The black SUV kept a discrete distance. The driver knew how to run a tail.

"That's my theory, anyway," Tina said.

"It's an interesting theory," I said, "but only if the mob's after all three of you."

"But I thought …" Tina said, as her voice faded.

"I'm not sure it's the mob," I said. "The people we're hunting for might never have made our radar screen."

Silence replaced the chatter after I said that. Henri took Central Avenue through town, passing shops featuring fudge, T-shirts, and trinkets. He pulled up to the gate at Shepler's and paid cash to park on the dock.

Henri pulled into a parking spot three rows away from the ferry ramp. "Michael, look," Henri said, pointing toward the street.

"I should have guessed," I said, watching Jimmy Erwin exit the black SUV and make his way through the parked cars.

"Is that the same man who was at the church," Tina said, "at Kate's memorial service?"

"That's him," I said.

The others headed for the ferry ramp.

"Save me a seat," I said, and went to meet Jimmy Erwin.

He stood next to an elegant Porsche Carrera S, slate gray over tan leather.

"Nice ride," Jimmy said, ogling the car. "Got to get me one of these someday."

"One-twenty large, my man," I said. "You'll have to be a gunman a long time."

"Yeah."

"So?"

"Nobody followed you up from Petoskey," Jimmy said.

"Comforting to know. You coming to Lenny's talk?"

Jimmy shook his head. "Next time. You'll be in good hands on the island for a couple of hours."

I wasn't sure what he meant. Jimmy didn't have much of a sense of humor.

"I'll be here," Jimmy said, "when you get back to the mainland."

"So you can keep an eye on us."

Jimmy smiled. "To keep an eye out for the shooters."

I nodded, and went to catch up with the others on the ferry.

36

've crossed the Straits to "the land of the great turtle" regularly since that first time when I was four years old. I've never tired of it, not once. The deep blue water with a scattering of whitecaps, the elegant Mackinac Bridge, and the quaint charm of the harbor at Mackinac Island.

The deckhand left the bow door open, allowing cool, refreshing air to push through the passenger's cabin. As we rounded the west breakwater, the captain sounded the horn and cut the throttle. The *Wyandot* slowed, settling into the water.

"Are we taking a taxi?" Lenny asked.

"No need," I said. "The hotel is a block away."

"Ah, too bad. How often can you ride in a taxi pulled by horses?"

The ferry pulled up to the ramp, and lines, fore and aft, were secured to the dock. Once the luggage carts were removed, a deckhand shouted, "All ashore folks. Watch your step."

We made our way slowly up the dock, through the crowd of people waiting to catch a ferry back to the mainland. At the top of the dock, the chaos of Main Street Mackinac Island opened up in front of us. Bicycles, horse-drawn taxis and drays, and people all competed for space on the street or sidewalk. Somehow, they managed to fit. Most of the time.

Across the street, leaning next to the Carriage Tours ticket window, I noticed a familiar figure, Santino Cicci, a lean six feet, with a weathered, chiseled face and a neatly trimmed goatee. I quickly understood Jimmy Erwin's quip that we'd be in "good hands" on the island. Cicci and his partner, Gino Rosato, were longtime bodyguards, first for Carmine DeMio and then his son. Joey brought in Jimmy Erwin and Bobbie Lampone when Carmine retired and he required his own protection.

"Henri," I said.

"I see him. Think something's up?"

"Well, why don't I find out? I'll meet you at the hotel."

Henri nodded, then set off down the street with Lenny and Tina.

Cicci watched me carefully as I crossed Main Street.

"People watching your new hobby, Santino?" I said.

Cicci fingered his goatee. "Always the smart-ass, aren't you, Russo?"

"Do the best I can. You our welcoming committee?"

"Something like that," he said.

Cicci kept an eye on Henri and the others as they slowly moved down the sidewalk.

"They're headed to the Iroquois," I said.

"Yeah," he said, and started across Hoban Street. "You coming, smart-ass?"

Being a savvy private eye, I assumed he was talking to me. "You bet."

We waited at the edge of the sidewalk for two dock porters, baskets piled precariously high with luggage, to pass by.

The Iroquois Hotel was built in 1900 as a private home by island blacksmith Robert Benjamin, whose descendants still call Mackinac home. In 1904, the Benjamin House was converted into Hotel Iroquois, which was eventually bought by the McIntire family, who managed the intimate 45-room hotel until 2020.

Cicci and I took the long brick walkway to the hotel's Carriage House Dining Room, site of Lenny Stern's luncheon presentation. The peaceful, spacious room, with large windows on three sides, offered a spectacular view of the Straits of Mackinac and the Round Island Lighthouse.

I went over, near the bar, and picked a spot with a good view of the room. Cicci remained at the entrance.

A few people were milling about, others enjoyed salads or sandwiches at brightly decorated tables. Women, mostly older, outnumbered men in the dining room, but all were dressed appropriately for a luncheon at the Iroquois (rather than, say, a hot dog at a picnic table next door at Windemere Point). Lenny chatted with two women near the bar. They held wine glasses, Lenny a cup of coffee. The two women smiled a lot and seemed to be doing most of the talking.

It was almost showtime. I looked over at Henri, who stood at the back of the dining room, near the kitchen. He nodded toward the door. I looked over.

Carmine DeMio.

The retired Don of the Baldini crime family was older now, perhaps slower, but he still commanded attention, standing erect, face tanned, in an elegant black suit, his thinning gray hair combed straight back. He surveyed the dining room as if he were a general about to issue orders to his troops.

A few feet behind Carmine stood Gino Rosato, longtime bodyguard for Carmine and partner of Santino Cicci.

Rosato was Oliver Hardy to Cicci's Stan Laural, overweight not trim, unkempt not fastidious, with a puffy red face and nose to match. Take it from me, the man knew his way around a .45 automatic.

Carmine gestured discretely. Rosato lumbered over to the windows and stood by the only open table, a four-top with a small silver stand on one corner. It held an elegantly written sign, which read, "Reserved." I'd seen this one-act play before, choreographed to perfection and implemented wherever other people were around, even in the dining room of Carmine's own hotel. Bob Fosse would have been proud.

When he was satisfied it was safe, Rosato nodded, and he was joined at the table by Carmine and Santino Cicci.

Lenny Stern, still with the chatty women, watched Carmine's table. He spoke to the women, handed off his coffee cup to a waiter, and made his way toward Carmine.

When Lenny reached the table, Carmine stood. I'd never seen that before. Other people stood for Carmine out of respect, or fear. But not this time.

"Well," Henri said as he came up, "what do you think of that?"

"It's a good bet there's more between them than just sharing gangland information in the old Windy City days."

The clock edged its way toward the noon starting time. Waitstaff cleared tables. Coffee was being consumed, along with an occasional glass of wine and slices of peanut butter pie.

"Good afternoon, everyone," a pleasant voice offered. "Good afternoon."

It didn't take long for the gathering to settle down as Lenny left Carmine's table.

"We're excited to have Leonard Stern with us today. Most of you know him as a reporter for the Petoskey *Post Dispatch*. But today, he's also author ..."

And, so, Lenny took over the room with charm, wit, and bold tales of Chicago crime and corruption. Just what the guests came to hear. After a rather brief and sedate Q&A, Lenny chatted with people while the Island Bookstore folks sold fresh copies of *Corruption on Trial*.

Carmine DeMio and Gino Rosato made a hasty, inconspicuous retreat as the session wrapped up. Santino Cicci stayed behind, by the doorway.

Henri whispered something in Tina's ear and moved past Cicci. We left the dining room.

"You tell Tina we'd wait out here?"

Henri nodded, but his attention was elsewhere.

"What?" I said.

"This," he said. "Look. The walkway."

He made a sweeping gesture at the beautifully decorated walk, all thirty feet of it, a combination of flowers, shrubs, and assorted greenery.

"Yeah. What about it?"

"I ought to have Barnwell Landscaping design my walk like this."

Besides his other endeavors, Henri LaCroix was an island landlord, with a small apartment building downtown and a house in the village.

"Henri, the walkway at your house is six feet long, if that."

"But wouldn't it ..."

"All right, let's go," Lenny said, interrupting Henri's gardening fantasy as he and Tina emerged from the luncheon. "We can make the next ferry, can't we?"

37

The line waiting for transport to the mainland at the Shepler's dock was, happily, short for a July afternoon. Our literary group found seats at the back of the cabin. Santino Cicci turned and walked toward Main Street as we sat down, his job done.

The *Miss Margy* cleared the west breakwater and picked up speed. The wind blew harder than it did on our trip over, so it pushed more water-cooled air into the steamy cabin than just a few hours earlier.

Lenny Stern sat Henri in the row behind Tina and me. They talked during much of the twenty-minute ride. I picked up a few words now and then, suggesting they were relieved that the final Michigan stop of the book tour went off without trouble. I felt pretty good about that myself. The wrap-up for the tour was in the Windy City, but that was a job for Bigelow's security people, not Henri and me.

Tina leaned against the portside window, scrolling through her phone. She occasionally let out a small laugh, then her thumbs danced around the screen. For a few welcome moments, she was lost on *Facebook* or email or *Instagram*.

I envied Tina, but Martin Fleener asked me to let him know when we were on our way to the mainland. I did.

"hendricks' office 9a?" Fleener texted back.

"tomorrow?"

"tomorrow morning"

Fleener usually offered more than cryptic responses. He was probably tied up with official cop business instead of chasing down imagined gang activity in northern Michigan.

But why meet in Don Hendricks' office? Kate Hubbell's murder was Hendricks' responsibility as Emmet County prosecutor. Maybe there were new developments, but that would have to wait until tomorrow.

I stared at my phone. I wanted to call her. Or text. Something. When I left AJ's house after a comfortable, pleasant night, the tension hadn't vanished, but it had been sidelined for a few hours. I wanted to see her, I always wanted that, but I didn't want the distance between us. The tension was going to hang around until we came back together, hopefully by resolving the issue's source.

"you home?" I tapped.

"work. you in mac city?"

I briefly explained where I was and that all went well at the Iroquois. She wanted to hear that, even if she didn't ask. I wanted her to know we were all safe.

"sandwiches, Toski Sands, meet you state park?"

I sent a thumbs-up emoji.

"at the beach house."

A second thumbs-up.

I put the phone away. We were closing in on the dock in Mackinaw City.

I couldn't get AJ out of my head. Not AJ exactly, but the stress, the tension. I remembered what she said, her worry that I might be hurt or killed. Her fear of a phone call in the middle of the night.... That started years ago when I chased down a killer at Cherokee Point Resort. We talked about her fears then, we'd talked about them since. Danger went with my job, and she just accepted it as best she could. Over time, the fear grew out of control, no longer manageable. For my part...

The ferry's horn sounded as the captain throttled back, and the *Miss Margy* settled into the water at the entrance to the Mackinaw City harbor. Several passengers left their seats and stood in the aisle, eager to be first off. Island workers anxious to get home. Young and old, women and men, many wearing the familiar cotton houndstooth pants of the kitchen. They all carried backpacks or large tote bags and had tired faces.

The passengers followed the workers and moved slowly, in a pack, off the ferry. They fanned out, some walking to a small four-car tram for a ride to distant parking lots, and us to Henri's SUV parked on the dock.

"Two rows over," Henri said, pointing, and we followed along.

"I'm meeting Fleener in the morning," I said, but Henri wasn't listening. He'd stopped; Lenny and Tina, too. His SUV, a gleaming white, had been unceremoniously desecrated by a red liquid splashed across the hood, both front fenders, and half the windshield.

"Son of a bitch."

I turned in time to see Henri unzip his lightweight nylon jacket. Never a good sign. It covered his shoulder holster.

Lenny, the veteran crime reporter, recognized the move and eased closer to Tina. Henri scanned the rows of cars, looking for anything out of place. I did, too. Nothing, no one.

Then I spotted Jimmy Erwin walking slowly toward us, his arms away from his sides, palms up.

"Henri?"

"Watch Erwin. I want to look around."

"They're gone, Henri," Jimmy said.

"You saw them?"

Jimmy nodded.

"Tell me."

"Two males, white."

"What age?" I said.

"My age, give or take," Jimmy said.

In other words, two teenage white boys again.

"Car?" I said.

Jimmy shook his head. "F-150, light green, good-sized dent on the left rear fender, cracked taillight."

"Why didn't you stop them?" Henri said.

"Sorry, man, not my job."

"What're you doing here, anyway?" I said.

"Keeping an eye on you."

"I meant . . ."

"I know what you meant," Jimmy said. "Santino Cicci told me you were on the way back to the mainland."

Henri glanced at his SUV.

"Your ride's okay," Jimmy said. "I poured water on it, came right off. Wash the car."

"See which way they went?" I said.

"I did better than that," Jimmy said, smiling. "I followed them."

I waited, figuring there was more.

"Carp Lake."

Carp Lake had been a dot on the map south of Mackinaw City since the 1880s. It sat between US 31 and Paradise Lake.

"One of those old, beat-up cottages down from the Post Office." Jimmy pulled a slip of paper from his pocket and handed it to Henri. "The number's hard to see, but it's there, on the doorframe."

"Thanks," I said.

"You going back to Petoskey now?" Jimmy said.

"Yeah."

"My car's over by the bakery," Jimmy said. "I'll meet you at the car wash."

38

"**W**as that supposed to be a threat, Henri?" Tina said. "That stuff on your car. Was it supposed to be blood?"

It took Henri ten minutes with a high-pressure hose to clean the surface of his car. Lenny and Tina sat patiently in the back seat while I texted with Sandy, telling her I wouldn't get to the office tomorrow until after I'd met with Captain Fleener and Prosecutor Hendricks.

We made our way back to Petoskey with Jimmy Erwin following along at a discrete distance. We knew he was there, and if the shooters tried something, Jimmy would spot them first.

"Not sure what it meant, Tina," Henri said. "A threat's a good guess." We picked up speed on 31 South. "Let's get Lenny and Tina home safe first, then you want to find those guys at Carp Lake?"

I thought about his question. The obvious answer was yes, particularly since Jimmy Erwin had handed us a good tip. But I wasn't sure.

"Is this about a new lead," I said, "or your car?" I knew Henri was pissed about the affront to his SUV.

"This isn't personal, Michael. It's business."

"You been waiting a long time to use that line, haven't you?"

Henri ignored my sarcastic reference movieland gangsters.

"Let's wait till tomorrow," I said. "I'd like to see what Fleener has to say first. Might be good to know if we are dealing with a gang."

"You won't have to be babysitters tomorrow," Tina said.

"What time do you head back to Chicago?" I said.

"First plane in the morning."

"How about it, Lenny, when are you going down?"

Lenny looked up from his phone. "No sooner than I have to."

Tina laughed. "Tomorrow, Michael. We're on the same flight."

"I'll get you to the airport," Henri said. "After that you're Gloucester Publishing's problem."

"I'm not looking forward to the Chicago stop," Lenny said. "I like Michigan events, the ones here. All the VIP small talk in Chicago, it's not my style. I'll be glad when this tour is over."

"Me, too," Tina said, a touch of resignation in her voice.

"Drop me at the office, Henri," I said.

After a moment or two, Henri said, "You seeing AJ tonight?"

"Uh-huh."

"Remember…"

"You don't have to say it, Henri." I knew what he'd tell me. I didn't need to be reminded again. I didn't feel like talking about AJ, particularly with our companions in the back seat.

"It's … I'll be fine," I said.

Henri dropped me in front of the office. The sidewalks were crowded with visitors about to transition from shopping in stores to menu shopping for dinner.

Sandy was gone for the day, but she'd left a sticky note on my desktop screen: "You should call AJ"

I laughed at them, Sandy and Henri. Were they sticking their noses into my personal life? Of course they were, but they weren't nosy people. Were they just worried about both AJ and me? Probably.

I wrote a couple of notes for the meeting with Fleener, stuck them in my brief bag and left for home. It was time for a break, time to play tourist, just AJ and me for sandwiches on the water. Once home I pulled on a pair of khaki shorts, a threadbare polo shirt and grubby Chaco sandals. I took the back way to the Harbor-Petoskey Road and turned in at the State Park.

I wound my way toward the beach house, left my car in the lot and walked toward the water. I spotted AJ at a table with a small blue-and-white cooler.

"This seat taken, lady?"

"I'm waiting for a guy I know … hey, it's you. I didn't recognize you in those clothes."

"You making fun of my summer wardrobe?"

"I am," she said. "Are you really a private eye?"

"Not right now," I said, and leaned in to kiss her hello. Her silly greeting felt comfortably familiar, loving.

"What's in the cooler?"

"Dinner courtesy of Toski-Sands."

Toski-Sands, a small market on the Harbor-Petoskey Road barely a half mile from the park entrance, had both a delicious deli and a knowledgeable staff.

AJ opened the cooler.

"J Lohr Chardonnay," she said. "Already opened." She put two glasses out, and I filled them.

She opened a bag. "Tuna salad and chicken salad. Take your pick. And a chef's salad to split."

We arranged everything on the table, and I raised my glass. "A toast."

"Yes, a toast," she said. "To what?"

I smiled. "To a summer dinner on the beach."

"Here, here."

We opened our sandwiches and salads and dug in.

"When did Toski-Sands start offering real silverware and cloth napkins?"

AJ grinned. "Smart-ass. I just thought the real stuff would be more fun."

"Elegance on the beach?"

"Exactly," she said, and lifted her glass. "Another toast … to elegance on the beach." We touched glasses, took drinks, and returned to the food.

"You said everything went okay on the island."

"It did."

"Was the Iroquois dining room full?"

"Lenny has his fans." I explained the afternoon, starting with the charm and wit of Lenny Stern.

"Good for him," AJ said. "And no trouble, right?"

I hesitated, and she caught it.

"What? What aren't you telling me?"

I wasn't hiding anything, but I felt the tension in her words, in the way she asked the question. I wanted to be careful, to edit my comments. We were having fun. I didn't want to lose it.

I gave her a condensed version.

"So you'll check out the two guys? You and Henri, I mean." "Best lead we've had since the Cavendish Company president lied about his father being alive long after he was killed in prison."

"At least you won't go charging over there alone."

"AJ, I told you I wouldn't do that. Henri went along to see DeMio, and to the Cavendish Company. He'll be there this time, too."

I probably should have kept my mouth shut, but there it was, right there on the beach, in the park, by the water.

"Don't get pissed at me again, Russo. I don't like it."

"I have a job to do, AJ. We've ... we've done this before." I rolled up the rest of my sandwich in the wrapping. "You're worried about me, Henri thinks I don't pay attention to the job ..."

"Are you blaming me for that?"

I shook my head. "No, but ... Henri says I don't focus on my job when I'm worrying about you, and that's dangerous."

"Henri's right, Michael."

"Did you talk to him?"

"I didn't have to." AJ folded up her half-eaten sandwich and shoved it back in the paper sack.

"Is it that obvious?" I said.

"Just do your goddamn job, Russo. Just do your job. I'll be here when you're done. I'll figure it out."

39

I woke up early. The sun had crept its way through the blinds, putting rows of light on the opposite wall. Dinner on the beach ended well enough. But AJ went one way, me another, neither of us at peace — or comfortable.

Do my job, AJ said. I tossed the covers back and sat on the side of the bed. Time to meet Martin Fleener at Don Hendricks' office.

I put water and coffee in the machine, punched the button, and headed for the shower. It was time to focus, as Henri would say. By the time I sat at the kitchen table with an English muffin, fresh raspberries and coffee, I had not made much headway with focusing.

I took a lightweight cotton blazer to cover the hip holster. I cut through the parking lot behind the Perry Hotel and went up Bay Street to the rear entrance of the County building.

"Morning, Sherry," I said. Sherry Merkel was assistant to Emmet County Prosecutor Donald Hendricks, and chief protector of his privacy.

"Mr. Russo," she said. "They're waiting for you."

I went through the door behind Merkel's desk.

"Morning, Russo," the prosecutor said. Donald Hendricks was in his third term, duly elected by the county's voters. In his fifties, the slightly overweight Hendricks looked rumpled no matter the time of day. Tie loose, collar open, shirt sleeves pushed up. "Take a seat," he said.

I did, and a tough decision it was between three worn-out metal chairs. At least they matched the faded institutional green of Hendricks' desk.

"Good morning, Marty," I said to Captain Fleener, who occupied his usual chair under a huge map of Emmet County.

"Morning," Fleener said.

"You've got the floor, Marty," Hendricks said.

Fleener flipped open a reporter's notebook.

"Ah, before we start," I said. "Mind if I ask why we're meeting here?"

"You don't like my office?" Hendricks said. The prosecutor was not known for his sense of humor, but he tried every so often.

"Just curious, Don," I said. "Didn't think a background check on gang activity would interest you much."

Hendricks leaned forward, elbows on the desk. "Everything in this county interests me, Russo." So much for humor.

"If there is a gang," I said.

"That's my cue," Fleener said, leafing through a few notebook pages. "When the idea of gang activity first came up, I paid attention, but nothing you said rang a bell. That's why I wanted to talk with my guy in Lansing."

"The one on the task force, right?"

"Yeah." Fleener hesitated, glancing at Hendricks. "Don, you want this one?"

Hendricks cleared his throat. "Some of our gang people, sometimes they work off the books."

They waited, letting that sink in.

I glanced at Fleener, then back to Hendricks. "They don't have, shall I say, proper authorization?"

"Something like that," Hendricks said, sounding purposefully vague. "They're not exactly dealing with conventional crooks..."

"Not like the Joey DeMios of the criminal world."

Hendricks nodded. "Nobody would use the word 'organized' to describe their activity. They're not very bright, their movements are too random." Hendricks shrugged. "They don't lend themselves to conventional means."

"So, you spy when you need to?"

"Marty," Hendricks said, ducking my question. "Give Russo what you know."

Fleener glanced at his notebook.

"Four men, white, late teens or early twenties. Oldest is twenty-four. Two work, two unemployed. Only one, a Samuel Dexter, graduated high school."

Fleener looked up from his notes. "By the way, the unemployed guys do not draw unemployment from the state."

"That's comforting," I said.

"All four have had run-ins with the law, small-shit stuff nobody cares about. No felony charges or arrests."

"Does this gang have a name?" I said.

Fleener shook his head and grinned. "It's a stretch to suggest they're anything more than four guys who drink too much and get in trouble together."

"Okay," I said, "then how did they get on your radar in the first place?"

"Wondered how long it would take you to ask," Fleener said.

"Well?"

"Dumb luck," Fleener said. "One of the guys, a Benjamin Jarvis, beat up his girlfriend. She filed a complaint, later withdrawn ..."

"Of course, it was," I said.

"...in Mackinaw City. The girlfriend called Jarvis a drug dealer, so Mac City cops alerted SANE."

SANE, an acronym for Straits Area Narcotics Enforcement, covers drug activity in Emmet, Cheboygan, and Otsego Counties.

"If they have drugs at all," Fleener said, "they sell them to their buddies for change. We didn't charge them for dealing."

"Why is it you think this is the bunch threatening Lenny Stern?"

"Dumb luck, again," Fleener said. "I was thumbing through the file, thin as it was ... the only real paperwork was on Jarvis."

"The one who beat on his girlfriend?"

Fleener nodded. "Mac City officer made a note about a tattoo on the kid's forearm."

"Really?"

Fleener nodded. "A 44 inside a circle."

"Do you believe in coincidences?" I said.

"You bet I do," Fleener said, "but I know you don't. Figured you'd want to see the file."

"You figured right."

"However." It was Hendricks. "We wouldn't be able to show you, since there is no official paperwork."

"So, I saved you the trouble of being a pain in the ass," Fleener said. "I dug a little deeper."

He had my attention now.

"The two guys who work, Dexter and Jarvis? They live together in Gaylord, downtown. That's where a familiar name popped up."

"Cavendish?" I said.

"Yep," Fleener said. "Wouldn't have meant a thing, but I'd just checked DMV about that old truck that took a run at LaCroix in Harbor Springs."

"The two guys," I said, "they work at Cavendish Company?"

"Yes, they do, and there's more. My guy in Lansing thinks Sylvia Cavendish is supplying the drugs."

"Mama Cavendish is a drug dealer?"

"No," Hendricks said. "Sylvia Cavendish supplies the drugs to Dexter and Jarvis. That's all, she doesn't deal."

I described my visit with Sylvia's sons, Daniel and Walter, in Gaylord, relating how Walter lied about their father and the vanity plate. Pieces of my puzzle were dropping into place. A few of them, anyway.

"The Cavendish sons run the family business," I said. "So why does Sylvia supply employees with drugs?"

"Good question," Fleener said. "I thought Cavendish might be connected to Lenny Stern and the Kate Hubbell murder investigation, so I took it to Don. But it's all pretty thin."

"Just out of curiosity," I said, "the other two, the unemployed pals? They live in Carp Lake, by any chance?"

Fleener shot a glance at Hendricks, then they both stared at me.

"What do you know," Hendricks said, "that we don't know?"

I told them about Henri's car, the phony blood, and the two guys who were followed to Carp Lake. I skipped that it was Jimmy Erwin who did the following.

"All right," Hendricks said. "Let's see what we've got here."

Hendricks tugged at his already-loose tie, then ran his hands over his head as if his hair needed rearranging.

"Ms. Hubbell's murdered," Hendricks said. "No leads…"

"No leads until Russo asked me to check with the DMV," Fleener said, "and maybe a gangbanger or two in our neighborhood."

"Then pieces started falling all over each other," Hendricks said.

"That prosecutor lingo, Don?"

Hendricks almost smiled. "You bet it is. Look, the pieces start with a number, 'forty-four.' A vanity plate, a tattoo. The same tattoo shows up on the arm of a guy yelling at Lenny Stern in a parking lot, on the arm of a guy whose girlfriend says he gets drugs at work. Then 'work' turns out to be the Cavendish Company, owned by the widow of a central figure in Stern's book. That company owns a truck with forty-four on a vanity plate."

Don Hendricks took a deep breath, let it out slowly, and looked at each of us. "The hell's going on here?"

40

"**I**t's got to be more than a license plate or a tattoo," I said.

"That's stating the obvious," Don Hendricks said as he returned to his desk with freshly made coffee. "Can't you do better than that?"

If I could have done better, I would have thrown it out there, I thought about saying. But it was a rhetorical question. Hendricks was starting to feel the pressure. Kate Hubbell's murder investigation was not following predictable patterns, not leading to the predictable culprits. Experience was less helpful than usual. Hendricks knew that; so did Martin Fleener.

"One more thing," Fleener said, "before we adjourn for the day."

Fleener tipped his chair back, leaning it against the wall.

"Nothing's come together on this one, Don. Kate Hubbell was killed. Since then, what? Leads? Suspects? Motives? Usually things start to fall into place with good police work."

"Tell me something I don't know," Hendricks said.

"That list you just ran off? The tattoo, the rest of it."

"What about it?" Hendricks said.

Fleener was good at this, adding things up.

"Remember where they found Kate Hubbell's body?"

"Behind a warehouse, wasn't it?" Hendricks said.

Fleener nodded.

"So?"

"It's amateur hour, Don," Fleener said. "That list of yours adds up, but we don't recognize it. We expected the usual, the familiar, and haven't gotten it. These aren't professionals, Don. They're careless amateurs."

"Go back to Kate's body," I said.

"The rope around her neck, remember?" Fleener said. "The kind of line used on boats?"

"But she was shot," I said. "One to the head."

"Right," Fleener said. "So we figured the rope was some kind of message, maybe another threat." Fleener shook his head. "Sloppy police work. I was sloppy. Stern's book was about the mob, about corruption. I jumped all over Joey DeMio. The mob killed her, the mob was sending a message ..."

"But you concluded DeMio isn't involved," Hendricks said.

"Right. That rope on Hubbell was an amateur's idea of the mob's code of silence. Violate *omerta* and you die."

"A red herring?" I said.

"It was a bad one, and I fell for it," Fleener said. "I was so eager to tag Joey I wasn't paying attention."

"You weren't the only one," I said.

"What're you thinking, Marty?" Hendricks said. "Now, I mean."

"All roads lead to the Cavendish Company. The truck, the plate ..."

"Yeah, yeah. Got that," Hendricks said. "Now what?"

"Cavendish is in Otsego County," Fleener said. "If we move on Sylvia or her sons, we tip them off. Besides, we have nothing solid that connects any of the Cavendish family to a murder in Emmet County."

Fleener looked my way. "What was your next move going to be, Russo, if we weren't having this little chat?"

"The two at Carp Lake. Thought we'd see what they're up to."

"'We' means you and LaCroix?" Hendricks said, with a touch of annoyance.

"Of course," I said. For several years the prosecutor, not to mention the State Police, had regarded Henri as trouble. Henri did nothing to dispel the idea.

"Just keep him in check, Russo," Hendricks said. I let it go. We'd had this debate before. It always got us nowhere. I changed the subject.

"Clear something up for me, will you, Don?"

He waited.

"Joey DeMio," I said. "The restaurant over on Lake Street. What do you make of it?"

"Pretty obvious to us," Hendricks said. "Joey's making his move to the mainland."

"Is he leaving Mackinac?"

"Our sources tell us no." It was Fleener. "Joey's expanding."

"You worried about that?" I said.

"Concerned would be a better word." And that was that. Hendricks drank some coffee, put the mug down and said, "All right, Russo, get on those two guys in Carp Lake, but keep Marty in the loop. Understand?"

I left the County building on the Lake Street side and headed for the office. I'd walked almost two blocks, lost in thought about our meeting, when I noticed the sun and the blue sky were lost in clouds. It was still July hot, but the edge was gone, at least for the moment.

"Morning, boss," Sandy said when I walked into the office. She was at her desk. Henri sat in a client chair over by the Lake Street windows. I grabbed a bottle of water from the small refrigerator near the door and sat next to Henri.

"So how did you and Hendricks leave it?" Sandy said.

I took a long drink of water. "First, did all go well at the airport, Henri?" Henri nodded. "Picked up Lenny first, then Tina. I waited in the terminal until their flight was in the air. Arrived at O'Hare early. They're Gloucester Security's problem now."

"They'll have an easier time covering him," I said. "Three days of meetings, cocktail parties, the hotel. Limos between the events. They'll wrap him up tight."

"He won't be very happy," Sandy said, "but he will be safe. Now what about Hendricks?"

I took another drink of water, put the bottle on the floor next to my chair, and gave them a quick recap of my meeting.

"Hendricks and Fleener don't want to tip off the Cavendish family any sooner than necessary."

"Well, if mother Sylvia's dealing drugs," Sandy said, "wouldn't they have their guard up anyway?"

"Hendricks doesn't think she's a dealer."

"Sell them or give them away," Henri said. "You do that, you're on edge."

"Did they speculate," Sandy said, "why Sylvia would give drugs to company employees, who then supply their friends?"

"She wants to be loved?" Henri said.

Sandy ignored his comment and said, "She's paying for something. Loyalty, maybe."

"That wasn't a question," I said.

"Wasn't meant to be. You give something of value, you expect something in return."

"A little cynical, don't you think?" Henri said.

"Got a better suggestion?"

Henri shook his head. "No, ma'am."

"For services rendered?" I said.

"Does that include murder, boss?"

"Could be," I said, "but we know the four buddies and Cavendish Company have something going on, or we wouldn't be having this discussion. Let's go see if the Carp Lake pair is home."

"They were there a while ago," Henri said.

"Yeah?" I said.

Henri nodded. "Swung up that way after I dropped our friends at the airport. Found the house, with the truck Jimmy Erwin described out front."

"I wonder how much drugs it takes to buy a murder?" Sandy said.

41

"You think Kate Hubbell was murder-for-hire?" Henri said.

He eased his SUV through traffic north on US 31 toward Carp Lake. He always insisted on driving if we were trying to be inconspicuous. Another SUV, no one noticed or cared. But my BMW? Inconspicuous?

The cloud cover cast a welcome gray dullness over the late morning. It wasn't much cooler or less humid, but hiding the sun for a while made it feel that way.

"Not sure what to think, Henri."

"If Sandy's right about the Cavendish woman ..."

"That she's paying for something?"

"Yeah. Could she be paying to threaten Lenny Stern?"

"Could be," I said. "Question is, why?"

"Maybe she doesn't want bad publicity for her dead husband."

"So she'd contract a murder?" I said.

We cruised by the Pellston Airport. The landing lights of the north-south runway sparkled in the gray day, and the parking lot was crowded with cars, as it always was in mid-summer.

Henri paid little attention to speed limits as he blew through the Levering blinker light. He eased off the throttle several minutes later and turned off 31, near the Carp Lake post office.

"It's a few houses down," he said, turning on a narrow tarmac road that paralleled Paradise Lake. "There. The green F-150."

"Someone's in the truck," I said. "Two guys."

Henri slowly drove past the house, pulling to the side of the road about sixty feet away. I turned to watch. Henri adjusted his mirror. The green truck went the other way.

"You recognize them?"

"Didn't get a good look."

"Shall we go for a ride?" Henri said, making a U-turn.

"Nothing better to do," I said. "Truck's headed south, toward Petoskey."

"Too bad we didn't get a look at them," Henri said.

"Let's see where they're going. Maybe we'll get lucky."

The green F-150 moved steadily along, not pushing the speed limit. Henri kept plenty of highway between us, and the road was straight. We'd pick up a turn easily enough. The truck went past C-66 at Levering.

"Not cutting to I-75 or the lake," Henri said. "Petoskey, here we come." He glanced at me, then added, "I'm curious why Hendricks was so eager to let you run interference for him and Fleener."

"Hendricks was clear, Henri. They can't tie the Cavendish family to Kate Hubbell's murder. But if they are involved, why tip them off?"

"You think the Cavendish brothers.... Hey, they're turning," Henri said. The green truck took a right about fifty yards ahead.

"Only one thing between here and the lake."

"Moose Jaw Junction," I said. "A burger and beer in beautiful Larks Lake, Michigan."

There were no vehicles between us and the F-150 on Van Road. Henri stayed well back, but another arrow-straight road through rural Michigan farm country made for an easy tail.

"Bar's another mile or so," Henri said. "The brothers ... you think they believed your bullshit story about a company truck driver witnessing a crime?"

"Don't know, but they must suspect something's going on. They didn't strike me as dumb, especially Walter."

"He the one who took over the conversation?"

"Yeah," I said. "I'll bet they're trying to figure it out."

The green truck slowed when it reached the restaurant. Cars and trucks lined the shoulder of Van Road and jammed the parking area in front of the one-floor roadhouse.

Henri drove on a bit and pulled into an empty spot.

"Get a look?" he said.

"Could be the kid from the parking lot run-in," I said. "Not sure."

"Jump out, I'll be there in a minute."

I moved quickly to the entrance, walking right behind a noisy group of four women. This was not their first stop of the day. They laughed, pointing at the huge, phony antlers above the door. The women gave me cover as we went through the door. The room was crowded, from the bar just inside the door all across a large room filled with tables and chairs. Wood paneling, a red brick fireplace, and an abundance of moose paraphernalia left little doubt about the theme of the popular place.

I eased my way to the bar, jammed three-deep its entire length to the back wall. Hard to order a beer, even harder to be spotted by somebody who wasn't looking for a tail anyway.

Henri came through the door and stood next to an older couple, scanning the room until he saw me.

"Can you find them?" he said.

"Look for yourself," I said, nodding toward the fireplace. "Recognize anyone?"

Henri picked them up quickly. At a four-top on the far side of the room were the two men I followed inside. But the other two men?

"Well, well," Henri said. "If it isn't the two bad boys we chased in Harbor Springs."

"We got lucky again, Henri. All because Jimmy Erwin tipped us off."

"How do you want to play this?" Henri said. "They just ordered food."

"How about a beer while we wait?"

We signaled a bartender, got a couple of beers and settled in with the noisy crowd around the bar.

"They're not watching for us or anyone else," I said.

"One guy," Henri said, "buzz cut and black T."

"What about him?"

"Pretty sure he was the dude in the Side Door parking lot, the one with the tattoo."

"The gang's all here," I said.

We finished our beer, paid the tab, and retreated to Henri's SUV. Henri moved to another spot to get a better view of the door. We didn't have too wait long. Our teenage diners did not savor a leisurely meal, though they had consumed their share of adult beverages.

They burst out the front door, laughing, shoving, with all the sloppy exuberance of four teens who'd been drinking after the big game. They stopped at the green truck, where the Carp Lake duo climbed in, then drove from the parking lot, scattering dirt and stones behind them.

"Hard to imagine one of them is a killer."

"Not the first time we've said that, Henri."

"Shall we chase down the green truck, or follow these other two?"

"We know how to find the Carp Lake truck," I said.

Henri started the SUV as the other two left the lot in a Chevy truck, a dark blue Colorado, headed toward US 31. They drove past the Pellston airport and went west on Riggsville Road toward I-75.

"Fleener told me the two who work at Cavendish Company live together in Gaylord. Downtown."

The truck took I-75 south, and we settled in for an easy tail.

"I suppose we could get lucky, if they stop at a bar on the way home."

I laughed. "A little sarcasm, Henri?"

Forty minutes later, we exited at M-32, Gaylord. We hid in traffic on Main Street until the Chevy truck went past the Otsego County build- ings, heading north on Center towards the hospital.

"Maybe they're sick," Henri said.

"You're full of one-liners today," I said. "I settle for wherever home is and call it a day."

"Got a hot date tonight, Russo?"

I let that pass.

After a moment, "You ignoring me, Russo?"

I was ignoring him. I knew where this was going, and I wasn't interested.

"You can't duck the question," Henri said. "Not for very long."

"We're here to do our job, Henri, leave it alone."

Even I didn't like the sound of that. I doubt that Henri did.

Timing is everything.

The truck turned off Center just short of Otsego Memorial Hospital, then into the parking lot of an apartment building. It was a three-floor faded red brick structure, of which the basement was no doubt referred to as the "garden level."

Henri pulled into an empty spot, left the motor running, and got out. "Back in a minute."

Henri moved slowly, approaching the entrance shortly after they went inside. One minute later, he returned to the SUV.

"Didn't you tell me the Cavendish workers were Dexter and ...'"

"And Jarvis," I said. "According to Fleener."

"Apartment 310."

I looked over the apartment building where the pair of teenage tough guys lived, rubbing at my jaw.

"First question," Henri said over the hum of the A/C. "You want to roust Dexter and Jarvis here and now, see what they know?"

"Tempting," I said. "But not now. Let's go."

Henri made his way down Center Avenue to Main Street, then headed west through the thick traffic of downtown. Once past the end of the retail congestion at the Meijer store, Henri took the Alba Road shortcut to Traverse City, and we were on our way home.

"Whatever we do next," I said, "will alert the Cavendish clan that we're on to them."

"Don't you think they're suspicious already?" Henri said. "You just happened to show up at the company offices asking questions."

"About a crime scene."

"Doesn't matter."

"Probably not," I said.

Henri motored along the two-lane, passing the occasional gawker mixed with locals, all heading somewhere.

"What's next?" Henri said. "Since you don't want to push those guys for some answers."

"I'm not against it, just not yet, not now."

"Now we got time," Henri said. "Lenny'll be in Chicago for a couple more days wrapping up the book tour. I'm not babysitting."

"Yeah, I know."

"How about the Cavendish brothers, then? We're stalled right now."

"I got your point."

Henri slowed for the blinker light, turned north on US 131, and we joined the parade of vehicles on their way to Petoskey.

"It's obvious the brothers know something, or they wouldn't have clammed up and escorted you out the office door."

"They might just be protecting dear old Mom. Think she knows more than her sons?"

"Hell if I know," Henri said. "But Fleener's got her connected to at least two of the guys who've been after Lenny."

"Time to see what Sylvia knows."

42

"You're in early this morning," Sandy said when she arrived at the office at her usual time.

I was at my desk, chair turned, feet up on the window ledge. I drank coffee and watched the sun dancing on the light chop on Little Traverse Bay.

"Restless night," I said.

Sandy put down her bag, poured a mug of coffee, and took her usual chair against the sidewall in my office.

"Did you run this morning, boss?"

"Didn't have the energy," I said, moving my chair back to the desk.

Sandy put down her mug. She hesitated for a moment.

"Did you talk to AJ last night?"

"Sandy."

"I'll take that as a no," she said. "You want to tell me what happened when you and Henri dropped by the Carp Lake house?"

I did.

"Well, I think you have it right," she said. "Sylvia's all that's left. There doesn't seem to be any point talking to the Cavendish brothers again. And they might not even know what mama is up to. You've ruled out, shall we say, encouraging the teenage bad boys to talk. So, Sylvia." Sandy picked up her mug and drank some coffee. "If it were up to me, I'd rough up the bad boys first."

"You and Henri," I said. "Were you a juvenile delinquent in another life?"

Sandy smiled. "I wanted to be, but Catholic girls start much too late."

"You doing Billy Joel, now?"

"Don't knock the oldies-but-goodies, boss. Where would we be without them?"

"Listening to Jay-Z, Billy Eilish, and *Hamilton*."

"I think I need more coffee," she said, faking a grimace.

"While you're up," I said.

"You want coffee?"

I shook my head. "No, thanks. Can you find Sylvia Cavendish?"

"Sure. It's with the Cavendish info I pulled up the other day."

I returned to my view of the bay. A small sailing skiff glided around the breakwater and picked up speed with fresh wind.

"I ought to get a sailing skiff, a high performance one," I said when Sandy walked in.

"Stick to high performance cars," she said. "At least you know what you're doing."

"Everyone's a critic," I said as Sandy handed me notepaper.

"Sylvia Cavendish lives just outside Gaylord. Use the nav system. The address is in the system, I checked."

I folded the paper and shoved it in a pocket.

"You want me to call her first?"

I shook my head. "Better if I just show up, see if she'll talk to me." I looked at my watch. "Think I'll stop at Diana's first, have some breakfast."

Diana's Delight was a mom-and-pop eatery in downtown Gaylord known for breakfast, although lunch wasn't bad either.

Sandy put her hands on her hips and glared at me.

"What?"

"You didn't run, you didn't talk to AJ last night, and no breakfast? Not even a banana? Did you think I wouldn't notice?"

"You playing my mother now?"

"You don't need another of those, but listen to yourself if you won't listen to me. Pay attention."

I pushed my chair back and stood. "Look, I know you mean well, Henri, too, but I'm tired of you jabbing me about this."

"Well, good luck," Sandy said. "Whatever's going on with you and AJ's eating at you, boss. It's always in your head. It's time to figure it out."

I went to the outer office, grabbed a lightweight blazer from the hall tree.

"I'm going to Gaylord."

I cut through Roast & Toast to the parking lot. I stopped in the middle of a row of cars, looking around: nothing. I beeped the door locks. I drove the back way, close to the North Central Michigan College campus, over to US 131.

The clouds, so welcome yesterday, had disappeared. The sun had returned undisguised high in the sky, alongside the humidity.

I shouldn't have barked at Sandy. I had been short on patience with both of them lately, her and Henri. They were trying to help, but bringing up AJ over and over again wasn't helpful. It hurt.

I was suddenly aware I was on the outskirts of Gaylord, about to join the congestion of downtown; I remembered little of the drive. Too preoccupied with AJ and me. More troublesome, I hadn't once thought of Sylvia Cavendish on the trip over either.

I stopped at Diana's downtown. I had no idea what Sylvia Cavendish would have to say, if she talked to me at all. But I decided to lead with the well-traveled story that a company employee had witnessed a crime. I finished some eggs and toast, took a coffee to go, and found my car in the lot.

O'Rourke Lake was a ten-minute ride east and a little south of downtown. I glanced at the nav screen. Off Kassuba Road, I turned on Lake Club Drive, a narrow stretch of tarmac that cut through the trees. Mailboxes were stuck at the side of the road. I watched for one marked "Cavendish."

I counted only four driveways in a half-mile from the main road. Folks out here in the toniest area of Gaylord didn't like to live too close to one another. Nor did they like to live where the common folk could see how they lived. It was the perfect refuge for the well-heeled from Bloomfield Hills, Evanston, or Shaker Heights.

I spotted the mailbox and turned in. At the end of the long drive, the trees broke into a large expanse of manicured lawn, elaborate flower beds and, in the center of it all, a huge cement statuary of a woman with water spouting out of wings on her back. At the far end of the lawn sat a two-story cedar-sided house at lakeside. A long porch stretched across the front. I counted six pairs of sash windows across the second floor.

I parked the car on the curved drive, walked up the stairs to the double front doors and punched the button. A familiar tune chimed my arrival. I knew it, but couldn't place it. It felt wrong here.

The door opened slowly.

"Mrs. Cavendish? Sylvia Cavendish?" I said. The woman was probably in her sixties, but looked older and harder. Her salt-and-pepper hair was more salt than anything else. It framed a triangle-shaped face with wide-spread oval eyes. Her clothes were straight out of Ann Taylor: tapered black slacks, a white linen V-neck shirt, and no jewelry.

"Yes?" she said, her mouth barely moving.

"Ma'am, hello. I'm Michael Russo. I'm a private investigator looking into a crime committed recently in Harbor Springs."

"No, you're not," she said.

I expected the door in my face. Instead, Sylvia opened the door wide, moved forward, and stood on the threshold.

"I know who you are. I don't understand … why are you here? What do you want with us?"

I caught the "us."

"My sons may have indulged you, Mr. Russo, but I have no interest in doing so."

She took two steps back and slammed the door.

I've had interviews like that before, so brief as to be non-existent and annoying. I didn't always learn anything helpful. I certainly didn't with Sylvia, but if there was a chance … .

I walked back to my car, leaned on the hood and looked back at the elegant lakefront house. A pleasant place to live. I guess Henri and I worried for nothing about arousing the suspicions of the Cavendish family. It wasn't that Sylvia was expecting me to show up, but she wasn't surprised when I did. I heard a vehicle and turned around. A truck — small, white, with "Cavendish" in large letters on the side panels — stopped behind my car.

The driver's side door swung open, and out came Walter Cavendish. Three long strides, and he stood in front of me.

"What are you doing here?"

"Funny, your mother just asked me the same question."

He shot a brief glance at the house.

"Who the hell do you think you are … bothering mother like that. You got no business, no business …"

He took a step forward, opening my car door. "Get in." Then, almost yelling, "Get the hell out of here, and don't come back!"

I pulled away from the house, watching the rearview mirror. Walter had already turned and was marching toward the house.

43

AJ didn't respond to my text. A call went to voicemail. I put my phone on the desk and looked up. Sandy stood at the doorway. She had that look, the one that signaled she knew very well what I was trying to do.

But when Sandy wanted to be diplomatic, she was good at it.

"Are you still wondering," she said, "how Sylvia Cavendish knew it was you?"

I shrugged. "Probably a waste of time."

"If the Cavendish family really is behind the threats to Lenny Stern..."

"Not to mention killing Kate Hubbell."

"And Kate. Don't you think they would have expected you or Henri to show up sooner or later?"

"That's the logical conclusion, sure."

"It's the only conclusion that makes sense," Sandy said.

"Where did you say Henri was? I know you told me, but I was distracted, I guess."

Sandy chose not to follow up on my comment. More diplomacy.

"He went to the island for the day. He said he needed to check on repairs. On his house, I think."

"Good time to go, since Lenny's still in Chicago."

I glanced at the time on my computer screen. "Aren't you here late?"

"I'm leaving in a minute," Sandy said. "Remember the Simmons file?"

"Uh-huh."

"Finished up. I'll drop it at the courthouse in the morning. Besides, Dad's playing bridge with some of his buddies."

"You don't have to make dinner?"

"Yeah, but he'll be late. A couple of beers after cards. He won't be in a hurry for dinner."

She hesitated at the door.

"What's up?" I said.

"Call her again, boss. Call no text."

I decided quickly to return her courtesy and chose diplomacy. I nodded. Sandy smiled, and returned to her desk.

I tapped AJ's number.

"Hi, Michael," AJ said. She sounded too formal, but she was at work. At least that was my rationale. I tried not to read any more into it.

"How's things?" I said.

"You know, how about you?"

Perhaps there was more to it.

"Okay," I said, skipping my friendly visit with Sylvia Cavendish. "Thought about making pasta and a salad. Want to join me?

"Ah … it's pretty hectic here," she said.

"I'm not starving," I said. "I can wait."

"How about a rain check. Is that all right?"

"Sure. A rain check it is." It didn't feel like I had much of a choice.

"All right," AJ said. "Got to go. See you."

I was uncomfortable the way it ended, not edgy or annoyed, just uncomfortable. We've had that same conversation dozens of times over the years. Most of the time we shared dinner somewhere. Occasionally, we did not. Either way was okay. But they used to be easier conversations.

I no longer felt like putting together dinner. I tapped the keyboard, went to Pallette Bistro's menu. I tapped out an order for crab cakes and a Caesar salad, and paid for it. I was only going a couple of blocks, of course, but some menu items tasted better than others by the time I got them home. I picked up my brief bag and left the office.

I tossed my bag in the car, went across the street to pick up dinner, and drove home.

I always liked dinner at home, on the couch, in old running clothes. By myself was good, being with AJ was better. I walked toward the rear entrance of my building, brief bag over my shoulder. My toughest decision was, wine or scotch. What sounded better with crab cakes?

I never saw them.

I hit the tarmac. Hard. Face down. A boot to the ribs. Again. A knee, low in the back. Jerked to my feet by two guys, one on each side, yanking my arms. Shoved forward into a big SUV, spun around. Held up, held back. A blow, straight to the midsection. No air.

"Listen, asshole." Elbow to the side of the head. Fist to the ribs.

It was Dexter, couldn't see the other two. Dexter swung low, to the ribs, swung high to the head.

"Stay away from Cavendish. Got it?"

Another to the ribs. "Not your business. You're a dead man you fuck with Cavendish." Two quick hits, the ribs, the face.

On the tarmac. They were gone.

44

Noise ... beeping? What? Beeping? Pinging?

"Mr. Russo?" A women's voice.

"That noise, what's that noise?"

"Mr. Russo? Over here, Mr. Russo. Look left."

I moved my head slowly.

"Yes, this way. Open your eyes a little."

"What's that noise?"

"It's a monitor, Mr. Russo."

"Where ..."

"The emergency room, Mr. Russo. You're safe. The emergency room in Petoskey."

My eyes began to focus.

A white coat, a name scribbled on the left breast pocket. A soft smile, brown hair.

"You were worked over pretty good," she said. "You can still take a punch, I'll give you that."

"You ... you ..."

"Look familiar, do I, Mr. Russo?"

I nodded. It hurt.

"I'm Dr. Rochelle Silverstein. Hospital staff."

I didn't place her.

"I was on duty the last time you were brought in. The time before that, too. Every couple of years, it seems."

"Give him the good news," another voice said. "And the bad news."

"Marty?"

"Having a rough evening?" Fleener said from the end of the bed.

"Is your head a little clearer?" the doc said.

I nodded. It hurt, but not as much.

"You can hear me okay?"

"Uh-huh."

"Mr. Russo," the doc said, "the good news is, no serious damage. You took a beating, mostly the ribs and the lower back. You were kicked in the groin, but they missed. A few shots to the head, but they look worse than they are."

"The bad news?" I said, my head not quite as fuzzy.

"I gave you something for the pain, especially your ribs. When it wears off, you'll be pretty sore for a while."

I looked around.

"She went downstairs for coffee," Fleener said.

"Mr. Russo," Dr. Silverstein said, "it's a busy night. I'll check back later, see how you're doing."

"What time is it?"

"Almost midnight," she said.

"Can I get out of here?"

"I'll check back," she said with a smile, and left the room.

I reached for the left side of my head. Sore, especially around the ear.

Fleener moved up closer. "Do you remember what happened?"

"How'd you get here?"

"One of the patrol officers recognized your name called."

"At the hospital?"

Fleener nodded. "What happened?"

"I left the office . . ."

AJ came through the door.

"Michael, hi."

"Hi," I said, trying to sit up.

AJ put down her coffee.

"Lift up a little," she said, pushing the pillows back and up. "Is that better?"

"Thanks." It was better, and easier to talk.

"I was asking our friend," Fleener said, "if he remembered what happened."

I described the evening's events, starting with a carryout dinner.

"He asked me to meet him," AJ said.

"Good thing you weren't there," I said.

"They wouldn't have jumped you if I'd been there. And even if they did, I could have done something."

"AJ," I said.

"I should've met you."

"Don't … don't feel guilty about it."

"You went to Gaylord alone? We talked about that, remember? Why didn't you wait for Henri?"

"Hold on, both of you," Fleener said. "Stop. Just … just take it easy. It's over."

The room went quiet, except for the incessant beeping. AJ picked up her coffee and drank some.

"Did you recognize them?" Fleener said.

"Dexter," I said. "Sam Dexter did the hitting."

"You're sure?" Fleener said.

"I'm sure. The guys who held me, don't know, not for sure. Good bet they were the others."

"Didn't you tell me there's four of them?" AJ said.

"As far as we know," Fleener said.

The door opened, we all looked. Henri came in, went around AJ and Fleener to the other side of the bed.

"Michael, you all right?"

"I'm okay."

"Sure?"

"Yeah, I'm sure."

"Cavendish do this?"

Before I could answer, Henri said, "How many?"

I told him.

He sized up the situation quickly. "The hitter Dexter?"

I nodded.

"The oldest thinks he's the toughest," Henri said. "Think I'll ask him about that."

"No," Fleener said. "Stay out of it."

Henri ignored what he said, and we all knew it.

"I've got a better idea," Fleener said.

Not expecting that from an officer of the court, we all looked his way and waited.

"Are we off the record?" Fleener said to AJ.

"Can the paper have the story first?" She was an editor these days, the one who got the digital edition of the *Post Dispatch* up and running, but she never stopped being a reporter.

"Yes," Fleener said.

"Then we're off the record."

Fleener turned toward me. "File a complaint against Sam Dexter."

"I could do that," I said, curious what he had in mind.

"We'll arrest Dexter, play him a little. Talk about him and his pals beating you up. Then say we know about the drugs, push him. Make it sound like we have hard info ... accuse him of dealing. If we can get him to talk drugs and Sylvia Cavendish ..."

"You'll bring her in," I said.

Fleener nodded. "I don't care about the drugs."

"What about her sons?" AJ said.

"Our information says Sylvia's been supplying drugs, they had nothing on her sons. We'll start with her and see where it leads."

"The prosecutor okay this?" Henri said.

"If Hendricks believes we have a shot at the people who killed Kate Hubbell," Fleener said, "he'll go for it."

Our conversation stopped when Dr. Silverstein returned to the room.

"I'll take care of that complaint, Marty," I said.

"How's your head?" the doc asked. "A little clearer?"

"Yes. Can I go?"

"Sorry, Mr. Russo," she said. "Whatever you had planned for 'later,' will have to wait. You can't drive. Even walking will be unsteady for a few hours. So, no, no plans for anything until morning. Understood?"

"But I can leave the hospital?"

She looked at the others crowded around the bed. "If one of you will take him home, he can leave."

"I'll do it," AJ said.

"Good," the doc said. "I have other patients to see, so I'll be off. Mr. Russo," she began, then paused. "Mr. Russo, I'd rather not see you in my ER again. Could you work on that, please?"

"I'll try," I said.

"He'll do better than that," AJ said.

"All right, then," Dr. Silverstein said, and left the room.

"I'll get a warrant for Dexter," Fleener said. "Will you go to the office in the morning?"

"He's going home with me," AJ said. "He'll be in your office in the morning if you need him."

"Okay. Russo, you take care," Fleener said, and walked away.

"Will you follow us to my house?" AJ said to Henri.

"Better than that, we'll put him in my car, meet you there."

"You'll come get him in the morning?"

Henri nodded.

"I don't need a babysitter," I said.

"You need somebody," AJ said. Then to Henri, "You had to go to the island?"

"It's late, AJ," Henri said, letting the question slide. "Let's get the two of you home."

Without another word, AJ turned and walked out.

Henri looked over at me. "I'll find a nurse, get you out of here. Meet you outside."

A nurse I had not met arrived with a wheelchair and put me in it. I was more unstable than I imagined, just getting into the chair. A slow elevator ride later, an awkward climb into Henri's SUV, and we were off to AJ's.

Henri pulled into the driveway at AJ's house and stopped at the side door. She was waiting for us.

"To the guestroom," AJ said, and the two of them clumsily got me into the house and upstairs, dropping me unceremoniously on the bed.

"What time?" Henri said.

"I'll let you know," AJ said. "Not early."

"See you tomorrow," Henri said, and went downstairs.

AJ sat on the side of the bed. Tears glistened around the corners of her eyes.

"This isn't good, Michael."

45

"**W**ould you like more coffee?" AJ said.

I sat on a long, slatted teak bench in the shade of the front porch. I vaguely remembered arriving at her house last night.

"Please," I said, and watched her add to my mug. She smiled, easily. The edge on her face had disappeared overnight.

"Is it really almost eleven?"

"Yep. By the time I dragged you out of the tub and tucked you in bed, it was late."

I awkwardly rearranged myself on the bench, sipping coffee.

"How're the ribs this morning?" AJ put the carafe on a side table and sat down.

"That ER doc was right, pretty sore. I think the hot water helped." "You can do that again this afternoon."

"I just might."

I noticed her paint-stained running shorts, loosely hanging T-shirt, and bare feet. "Aren't you late for work?"

She shrugged. "I talked to Maury. They can lose me for a day. There's more coffee cake, want another piece?"

I shook my head. "I need to think about getting to the office. You heard from Henri?"

"He'll be along, but you're not leaving the porch quite yet."

"Why is that?" I said. "Just curious."

"Marty Fleener's on his way. Should be here any minute."

"Did he say why?"

"Because you're here. He told me to see that you stayed put until he got here."

I drank some coffee and set the mug down.

AJ took my hand, leaned over and kissed my cheek. "I love you."

"I love you, too. You were upset last night, I think. Hard to remember."

"Upset and angry, Michael."

"Angry at me?"

"Of course, at you."

We slid from the easy comfort of coffee together into something else. The teak bench felt longer.

"At you, at me. I don't like being scared."

Her soft smile had faded into...not sure what it was. Anguish? It didn't feel like being irritated or annoyed. It almost felt like impatience.

"I don't know how to deal with it...how...to..."

"Maybe it has to run its course."

"You mean get used to it? That's easier said than done. Sometimes I think...is that Marty's car?" AJ said, pointing up Bay Street.

A black sedan moved toward our end of the block, going faster than it should have in a residential area. It stopped at the curb in front of the house, on the wrong side of the street.

Marty Fleener swung both legs out of the car, put his feet to the ground, and pushed himself up. He came up the front walk, slowly.

"You got any more of that coffee?" he asked, pointing at AJ's mug.

"Just made a fresh pot," she said. "You look tired."

"I am tired. Mind if I sit?"

"Sit here," AJ said. "I'll get your coffee."

Fleener took off his suit jacket, put it over the porch railing, and dropped himself on the bench. He loosened his tie and opened his shirt's top button.

"Good morning," I said.

"Morning."

AJ returned, handed Fleener a mug, and sat next to him.

"Thanks," he said, and drank some.

"You look like you haven't slept," AJ said.

"That's because I haven't slept."

"Would you like some coffee cake? Made this morning."

"No, thanks. I don't want to encourage my stomach to expect food on a regular schedule."

"You haven't slept all night, and you're doing sarcasm?" I said.

Fleener took a breath and drank more coffee.

"We picked up Sam Dexter around four o'clock this morning."

"You found a judge to give you a warrant in the middle of the night?"

"Called in a favor."

"How about Hendricks? He know about this?"

Fleener almost laughed. "First one I called. Got him out of bed."

"My ID at the hospital was enough then?"

Fleener nodded. "Hendricks said, and I quote, 'If Russo's messing with me, I will fuck with him for the rest of his life.'"

"What about Dexter?"

Fleener turned to me. "You sure you aren't screwing around with your ID?"

"Man stands three feet away, gives me shot after shot while his buddies hold me down — yeah. I don't get it wrong. Now what about Dexter? When do you sit him in the room?"

"Done."

"Seriously?" I said.

Fleener nodded.

"He have a lawyer?"

"Court-appointed."

"In the middle of the night?" AJ said.

"Called in another favor," Fleener said. "Mind if I have some more coffee?"

AJ refilled Fleener's mug. "Thanks." He drank some and said, "We scared the liver out of the guy, had him believing we thought he was the next worst thing to a Mexican drug kingpin."

"He say anything about Sylvia Cavendish?"

"Gave her up," Fleener said. "She's been supplying drugs to Dexter and his roommate, Jarvis, Ben Jarvis. They made a few bucks selling stuff to their Carp Lake pals."

"Did you talk about Kate Hubbell?"

"Not a word, nothing about Stern or you either. Nothing." Fleener smiled. "We're going to save all that. The threats, Stern's book, all of it, especially Kate Hubbell."

"Saving it for?" AJ said.

"Are we still off the record," Fleener said to AJ, "like before?"

She nodded. "Off the record, like before, and I get the story."

Fleener smiled. "Sylvia Cavendish. We're saving it all for her."

"You'll talk to Hendricks?"

"Done. He liked it."

"Are you going to arrest her?" AJ said.

Fleener shook his head. "Don made some calls, talked to a few people, called in a favor."

"There certainly are a lot of favors being used up on this," AJ said.

"Murder will do that," Fleener said. "A killing's bad for everyone. City Council, County Commission, they call special meetings, issue statements. Very predictable. Can't risk our northern Michigan image, summer tourists will stay away. Whatever, just solve it fast."

"Back to Sylvia?" I said.

"She'll be here tomorrow."

"She just going to drop by for a chat?" I said, intending the sarcasm.

Fleener ignored me. "Hendricks set it up. Otsego Sheriff will talk to her. Let her come in voluntarily in the morning. Probably have a lawyer or two with her."

"She thinks this is about drugs?"

"I have no idea what the lady thinks," Fleener said. "Hendricks only talked drugs. I know that."

"You doing the interview?"

"I am."

Fleener's reputation as an interviewer, the man with the right questions and the right strategy, was a legend built over the years. No one was better. Cops, even prosecutors, did their best to watch him and learn.

"You want to be there?" he said.

"You bet I do."

Fleener gave me details.

"I assume Hendricks will be there."

"Oh, count on it."

Fleener glanced at his watch. "All right," he said, and stood up. "Thanks for the coffee, AJ."

"You're welcome."

He went down the front steps, walked to his car, and drove away.

"Did you ever wonder why they call it an interview?" AJ said.

"Not when Fleener's in the room."

46

After a decent night's sleep in my own bed, I hauled my stiff body up early to get in a light run. I needed to clear my head of the events of the last couple of days. No Lenny Stern, no Cavendish family, no tension with AJ.

The run turned out to be less helpful than I expected. One hundred feet, maybe. That's as far as I got. I thought my ribs had exploded. So, I walked. Not as energizing, but I was outside in the summer air. Better than nothing at all.

I sat at the kitchen table with scrambled eggs, an English muffin and water. If Fleener employed his talents this morning, we might have a clue to the identity of Kate Hubbell's killer. Fleener seldom walked away from an interview empty-handed. He didn't always solve a crime, but he often came away with good leads, good suspects, or good ideas about what to try next.

I left a few minutes early, cut over to Bay Street and walked up the short road that ran next to the side entrance to the sheriff's office in the Bodzick building.

I spotted one man in his fifties, round and soft, unfamiliar with exercise, pacing up and down, up and down. As if he were waiting for someone. Parked cars lined the road, so I put myself out of sight between two trucks. I had a clear view of the side door.

I hadn't waited but a few minutes when a dark blue Lincoln Continental pulled to a stop at the side door. Walter Cavendish got out from behind the wheel, went around the car and opened the passenger door.

The round man moved forward to greet Sylvia Cavendish as she exited the Lincoln. He shook hands with mother and son.

The three of them chatted, if that was the right word, for a few minutes. I was close enough to pick up a word or phrase. It was not a friendly conversation. At first, round man did most of the talking, head moving, hands gesturing. Sylvia stood rigid, hands on hips, or arms folded across her chest. Walter leaned back on the Continental, more observer than participant.

Round man said something I couldn't hear, but I had no trouble hearing Sylvia. "Bullshit," she said, taking a step toward round man, her index finger inches from his face. "Don't you tell me what to do."

Walter came off the car, said something I didn't catch, but Sylvia certainly did. She swung in his direction, her finger pushing against his chest, "Shut up, Walter. I'll let you know when I want to hear from you."

Sylvia's voice dropped but she continued to hold the stage, looking at each man, finger moving as she did. I'd bet five bucks she told them ... no she instructed them, how things would go.

Round man glanced at his watch. "We have to go," he said to Sylvia. Her hands returned to her hips, she said something. When the round man replied, Sylvia threw her arms in the air. "Let's get this over with," she said.

Round man apparently had won the moment, and escorted Sylvia through the side door of the building.

When Walter Cavendish drove off and found a parking spot down the road, I walked around the block to the Lake Street doors. I made my way through the hallways to a long corridor with several doors spaced evenly along the hall. I tapped on the last one and walked in.

"Morning, Russo," Don Hendricks said. "Thought you might not make it." He occupied a chair to one side of a large rectangle of glass. The interview room, on the other side of the glass, held an ancient metal table and four equally unappealing metal chairs. The room was empty.

"How are you, Don?"

He shrugged. "Okay. You know, after all these years, you'd think I'd know if it was adrenaline or nerves."

"Maybe it's both."

"What are you, a shrink?"

I shook my head. "Today, I'm just a spectator."

"That'll be the day. When's the last time you sat in this room and shut up voluntarily?"

I never had a chance to answer, even if it hadn't been a rhetorical question. The door to the room opened and in walked Sylvia Cavendish, accompanied by the round man from the parking lot.

Sylvia was dressed for an afternoon of bridge with the girls: linen slacks, tank top, no jewelry. No doubt in deference to the air conditioning, she had covered the tank top with a light cardigan sweater.

"Did you talk with Walter Cavendish?" I asked Hendricks.

"Uh-huh, after the Otsego Sheriff arranged for her appearance today."

"Any reaction?"

"From the son?" Hendricks shrugged. "Seemed mystified why we wanted Sylvia to come in. He tried to sound surprised we wanted to talk about drugs with mama."

"Is that right?"

"Yep," Hendricks said. "Insulted, he said. He was insulted we'd even suggest such a thing."

"Is he telling you straight?"

"Doubt it," Hendricks said. "Asked him flat out, if he and his brother were giving drugs to their employees."

"And he denied it."

"Of course, he denied it," Hendricks said. "But he's an amateur. Doesn't know how to lie with a straight face."

"What're going to do about the brothers?"

"Not sure, yet. Let's see how it goes in there," Hendricks said, nodding toward the room.

Sylvia sat down first. The round man, in an awkwardly fitted suit, sat next to her. He opened a briefcase, took out a yellow pad and pen, and put them on the table.

"That's her lawyer, I assume?"

Hendricks nodded. "Name's Randolph Bakersfield. He's a partner in a white-shoe firm in the Chicago burbs. On the West Side, I think."

"He any good?"

Marty Fleener came in the door, stood behind us and looked through the glass. "Good morning, gentlemen," he said.

"Russo was asking about Bakersfield," Hendricks said, "if he was any good."

"Good reputation, solid firm, but not a criminal attorney," Fleener said.

"Family friend?" I asked.

"Probably."

Hendricks said, "You ready, Captain Fleener?"

"I am," he said, "but let them sit a few."

"See if they get impatient?" I said.

Fleener nodded. "She has no record, Bakersfield doesn't do criminal law. They got to be uncomfortable."

Several minutes passed; neither Cavendish nor her lawyer said a word.

"Doesn't look like they even know each other," I said. "No idle chit-chat, nothing."

"Could be nerves," Hendricks said.

"Don, did you tell Russo about the library?"

Hendricks shook his head. "Forgot."

"Remember," Fleener said, "when you couldn't figure out how Sylvia knew about Stern's book?"

"I thought somebody at Gloucester Publishing leaked it."

"Nope. Sylvia's a Friend of the Petoskey Library."

"She doesn't like Gaylord's library?"

"Gaylord does not have a Carnegie Library," Fleener said. "She's a big donor."

I turned toward Fleener. "So Sylvia got advanced notice of Lenny's first event for the book tour."

Fleener nodded. "Yes, she did."

"Ready, Marty?" Hendricks said.

Fleener picked up a folder and said, "Yep."

Hendricks turned in his chair. "Break a leg."

47

Fleener left us, appearing moments later on the other side of the glass. "Good morning," he said, introducing himself to Cavendish and Bakersfield.

Fleener put the manila folder on the table, followed by his legal pad and pencil. He removed his suit jacket, hanging it over the back of the chair.

I'd watched Fleener in the room several times over the years. His routine was always the same — methodical, deliberate, paced. People at the table could not help but watch him. Martin Fleener was in charge, and every move was choreographed to convey that feeling.

He sat down, placed a digital recorder in the middle of the table, and opened the folder.

"For the record…" Fleener began with a series of basic questions, all about the Cavendish company, Sylvia's sons, her life in Gaylord.

"Captain Fleener," Bakersfield said. "You have all this, there's no need for these questions."

"Mistake number one," Hendricks said, leaning toward the glass.

"Uh-huh," I said. "The guy doesn't understand the formalities."

"Just a few more things," Fleener said, faking a friendly smile.

Fleener carried on as if every question were a matter of grave importance.

Sylvia was restless, but she managed to deliver answers in a flat, uninterested voice. Bakersfield was growing impatient, too, constantly rearranging himself in the chair.

"Can we move this along?" he said. "Mrs. Cavendish is here out of a desire to help, to be a good citizen."

"No, she's not," I said. "Doesn't he remember the Otsego County Sheriff didn't offer her a choice?"

"Neither did I," Hendricks said. "He's annoyed now. Think that'll carry over to his client?"

"Now, Ms. Cavendish..."

"Captain," Cavendish said, and Fleener stopped. "Please call me Sylvia, if that's all right." She smiled and turned to her lawyer. "You, too. Sylvia's fine."

"Guess they're not old friends," Hendricks said.

Fleener smiled. "All right. Sylvia, do you know Samuel Dexter?"

Sylvia shrugged. "I might have met him, you know, around, I don't remember."

"He says he knows you."

"Well, okay."

"How about Benjamin Jarvis, you know him?"

Sylvia shrugged.

"They both work for you," Fleener said.

Sylvia leaned forward. "They do not work for me, Captain. They work for the business."

"Well, well," Hendricks said. "Do I detect annoyance?"

"In fact, Dexter and Jarvis do handyman work at your house, don't they?" Fleener said.

"Well, I suppose..."

"Fairly frequently?"

"I don't see what this..."

"Sam Dexter says you supplied him with drugs," Fleener said. "Is he telling the truth?"

"Captain." It was Bakersfield. "We know about the allegations that brought us here today. I will not let Sylvia answer that question."

"Nothing like stating the obvious," Hendricks said. "This guy belongs in probate."

"Did you supply marijuana, amphetamines …"

"Don't answer that," Bakersfield said.

"Dexter said you …"

"No, Captain," Sylvia said before her lawyer could intervene. "Why do you believe him and not me? Is there evidence that he's telling the truth?"

"Maybe Sylvia should represent herself," I said.

"Let me ask you about Benjamin Jarvis," Fleener said, pushing on.

He softened the questions, but always returned to drugs.

"Do your sons give drugs to Dexter and Jarvis?"

"I don't know," Sylvia said. "Why don't you ask them?"

"I might just do that."

Fleener's questions grew repetitive intentionally. Bakersfield cut some of them off. He and his client were still annoyed, struggling to stay focused.

"Now, Sylvia," Fleener said, pausing.

"Here we go," Hendricks said.

"Tell me about RC 44."

Sylvia Cavendish sat bolt upright, her eyes wide open.

"Ma'am?" Fleener waited. "RC 44?"

"What do you want me to say?" Sylvia said, glaring at Fleener.

"Hold on a second," Bakersfield said. "Where are you … what is this line of questioning?"

Fleener ignored him. "It's a simple question, Sylvia, RC 44?"

"I don't know what you're talking about."

"I think you do," Fleener said.

"Would you like to explain the meaning of the question, Captain?"

"I'd rather hear from Sylvia, if you don't mind, Mr. Bakersfield."

"Well, I do mind, Captain. What's the purpose of the question?"

Without serious objections from Bakersfield, Fleener continued. "Have you seen RC 44 anywhere?"

Sylvia shook her head.

"How about at the Cavendish Company? Maybe on a truck or car?"

"Captain, that's enough," Bakersfield said, "until you tell me where this interview is going."

"How about a tattoo," Fleener said. "A 44 inside a circle?"

"Why do you make things up," Sylvia said, still glaring at Fleener.

"I think annoyance has morphed into anger," Hendricks said. "What do you think, Russo?"

I just stared, riveted by the people on the other side of the glass.

"A tattoo, a circle around the number 44. Seems pretty simple to me. You've seen it, haven't you?"

Sylvia sat stone-faced, but clearly angry.

"An odd tatt, don't you think?" Fleener said. "What does it mean, Sylvia?"

"Why isn't Bakersfield cutting off the questions?" I said.

"This isn't his ballpark, Russo. He doesn't understand. Of course, his client isn't helping any."

"Tell me about RC 44."

"You have no … I don't know what you mean," Sylvia said.

"Sam Dexter says you know all about the tattoo, Sylvia."

"Whoa, Don," I said. "I didn't know that."

"Neither did I," Hendricks said.

"Dexter's lying," Sylvia said, raising her voice.

"Lying about the tatt?" Fleener said.

"Yes, of course," Sylvia said.

"Lying about drugs?"

"Yes." Her voice grew louder.

"Tell me about the Cavendish Company truck with the vanity plate, 'RC 44.'"

Sylvia never hesitated. "I don't know anything about company trucks." But her response had no weight behind it.

"A vanity plate, RC 44, on a company truck, your company truck."

She shook her head. Shook it with dramatic flair, like that was more convincing.

"The RC," Fleener said, "it's for Ramsey Cavendish, your husband, isn't it?"

"Yes, my husband," Sylvia said, clearly angry. "My husband's dead and you know it."

"What's the connection, Sylvia? Ramsey and 44?"

"Captain," Bakersfield said, but Sylvia cut him off.

"Shut up," she said, her head only inches from Bakersfield face. "Shut up, just shut up. Both of you." She turned Fleener's way, "You have no right…"

Fleener pressed on. "What does the 44 have to do with your dead husband, Sylvia?"

Fleener flipped a few pages in the manila folder. It was show. He already knew what it said.

"Ramsey Cavendish died in prison. Says here he was beaten to death, Sylvia. Did your husband know about the 44?"

"Where's Fleener going with this, Don?" I said.

"Don't have a clue."

"Leave Ramsey out of this, damn you," Sylvia said. "He's dead. I don't want you talking…" She couldn't finish the sentence. Tears fell down her cheeks. She wiped them away with a finger.

"Why did Sam Dexter and his buddies threaten to kill Lenny Stern?"
"Damn," Hendricks said.

"What?" Bakersfield said. "No, Sylvia. Don't answer."

"Sylvia." Fleener paused. "Did you tell Dexter to kill Lenny Stern?"

"That's it, Captain. We stop. Now."

"What about Kate Hubbell? Did you tell Dexter to kill Kate Hubbell, too?"

Sylvia Cavendish came out of her chair, leaning on the table toward Fleener.

"You're damn right I did. That man killed Ramsey!" The tears ran freely down her face now. "The woman got dead, so Stern knew he was next. I wanted him to sweat it out…every…single…day." Sylvia drew the words out. "Like me when Ramsey went to prison. I want Stern dead. You hear me, *dead.*"

Bakersfield was out of his chair. "No. Sylvia, not another word. Captain, we're done. I need time with my client. Now."

Sylvia sat down, crying hard. Bakersfield put a hand on her shoulder. She swatted it away.

Fleener closed the manila folder, took his jacket, and left the room to Sylvia Cavendish and Randolph Bakersfield.

Fleener came in with us.

"Well shit," Hendricks said. "Did you have any idea…?"

Fleener shrugged.

"She gave it up pretty easily," I said.

"She didn't give anything up," Fleener said.

"But Sylvia admitted she ordered Lenny killed."

"All Sylvia cares about is her hate, Russo. Getting even for her husband's death. Somebody had to pay. Lenny Stern, Kate Hubbell, anyone related to the book project."

"That thing about 44," I said. "That sent her over the line."

"Took me a while to figure it out," Fleener said. "The 44? That was the number of days Ramsey Cavendish survived in prison before he was killed."

I shook my head. "Jesus…"

"What do you want to do about the sons?" Fleener said.

"Pick 'em up," Hendricks said.

A veteran criminal attorney once explained Martin Fleener this way: "Fleener is like LeBron James. The game looks the same because it is. But Fleener plays at another level. His experience and instincts work seamlessly. Fleener trusts his instincts, even if they conflict with logic. It takes him places others can't conceive of, not on their best days."

48

"What'll happen to Sylvia Cavendish?" AJ said. We sat with Henri and Sandy at a table near the front windows at City Park Grill. Lenny Stern was there, too, after wrapping up his grand book tour in the Windy City. Lenny, Sandy, and Henri drank beer, AJ and me, chardonnay. We'd ordered crab-spinach dip and sweet potato fries for the table.

"That's up to Don Hendricks," I said. "Fleener said it'd be a few days yet."

"What about Sam Dexter and Ben Jarvis?" Sandy said. "And the two from Carp Lake?"

"Dexter will be charged with killing Kate Hubbell," I said.

"It still doesn't seem clear why he killed a woman he didn't know," Sandy said.

"But it mattered to Sylvia." I put down my wine glass. "From what Hendricks said, Sylvia could be pretty persuasive. The bad boys weren't the savviest bunch either. Toss in the free drugs, they were easy marks for Sylvia."

"The others?" Sandy said.

"All of them were in on it," I said. "The threats, everything. Pretty gullible. Give them a free tattoo, it's like a club."

"I still don't see ... I have a hard time with Sylvia," Lenny said. "I know she blamed me. But that was a long time ago."

"She wanted revenge, Lenny," Sandy said. "She figured you were responsible for her husband's death. If he hadn't gone to prison ..."

"I understand that," Lenny said. "But why wait all these years? We only lived fifty miles apart. Why now?"

"Your book, Lenny," I said. "*Corruption on Trial* brought the anger and hate home, to her backyard. The book got publicity where she lived. She never forgot, never let it go. Her hate lived just below the surface. Then, one day, there you were with the book."

"A lot of hate to keep bottled up," Sandy said.

"I worry sometimes," Lenny said. "Is hate intrinsically evil? Is hate always evil?"

"No answer for that one," I said.

"It lured in those boys," AJ said. "Or maybe it was just Sylvia who did that."

"That's not much of a choice, if you ask me," Sandy said.

"No, it's not," AJ said, shaking her head.

"We worried about all the wrong things," Lenny said. "It wasn't about the documents after all. Sylvia never knew about them. It was all about revenge, about getting even. In Sylvia's mind, even killing Kate was getting at Lenny."

"Do you think the sons really didn't know what drug mama was up to?" Sandy said.

"I don't know," I said. "But Hendricks'll find out."

"All right, that's enough," Sandy said, finishing her wine. "Time to go home."

"If I hustle," Henri said, "I can catch the last ferry to the island. See how the new roof is coming along."

"I'm out of here, too," Lenny said.

We said our good-byes, and AJ and I remained at the table.

"You look tired," she said, putting her hand on mine.

"Weary, worn out, I guess. How about you?"

AJ thought for a moment. "We've had a lot going on."

"Yes."

"Not just with Lenny," AJ said. "You know what I mean?"

"Uh-huh, I do."

"We have some work to do, Michael. Maybe more me … some things to figure out. You know?"

I nodded.

ACKNOWLEDGMENTS

Most important, I thank the authors in my writing group, Marietta Hamady, Winnie Simpson, and Aaron Stander. Our discussions and their detailed critiques helped make my writing clearer and the mystery more exciting. I treasure their friendship and support. I missed, however, the easy camaraderie of our sessions together during the year of the pandemic when Zoom took over. While we would have preferred to be together, we remained healthy, safe, engaged in our writing.

Several other folks also willingly made Michael Russo's latest adventure a better read. I'm grateful for their time and energy. They include Frances Barger, Mary Jane Barnwell, John Mulvaney, Tanya Hartman, Mary Beauchamp, Fuller Cowell, Jeri-Lynn Bailey, Leigh Ann Klay, Justin Dempsey, and Joe Sandri.

Heather Shaw and Scott Couturier edited the manuscript and took it apart over and over again. Plot, characters and dialog. I look forward to their evaluations because they make the manuscript better. Because of Heather and Scott, I've learned new things about my characters and the situations I've created for them. Hart Cauchy proofread the manuscript, and made me look much sharper than I really am. I've also learned new things about myself as a writer. I appreciate their encouragement and support.

Since this is a story about a reporter, I envisioned the cover as a homage to gangster films (think, *Little Caesar* or *The Godfather*) that used a montage of newspaper headlines to convey gang warfare. I tossed some of that at Heather. Create a cover, I said. She did. Wow.

As I've said before, I made stuff up, all of it. The characters, events, and plot twists. Just like the earlier Russo adventures, I invented everything at the kitchen table with coffee, by the fireplace with a nice single malt, or on a relaxing run on the trails on Mackinac Island.

Peter Marabell grew up in Metro Detroit, spending as much time as he could street racing on Woodward Avenue in the late 1950s and visiting the Straits of Mackinac. With a Ph.D. in History and Politics, Peter spent most of his professional career at Michigan State University. He is the author of the historical monograph, *Frederick Libby and the American Peace Movement*, soon to be published by Kendall Sheepman Company. His first novel, *More Than a Body*, was published in 2013. The first of the Michael Russo mystery series, *Murder at Cherokee Point* (2014) was followed by *Murder on Lake Street* (2015), *Devils Are Here* (2016), *Death Lease* (2018), and *The Final Act of Conrad North* (2019). As a free-lance writer, he worked in several professional fields including health care, politics, and the arts. In 2002, Peter moved permanently to northern Michigan with his spouse and business partner, Frances Barger, to live, write, and work at their Mackinac Island business. All things considered (Peter still says), he would rather indulge in American politics, or Spartan basketball, after a satisfying five-mile run on the hills of Mackinac Island. Find out more about the author at **www.petermarabell.com.**

OTHER BOOKS BY PETER MARABELL

Made in the USA
Monee, IL
25 September 2021

78748211R00152